His Third Wife

Grace Octavia

Kensington Publishing Corp.

www.kensingtonbooks.com

DAFINA BOOKS are published by

Kensington Publishing Corp.
119 West 40th Street
New York, NY 10018

ISBN-13: 978-0-7582-8881-3
ISBN-10: 0-7582-8881-6
First Kensington Trade Edition: November 2013

eISBN-13: 978-0-7582-8883-7
eISBN-10: 0-7582-8883-2
First Kensington Electronic Edition: November 2013

10 9 8 7 6 5 4 3 2 1

Printed in the United States of America

His Third
Wife

Also by Grace Octavia

What He's Been Missing

Should Have Known Better

Playing Hard to Get

Something She Can Feel

His First Wife

Take Her Man

Reckless (with Cydney Rax and Niobia Bryant)

Published by Dafina Books

To my beloved Atlanta University Center.
To my beloved Atlanta.
To all those readers who've been emailing me since 2008 asking
what happened to Kerry and Jamison . . .

Acknowledgments

Thank you to the entire team at Kensington for helping me keep this here show on the road. Thank you all for believing in what I have to say and how I like to say it. To my busy, patient editor, Mercedes Fernandez, who once said, "I don't want you to lose your voice": I hear you. I won't.

My Dearest Reader,

Wow! It's been five years since I wrote *His First Wife*, and let me tell you, not a month has gone by when I didn't receive an email, letter, or phone call from readers from Weed, California, to Jacksonville, Florida, wanting to know what happened to my most chic, blue-blood Atlanta couple, Jamison and Kerry. Like I did as I wrote their emotional tale of love found, lost, and reclaimed, readers fell in love with this pair. And not because of their endless drama or insider's peek at elite black Atlanta, but because of their intense vulnerability, rawness, and sincere dedication to love. Perhaps that's what made me tell Jamison and Kerry's story in the first place. Like all of you, I wanted to see reflections of the loves I've known. What it feels like to be lied to. How it feels to be the liar. What it's like to move on. And, yes, why so many times we return to our lovers with open arms. Maybe we want to believe it will last forever. Maybe we know it just won't. But . . . maybe . . . it will. . . .

Of course, before I'm a writer, I'm an enthusiastic reader of these stories. So, like many of you, after reading *His First Wife*, I too wondered, "What happened to them?" And my need to fill this desire (and answer your requests) led me to give loyal readers random "Jamison and Kerry" updates in my other Southern novels like *Should Have Known Better*. Even then, I still got more letters and even when I responded, I still received more questions asking, "What's next for Jamison?"

That's what leads us, dearest reader, to this novel, the sequel to *His First Wife*. It's my answer to those emails and my needs. It's not just an update; it's a visitation with old friends, a resolution, a final chapter (hum . . . maybe not). What you'll find in the next installment in Jamison and Kerry's tale is scandal, secrets, sincerity, and faith. These characters demanded much from my imagination. And through the writing, as I discovered and rediscovered what made them tick, I kept thinking, "Well, wouldn't it take this kind of imagination to even dream up what actually happens in our real love lives? How it happens? How it feels? How it never lets us go?"

I really hope you enjoy this next step in the journey with Jamison and Kerry. I look forward to reading those letters and taking those calls. :)

Yours, of course,

Grace Octavia

"The New South"

After a predictable rising sun had rolled through hopscotch maps of plantations, crawled along the tips of decaying steeples in suburban enclaves, and made its way to the ambitious stacking skyline that marked Atlanta's city center, a body was found all akimbo in the middle of Peachtree Street. People who'd come from pollen-covered cars that had been slowed to a crawl in both directions along the venous strip, which connected all of what was being called the official "capital of the New South," looked to the sky, like maybe the bloody brown mess had fallen from the sun's fiery rays. One person pointed. Then two pointed. Three. Then four. A reporter arrived. And then a police officer. All pointed to the top of the Downtown Westin. The body in the street in the bloody gray suit had come from there. Had to have.

One pointing son asked his mother, "Was that a woman up there looking down at us?" Further along in the crowd, a co-worker asked a driver, "Was that a man dressed as a woman standing at the top of the Westin?" A wife said to her husband and then later to a police officer, "It was a woman. A woman in a dress." Her husband disagreed: "It was a man dressed as a woman. The shoulders were too broad." Then they started arguing about there being two women up there. Well, a woman and a man dressed as a woman. But some hadn't seen anything. Just a shadow. Maybe a bird sitting on the edge looking down at the body like prey.

Soon it was a scene. And someone in a white cloth jumpsuit lifted what was left of the head that had been crushed by the weight of the fall, and in the pieces and fragments of a once familiar face made out a truth. This was no angel that had fallen from the sun to halt rush-hour traffic. It was the new mayor.

That was when the talk started. When it would never stop. Because that man, the mayor who'd fallen from the top of the Westin to the black tar, was Jamison Taylor. Everything the chocolate side of the city could be proud of and the white side could use as an example of Southern progress. Born poor in the SWATS. A Morehouse man. Fraternity guy. Self-made millionaire. A heart that won the old guard. A voice that had vowed to repave the very street that had become his deathbed. A soul that wanted everything he could imagine. And he was dead. The city dressed in black for the funeral. And from the boardrooms in Buckhead to the lunch counters at the Busy Bee and Chanterelle's in the West End, chatter was king. There was a first wife. A new wife. A mother. A son. A fat pig's belly worth of secrets. A mess of shadows that everyone thought they could see clearly. Politics at its finest. Headlines.

But that was just the tipping point of it all. Stories like that never begin with a body falling from a mid-level hotel.

PART I

". . . to have and to hold, from this day forward . . ."

"His Next Wife"

Everything started when a mother came to town. Quiet and all alone, she got off a Greyhound bus across the street from a conveniently placed strip club. Had on fake pearls and a red lace-front wig. Her daughter picked her up in a shiny new Jaguar with two seats and the top down.

After maybe thirty minutes of silent riding, the mother was standing at the window in the big house—there were pillars out front and all. She was looking away from everything beautiful behind her. Clutching her purse like she wasn't staying. Thinking. Trying to decide how she should tell her smiling baby girl, who always wanted more than she could hold in her arms, that she ought to get on the next bus and go back to Memphis with her.

"I don't know why you didn't accept the tickets I sent you. First-class flight? I thought you'd like that," Val, her daughter, said. Maybe she was sipping her mimosa or waiting for the maid to pour her another glass.

"Memphis ain't but a stone's throw away," the mother mumbled. Her name was Mama Fee—everyone had always called her that, even before she'd had children. "Takes more time to get on the plane and fly than it does to get on the bus and ride. And I don't do big birds. Like to see the earth."

"That's old talk. This is a new world."

"Is it? Is it really, Val? You tell me."

"Yes, Mama Fee. You still act like flying is just for white folks. Or rich folks—"

"Ain't said nothing like that."

"Well, that's good, because it isn't. As long as you can pay, you can play. That's the Atlanta way." Val chuckled and looked at Lorna, the maid holding the pitcher of mimosa to her glass, to support the comedy of her play on words with laughter. "I'm just saying, it's 2012—not 1902!"

"What does that matter?" Mama Fee asked. "Po' folks *still* the same. Rich folks *still* the same."

Lorna was only able to produce a half smile before Val shooed her away with a tired wave. As soon as Lorna stepped over the threshold, the mother turned and looked at her daughter.

"Seems like you shouldn't be drinking," she nearly whispered before turning back to the window. "Not in your condition."

"Condition? Please! What do you know about it?"

"Plenty. Had you and your sisters. Doctor says it's bad."

"No. Doctor says it's good. Helps to relieve stress. A little won't hurt the baby at all." Val downed the last of her drink. There was an audible gulp that resonated with pangs of short nerves or anxiety. "And I need it today—with it being my wedding day and all." She looked at the big blue diamond on her ring finger. She'd purchased it a week ago with her fiancé's credit card and full blessing. "I need to relax."

Mama Fee was still looking out the window and thinking. The shiny Jaguar was resting in the middle of a circular drive that was filled with perfectly shaped creamy stones and purple pebbles that made the whole world outside the house look like a giant fish tank.

"Maybe you should've waited until the baby was born," she said. "At least until we could've had a proper wedding—your family come. You know? Like Patrice and Rhonda did. Still don't see why you couldn't invite your own sisters to your wedding."

"Would you stop it? I didn't invite *you* hear to go drilling me about everything."

"I ain't drilling you. They're your sisters. You were in their weddings."

"Yeah, and they married big fat losers. Is Patrice's husband out of jail yet?"

"You watch your mouth," Mama Fee said, finally turning to look at her daughter again. But she needed no confirmation that it was Val who could bring up such a thing. Her youngest child had been born spitting fire at anything that didn't seem to pick her up in some way that she deemed acceptable. This might've been considered gross ambition or maybe even unapologetic drive if it weren't for the fact that sometimes Val's desire for uplift went beyond frustrated tongue lashings and straight to unmitigated evil— well, the kind of evil a girl from Memphis who'd barely graduated high school could spin.

When Val was fifteen, Patrice had just finished beauty school and her prized graduation gift was a beauty box filled with emerald and sea foam and lavender and canary eye shadow. Lipsticks of every shade of red and pink. After Val had begged to sit and try just one shadow, paint her lips in one red, Patrice balked and hid the box beneath her bed. The next morning, the rainbow of shadows and lipsticks were floating in a river of bleach on the bathroom floor. Mama Fee nearly killed Val with her switch in the backyard after that incident, trying to teach the girl a lesson. But Val didn't cry one tear.

"Patrice's husband is a fucking jailbird. Don't blame me for that," Val said nearly laughing.

"And what about you? What about your husband?"

"Fiancé. And what about him?"

"Well, where is he?" Mama Fee asked, fingering a small Tiffany frame she'd found in the windowsill. It was a picture of a handsome brown man standing beside an older woman at what looked like his college graduation.

"He had to work this morning," Val replied.

"On your wedding day?"

There was a pause. And then, "You're picking again."

"I'm not picking. I'm just asking. It's an obvious question." She held out the picture to Val. "This him?"

"Yes. Him and his raggedy-ass mama," Val snarled. "Hate that old bat."

"At least you've met her. I can't say the same about her son. Don't seem right neither. Got to read about him in all those articles you send me. Can't tell enough about a man just by reading about him. Words don't make a man."

"Damn, Mama Fee! What's that supposed to mean? Because you've never met him, something's not right? You don't trust me?"

"I didn't say that either, girl. It just means I would like to have known him first—before he married my youngest daughter. Known what kind of man he is. Stuff your daddy would've done."

Both mother and daughter paused at the mention of a daddy. He'd been long gone. Had been a good man. But had disappeared one evening after leaving a bar following a fight with one of his white coworkers. Everyone had cursed him for leaving Fee alone to raise three girls. They'd never eat right again. There had been rumors of another woman, another family in Kentucky. Soon, Fee had believed these rumors, but then his body had floated to the top of a forgotten old swimming hole at the back of town. There'd been a noose tied to his neck. No genitals left on his body. No one had ever been interviewed, interrogated, or charged.

"A rich man. A powerful man. That's what kind of man my fiancé is. That's what you need to know," Val finally said in a voice so vindictive it promised some secret punishment for a private vendetta.

"A man who works on his wedding day?" Mama Fee asked.

"God, would you just leave that alone? Look, Jamison didn't want anything big. He just got elected to office. I'm his former assistant. I'm pregnant. The press, they'll run all over it. They're still running pictures of his first wife in the newspapers here. 'Kerry Jackson.' Fucking press."

"The press?"

"The press. Yes, the newspapers. The fucking websites. I have to think about that. *We* have to think about that. I'm marrying the fucking mayor of Atlanta, Mama Fee. Jamison Taylor. Not some jailbird like Patrice did."

"I know, baby. I heard you a million times before."

The sound of the beautiful stones and pebbles cracking beneath tires in the driveway announced a new arrival.

Val jumped up from her empty champagne flute with amazing ease and stepped quickly to the mirror over the fireplace. She puckered her lips, cleaned her teeth with her tongue, smiled, and was out the front door.

Mama Fee looked back out the window in time to see the soon-to-be son-in-law she'd never met close his car door and lean into Val's open arms with a stiff back. He was carrying a laptop in one arm. Had a gym bag draped over the other shoulder. Was wearing sweats. Mama Fee looked from him to the picture in her hand. Alone in the silent room, she looked over her shoulder for the maid and then slid the picture into her purse.

"You're late, Jamison," Val said outside. "We're going to have to hightail it downtown if we're going to do this today." She paused, but he didn't say anything. "We *are* doing *this* today. *Right*?"

"Jesus. A million questions. I just got here."

"My mother's here."

"I know," Jamison said. "I bought the bus ticket."

Val stood in front of him with her feet firmly planted in the pebbles and stones like a little girl about to cry.

"So, we're doing it?" she repeated after recovering with a hand on her hip.

"Yes."

"I'm just asking because we were supposed to go before the judge earlier and—"

"We're going to Forsyth."

"Forsyth County? Why? That's too far away."

"It's just far enough. I can't risk everyone knowing about this."

"They're all going to know soon. Right?" Val asked, setting off a conversation they'd had most every day since she'd announced she was pregnant.

"Yes. I just need to keep this quiet now. Until we're married. Then I can release a statement about you and the baby. I need to control the situation. Get in front of it. I'm still dealing with Ras's shit. And Jeremy with those hookers in Biloxi. I need some time out of the headlines."

"Fine. Well, where's your mother? Where's Tyrian?"

"Mama said she'll meet us at the courthouse," Jamison explained. "She didn't want to risk blowing my cover."

Val smiled at this lie. She knew Jamison's mother didn't like her. His mother actually told Val herself just days after Val started working as Jamison's assistant. She'd caught Val and Jamison having sex in the bathroom at his office. She didn't even leave. Didn't blink at the scene of blushing flesh and scattered office attire. She stood there like a pillar, glowering until Jamison had run away like a little boy. Val tried to be more defiant. It wasn't her mother. She excused herself out of the stall and went to the mirror to fix her lipstick. Mama Taylor walked up behind her and said two short sentences to Val's reflection in the mirror: "I smell your shit. More like diarrhea."

"What about Tyrian?" Val asked Jamison again.

"My son's with his mother."

"He's not coming to the wedding?"

"No."

You give a man everything. All of you. Out on a table. Every-thing. Appetizers. Sides. Drinks. An entrée. And dessert. Just every-thing you have to give.

For this, you ask for something. A small thing.

You get nothing.

I was tired of getting nothing. Nothing from every man. I'd bend like this. I'd turn like that. They'd notice and smile. Follow me for a little while. And then, I was alone again. Back and broken. Worse off than I was before. Poor. And black. And a woman. And I don't need to have gone to college to know that shit ain't fair.

So, you're damn right, when I met Jamison I was tired of getting nothing. But I gave him everything anyway. I wore high leopard-print heels and shit. I dusted my nipples in Ecstasy. I fried chicken in my thong in the middle of the night. Whatever he wanted. He noticed. He smiled.

Then I asked for something.

He got real quiet. That man-not-answering-the-phone-or-email quiet.

That's when I realized I wasn't being left with nothing this time. I was taking what I wanted.

It's funny what a man will do to keep what he has. When I told Jamison I was pregnant, his first question was how far along I was. I knew what that meant. I lied. Fifteen weeks. Too late for an abor-tion. He told me to take his credit card and pick out an engagement ring. Mr. Mayor had to marry me to keep everything he has. And that's no trouble for me. I wanted to marry him because of every-thing he has. Because now I have it, too.

The bride and groom took the long drive to downtown Forsyth in separate cars.

Mama Fee sat beside Val in the Jaguar trying to decide how to say what she needed to say and ask what she needed to know. What she wanted to say was, "This is crazy! This is ridiculous!" What she wanted to ask was, "Why are we in separate cars? Why hasn't your fiancé spoken to me?" But seemingly having her thoughts read, at every peak of possibility of internal eruption, Val would offer statements that made any claims or interrogations irrelevant in her new world: "Jamison likes to think in the car. He likes to ride alone. . . . I love driving my new car. . . . I don't mind driving myself around. . . . Soon, I'll have a driver anyway. . . . He can't wait to meet you. . . . Don't worry, Mama. . . . This ain't Memphis. . . . This is Atlanta. . . . Things are done differently here. . . ."

Jamison's new assistant, a white boy with strawberry-blond hair and emeralds for eyes, met the two cars in the parking lot at the courthouse, whisked Jamison into the back of the building one way and Val and Mama Fee into the back of the building another way nearly thirty minutes later.

So much rushing. So little talking. Mama Fee pretended she was having trouble walking just so Val would have to hold her hand.

"I love you, Val Denise. I want the best for you. Always have," Mama Fee said softly to Val just before the assistant pulled them into a holding room where Jamison was waiting on his cell phone.

Val smiled, kissed her mother on the cheek and let go of her hand.

Jamison was barking commands at the someone on the phone and signaling for his assistant to seat Val and her mother. He forced his free hand into his pocket and stood tall with his shoulders perfectly squared. The stance announced that he was a man handling business.

"Tell Darth the contract isn't negotiable. He can bring anyone he wants to the table," Jamison said. "I won't move. The people

ally the shortest and roundest person in any room. At one moment she could look like one of those old school inflatable punching dolls. At another, an overgrown obese toddler. It didn't seem to bother her though. She wore her weight and stature like war garments. It made people move out of the way and stare. And that's just what she wanted.

Jamison was up on his feet and had his mother in his arms before Mama Fee could get a good look at her.

Val seemed to have disappeared into a corner and was clinching her teeth tightly. Not necessarily in fear of what Mrs. Taylor would say to her, but what Val might say back. Since the scene in the bathroom at the office, Val came to realize that Jamison had a firm belief that his mother was the incarnate manifestation of Isis, Mother Nature, Yemaya-Ogun, and Sojourner Truth wrapped up into one wicked widow. Those who spoke against her were outcasts, never to be heard from again. Val just, simply, knew better than to rumble with this robust reincarnation. And that was no easy task for anyone. "The wicked witch returns," Val mumbled.

"My handsome, brilliant baby boy," Mrs. Dorothy Taylor said so fervently everyone in the room knew Jamison had heard these words a billion times since he was born.

Mother and son exchanged elegant words as if they were alone in the room before Jamison pulled his mother and her bouncing Malaysian curls to Mama Fee.

"Mama, I have someone I want you to meet." He pointed down to Mama Fee, who hadn't moved from her place on the couch. She was still taking in the real pearls and Malaysian hair. "This is Mama Fee, Val's mother."

"Oh, wonderful," Mrs. Taylor said. "Hello, dear." She reached down and offered half of her hand to Mama Fee in a half-friendly, non-palm-touching handshake that revealed that she was more of a politician than her son. Her voice was desperately detached though, and nearly patronizing, as if Mama Fee was a little dear twenty years her senior and on her way to a nursing home; however, they were clearly the same age. "And how are you enjoying our fine city?"

"It's not my first time here. We're from Memphis." Mama Fee deferred to her daughter, who was still hiding in the corner.

"Oh, yes, I've heard—" Mrs. Taylor nodded at Val and accepted a fake hug when she finally emerged from the darkness. "But you certainly haven't seen it with my son, the mayor." She nearly pushed Val from her side and pulled Jamison to her. "He can get anything done at the snap of his finger. Right, baby?"

"Yes, Mama." Jamison feigned embarrassment, but really his tone was set to cheer his mother's petty praises along.

Mama Fee looked on and smiled with tightly pursed lips as if she was listening to a pastor's wife brag about her new Second Sunday hat.

Leaf, who'd stepped out of the room and was now standing at the door with it halfway open, announced that everyone was to follow him to the judge's chambers. His voice was productive, punctual, as if he was seating them at the local burger joint and certainly not preparing them for what was commonly a Southern sacrament filled with all of the pomp and circumstance, ritual, and tradition of a pope's beatification. At that very moment, in a black Southern wedding, the bride was to be buried beneath a cloud of virginal whiteness in silk, lace and taffeta; her adoring father and loyal sorority sisters were to be at her side; a church should've been draped in two tasteful, season-friendly colors; a unity candle should be placed at the altar; a broom decorated by some old, or wise, or creative spirit should've been hidden in the front pew; three beautiful brown little girls with long pigtails and clear, ambitious eyes should've been walking down the aisle; a groom, nervous, but so proud should've been standing at the front of what seemed like a mile long line of envious spectators as a woman from the church sang "Ave Maria" out of tune. But there was none of that here. Jamison had asked Val not to wear white, so she wouldn't draw any attention to them, so she was in a beige Chanel suit that might make coworkers envious at an office luncheon, but seemed par for the course in the back breezeways at the courthouse. Jamison was straggling behind her in a navy suit his first wife had picked out for him just months before they'd divorced.

The small group of celebrants gathered to file out of the door like they were stepping into a teller line at a bank. The only person who might have appeared confused as to whether she was preparing for a deposit or withdrawal was Mama Fee, who was in the front of the line. Holding down the back was the one who was certain—Mrs. Taylor. She grabbed Val's hand just before she stepped over the threshold.

Jamison saw the tug. "Mama, we have to go," he said, his eyes now as troubled as Val's. "The judge is ready."

"I know who's ready and who ain't," Mrs. Taylor replied, unmoved. "I just need a moment alone with my soon-to-be daughter-in-law." She pulled Val farther back from the threshold.

"But, Mama—"

"Jamison Taylor, you know I don't care for people minding my business. I said I have to speak to this here gal about something and—"

"Excuse me, Mrs. Taylor, but we are on a tight schedule," Leaf tried, cutting Mrs. Taylor off with a voice drenched in authority.

Mrs. Taylor smiled and paused before answering, "White boy, you ain't worked for my son long enough that I should even know your name. Don't make today your last day on the job. Because I can make that happen. Ask that last white boy who was looking for a job."

Leaf, a Harvard University graduate whose perfect resume made him so overqualified for the job, Jamison thought it was a joke that he had applied and was willing to take a pay cut when he showed up out of the blue at Jamison's door the day after he'd had to fire his last assistant, seemed spooked by Mrs. Jackson's threats and went into action, nearly pulling Mama Fee and Jamison out of the room and sealing the door behind them. He wouldn't let anyone open that door until he heard Mrs. Taylor give the okay.

"You about to call me a bitch? A whore? Diarrhea again?" Val asked inside the room. She'd expected some kind of confrontation from Mrs. Taylor. Something just like this.

"Nonsense," Mrs. Taylor answered, tucking her blond hair behind her ear like a decent woman would. "I just wanted to congratulate you. That's all. Welcome you into the family."

Val stepped back and took in all of Mrs. Taylor again. "Really?"

"But, of course. Baby, this is the South. And family is family. And you're about to be family. So, we've got to move on."

"Really?"

"Now, I know I have my feelings. And you know my feelings. But we're right here, right now," Mrs. Taylor went on. "And you're marrying my boy. And it ain't in any way I ever would've wanted to, but you young girls have your ways." Mrs. Taylor's eyes went right to the little bump in Val's stomach.

"I know. He's marrying me because I'm pregnant. I'm not stupid."

"You at least love him?"

"Actually, I do. Jamison's a fighting man. Strong. He ain't nothing like any man I've ever been with."

"I know. I made him everything he is." Mrs. Taylor came in so close to Val, only the bump separated their lips. Her next words came like fire from her thorax. "And everything he is better stay the way it is. And if it doesn't . . . you see where the last wife is."

"Understood."

"Good. Glad we could have this talk." Mrs. Taylor stepped back and perked up on cue. "Now, congratulations." She bowed a little to Val and called for Leaf to open the door. Before Val could make it outside, Mrs. Taylor whispered in her ear, "And we'll see about this baby when it's born and we can get the blood results."

The wedding was nothing to remember. It couldn't even be called a wedding. Maybe a marriage meeting. A contract signing. A man read words from a book. Two adults agreed. Papers were signed. No one took pictures. It was done. Mama Fee wondered why she'd taken her fake pearls out of the box in her undergarments drawer.

Just before the meeting, Leaf dismissed himself from the exchange on account of some of the mayor's fires needing tending at his office downtown and a bank check for ten thousand dollars Jamison had ordered Leaf to overnight to a post office box in Los Angeles, so the foursome was alone afterwards. Jamison, being anxious to get back downtown himself, thoughtlessly led everyone right out the front door, thinking the exit would be so swift no one would see his irregular party.

But, even in Forsyth County, a black mayor is still a black mayor and most black faces that passed Jamison, his new wife, his mother, and his mother-in-law, smiled as if they'd discovered some new secret.

Jamison caught on fast and just before the softened wood on the bottom of his shoes tapped the last step in front of Forsyth's courthouse, he knew he'd made a mess.

A voice came calling to confirm this.

"And here he is—Mayor Jamison Taylor." A reporter holding a microphone materialized from nothing and was standing right in Jamison's tracks with a camera crew behind him. He was a young black reporter who'd graduated from Morehouse just a year ago and had his eyes on an anchoring seat at CNN. He was one of those ambitious reporters whose talent was desperation. He didn't sleep. He'd do anything for a lead. And almost everything led him to Mayor Jamison Taylor. This smelled like another such incident. "Care to make a comment?"

"A comment?" Jamison smiled like he should have, but anyone

who was watching the live feed on the news saw the emotional collapse in his eyes.

"Yes. About your new wife. Your marriage." The reporter looked at Val and smiled.

Jamison was suddenly very aware of Val's clothing. How tight her suit was. How red her lips were. Those big diamond earrings. How she was holding on to his arm.

"No comment," Jamison said.

"Reports say you married Val Long this morning. Are you denying that, Mayor Taylor?"

The microphone was pressed back into Jamison's face. The woman at his side was quiet and listening for his response. The women behind him had parted and were nearly leaning over each of his shoulders to hear anything.

"I haven't denied a thing. I just said no comment," Jamison said surreptitiously.

"So, you *did* get married?" the reporter asked.

"Yes."

The reporter grinned and pivoted to face his crew and into the cameras he spoke: "You heard it here first. Mayor Taylor marries his former assistant, ex-stripper Val Long. More later."

Someone in the crew yelled, "Cut!" and the women around Jamison erupted into a massive storm of curses and impolite commentary ranging from the reporter needing to mind his fucking business to suggestions that he was an Uncle Tom trying to ruin a black mayor's reputation.

Mrs. Taylor was about to beat him over the head with her clunky Louis Vuitton purse when Jamison got control and ordered the women to march ahead to the cars in the back of the parking lot and wait for him there. A crowd was gathering and he couldn't risk giving that situation any more weight.

Mrs. Taylor departed, walking backwards and making promises of vengeance against the reporter with each step.

When they were gone, Jamison grabbed the reporter by his shoulder and pulled him away from the camera crew.

"Do we have a problem here?" Jamison asked.

"No problem. I'm a reporter. I was reporting. Everything I said was fact. Right?" The reporter tried to pull away, but Jamison's hold was unbreakable.

"What's your name?" Jamison knew the man's face well. He'd answered some of his questions at a press conference about the bursting pipes downtown last winter. Still, he couldn't recall his name.

"You don't know that?" the reporter laughed. "I've been following you around for months and you don't know that?" He seemed insulted, though he knew big dogs like Jamison Taylor seldom remembered the names of street reporters. "I'm Dax. Dax Thomas. Fox Five News." He put out his hand to shake Jamison's, but it was left hanging there.

"How'd you know I was here, Dax?"

"I didn't. I sit out here every day and wait for something to happen. It's my job."

"Bullshit. You sit outside the courthouse in Forsyth County?" Jamison would've laughed if he hadn't been the target of Dax's investigation.

"Plenty of celebrities come here to—"

"Man, don't play games with me," Jamison said, suddenly sounding more frustrated by Dax's play. "I don't have to tell you who I am, what I can do. We both know you weren't just sitting out here with a full crew for a possibility. You got a lead. Just tell me—who sent you here?"

"Can't tell you, man. You know that. I can't make it in the business if my snitches find out I'm a snitch."

"So this is about making it?" Jamison asked. "You come out here to interrogate a man and drudge up some innocent woman's past so you can make it?"

"Everything's about making it. Right? That's how you got where you're at. That's how I'm getting to where I'm going."

I was itching something awful waiting in the back of that building for Jamison to come around the corner. The only thing that kept me from going back around to the other side and stabbing that reporter with the eyelash blade I keep in my purse was knowing Jamison knew just how to handle the situation. I've been called most anything to my face—bitch ain't nothing but a common noun in the circles I've traveled in. But in those same circles, you have to be prepared for what a bitch is serving back to you if you call her out. I wanted to serve something serious to that reporter. He hadn't called me a bitch, but that was what he'd meant.

"Here he comes," Mrs. Taylor said when Jamison finally came walking toward us. She headed toward him with me and Mama behind her. We were standing in the back of the lot beside my car.

Jamison was pulling off his tie and already on the phone yelling at someone about what had just happened.

"Son, who was that reporter? You need to have him fired!" Mrs. Taylor was repeating what she'd already told Mama that Jamison had the power to do when we were waiting for him to meet us in back of the building. "The nerve of him—to disgrace the mayor! And on television! I was about put him over my knee, and I would've if my heart could take it! You know I got this bad heart." She placed a dramatic Southern hand over her heart.

Jamison didn't acknowledge his mother. He was still spitting into the phone about a leak and his office putting out an official statement announcing our marriage within the hour. His eyes were cutting through me. I felt the fucking blades.

Mama and Mrs. Taylor continued begging Jamison for a response until he got off the phone, but I was quiet. This was everything Jamison had been afraid of. Everything any man I'd ever dated had been afraid of. My past.

Jamison stopped his call and pointed at me. "You're riding with me," he ordered.

"I drove Mama here," I reminded him, but he didn't respond. He kissed his mother on the cheek while ignoring her steady questions

and smiled politely at my mother before walking off to his car expecting me to follow. Instead, Mrs. Taylor was on his heels with more words and nagging that wouldn't likely stop until Jamison promised to kill that reporter himself.

"Mama, I need to meet you back at my house," I said, trying to hand my mother my key fob for the car.

"But I can't drive this car," she said, looking at the shiny car that was probably the only new car she'd ever been in.

"It's fine, Mama. Don't worry," I said still holding the fob.

"But I don't know where you live."

"There's a GPS system. It'll take you right to the house. Just press, 'Home.'"

"But—I—"

"Mama, this isn't a game. I need you to do this shit. Jamison needs me—my husband needs me."

She wanted to complain some more, but she didn't. Heavy histrionics aside, I meant what I was saying and she knew it. She took the key fob.

"I'll be home right behind you," I said as Jamison pulled up beside us in his car. "Lorna will let you in."

"Val," Mama started when I turned to get into the car with Jamison.

I turned back to her.

"Don't get in that car," she said so desperately I actually felt sorry for her.

"Don't worry, Mama," I said. "I'll be fine. I'll meet you at the house. He just wants to talk."

I was barely in the car before Jamison pulled away. He'd thrown his suit jacket in the back seat and his shirt was open.

"You're sweating," I pointed out, looking at beads of sweat on his forehead.

"Val, I need you to answer a question," Jamison said. The veins on his hands were popping out as he held on to the steering wheel.

"What?"

"And don't lie. Because if you lie, I'll know you're lying. And that won't be good." Jamison turned around a corner so quickly the butt of his car sputtered loose gravel everywhere behind us.

"Slow down," I said.

Jamison looked at me.

"I'm just saying, we don't want to get pulled over, too."

"Val!"

"What? What do you want to know?"

Jamison jammed the gas pedal and sped through a red light before gliding onto the highway toward Atlanta.

"Did you call the reporter?" he asked.

"Call the—? You think I—? Really?"

"Don't lie to me!"

"Jamison, you know better than that. Why would I call a reporter?"

"You've been upset about this whole thing. You wanted a big wedding. Wanted it all on the news. You—"

"I wanted to marry you. I got that. I'm not trying to mess that up on the day I get it." I couldn't even believe he was trying to pin the reporter on me. Why would I want that kind of heat? But Jamison wasn't easy to trust anyone. He'd lost a lot of good friends since he'd entered into politics. Apparently, anyone could be bought. And some of his closest friends had the lowest price tags.

"Don't lie to me!" Jamison tapped the gas pedal and we jerked forward as the wheels raced ahead.

"I'm not lying. I've seen that reporter before, but I don't know him. He's not exactly my kind of company."

Jamison banged the steering wheel.

"I know how this looks," I said. "But it's not me. I'm trying to leave my past behind. Not put it on display in front of my mama in front of a courthouse."

"Your past—" Jamison repeated my words in a way that made them sound like a death sentence.

"I never danced at Magic City," I said. "You know that. You met me there. I was not a stripper. That reporter just found my name in the permit book and he's sniffing the wrong pot of piss."

"No one's going to care that you never stripped. They're just going to care that you were going to and that you're married to me now," Jamison said. "I can't believe I got myself into this shit!" He banged the steering wheel again.

"Into what?" I looked down at my belly. "This?"

"Yes—that. And you. This whole thing. It never should've happened. You were my assistant, Val. That's a fucking cliché. I'm going to be a fucking joke. And I'm trying to get ahead of this, but I can't seem to keep things in line. Someone's working against me."

"Well, it ain't me," I said, feeling my eyes get hot. Every time Jamison looked at my stomach, the regret in his eyes made it seem like he'd do something drastic to get rid of me and the baby. He wasn't the only one sleeping with one eye open. I was just holding out for things to get better once the baby got here. Jamison loved his son, and if he loved my baby that much he'd know that I had given him a gift and just maybe he could love me for that gift. Just enough. Love me just enough.

I put my hand on Jamison's knee and started talking softly about him needing to let go of all of the tension if he was going back to the office to handle the situation with the reporter. He couldn't go in there angry. He needed to be calm. Relaxed. He resisted me, but then I started moving my hand in closer to his crotch and joking about us needing to consummate the marriage. I reminded him of the time I gave him head in his office just before he had a press conference to discuss plans to launch the city's first meth addiction hotline. He'd gone to the podium and one of the reporters had immediately pointed out that Jamison's zipper was open.

Jamison laughed at the memory and by then my hand was on his hard penis.

"Pull over," I whispered in his ear.

"Where?" he asked with his voice just as soft as mine then.

"The next exit. I can calm you down."

We stopped at the end of a long driveway that led to the back of a thick wooded area behind a farm. I tried to unzip Jamison's pants in his seat, but he pushed me away and got out of the car before slamming the door so hard the thing shook.

"What are we doing here?" I looked around.

"Get out of the fucking car," he ordered, walking to my door with threatening steps.

"Get out here? But I thought we were—"

"Get out of the fucking car!" He pulled the door open and grabbed my arm before I could get my cellphone from my purse.

"Why here? What are you doing?" I struggled to get away from him, but he managed to get me out of the car and pushed me, chest forward, into the back door. "What are you doing?" I asked and I could hear the fear in my voice.

He came up behind me and started pulling at my skirt with one hand as the other held me in place by the back of my neck.

"This is how you're going to calm me down," he whispered in my ear as I heard him undoing his pants.

My skirt was up over my hips then and he tore through my underwear angrily. I could hear birds chirping in the trees around us; the car's open-door indicator blaring because he'd left it wide open.

"You think you're running this shit, Val?" he said after he'd entered me and was squeezing my neck so tightly I couldn't think of moving. "I control you. You don't control me."

He stroked me in a fight and I panted to control the intense sensations of fear and mysterious pleasure storming through my body.

"You hear me? You fucking hear me?" he demanded.

"Yes," I said in a soft pant.

"Say that shit louder," he ordered. "Say it."

"Yes."

He stopped and pulled me toward the open car door and cocked my right leg up onto the empty seat where I'd been sitting.

"You're gonna scream that," he said, entering me again and stroking harder. His hand went to my hair and he pulled it. "I control you," he said. "Say that shit."

"You . . ."

"Louder!"

"You control me!"

Jamison's hands fell to my hips and he continued his strokes until his breath sounded like a cry and he shook from his waist to his knees.

He backed away from me coldly. Pulled up his pants and went back to his side of the car.

"His First Wife"

"You can't make a man do nothing he don't want to do. Not a thing. You can try. But you can't make him do it. Mark my words! My mama told me that. Her mama told her that."

Kerry was sitting beside Marcy in a hot-pink Adirondack chair. Marcy's chair was painted neon green. Their children—Kerry's son, Tyrian, and Marcy's daughter, Millicent—were steps away in a pool, engaged in a fiercely competitive game of Marco Polo. While six-year-old Tyrian was nearly ten years younger than Millicent, he was a better swimmer and he didn't mind getting his hair wet.

"I know that. But it just doesn't make sense. His assistant? Val?" Kerry responded to Marcy's declaration before adding in a lowered voice, "She's a fucking hoodrat, Marce! A fucking hoodrat."

"A hoodrat Jamison chose!" Marcy pointed out before Kerry tapped her arm to remind her to lower her voice so Tyrian couldn't hear them talking about his father.

"I hear you, but I know what Jamison is capable of. I was married to the man for ten years. This just doesn't fit. Something's up."

"Humpf," the two old friends said together, and both took the moment to reflect on what added up to those ten years that Jamison had been Kerry's and, more importantly, she had been his. Fanning away the summer heat that had them in bikinis and acceptable mommy cover-ups, the women looked up at the behemoth of a house that cast a cooling shadow over the pool. This had once been Jamison's home too. He'd claimed he wanted to live out the rest of his years with his college sweetheart in that Cascade Tudor. But where was he now? And how had he gotten there?

"You think she's pregnant?" Marcy posed the question Kerry had been considering ever since she'd seen the now-infamous news footage of Jamison walking outside of the courthouse with Val beside him in a white suit on their wedding day. It had since gone viral on the Internet, and in days the shotgun interview had been chopped up and bloggers and political gawkers had commented on everything from Mama Fee's terrible wig to Mrs. Taylor's jaw dropping to the cement when the reporter had revealed that Val had been a stripper.

"No," Kerry said solemnly. "He wouldn't sleep with her without a condom." She paused and listened to the children calling "Marco!" and then "Polo!" to one another and then turned to her best friend. "You think he would?"

"I don't put shit past a man—not even my own husband," Marcy said, pulling her sunglasses down beneath her nose and sitting up to look at Kerry. "And you know what happened with that shit. Thank God for late-term abortions and stupid office temps."

Kerry laughed uneasily.

And picking up on her best friend's discomfort, Marcy added, "I don't know though. Not Jamison. Not with that girl. Didn't you say she was damn near illiterate? He likes the smart types. The deep girls." Marcy sat back in her chair and looked back up at the house with Kerry. She had been there when Jamison and Kerry had met. She'd put them together.

Kerry Ann Jackson had been Marcy's roommate at Spelman.

The girls had had nothing in common—Marcy being a loud-mouthed, loud-dressed, big-haired New Yorker and the first in her family to go to college when Kerry was a third-generation Spelmanite and heir apparent of a blueblood, old black Atlanta dynasty that dated back to black men who'd passed as white and owned slaves. Kerry Ann was everything Marcy was at Spelman to become. A legacy. Someone who was "in." Had a good name and good blood. Marcy just needed somewhere to begin. The beautician's daughter decided to set her course to being and mattering on the traditional route that most new to the Atlanta socialite scene took—get the right clothes, join the right sorority, and marry the right man with the right family name. "Right" wasn't subjective here. And Marcy had been making all of the right decisions—all the way down to the man of her dreams. Morehouse man of honor and frat boy supreme was Damien Newsome—the spawn of a select bloodline of Atlanta tradition that crisscrossed both the white and black sides of Peachtree Street. He was bright light beige, had features like a white man, and hair that curled without a curlkit. What the women on campus called a "Good Breed." Pre-med. Smooth. A ticket to something spectacular. Marcy dug into him and wouldn't let up. By senior year, she was getting desperate and needed to drag Kerry to the annual Valentine's ball to act as a decoy to distract Damien's frat brothers while she got her last chance for romance. Back then, there was a belief that a Spelman girl needed to snag her Morehouse man by graduation. She needed her ring by spring, so she'd be jumping the broom that next summer. If she waited, she could lose him—or worse, go back to New York empty-handed. She couldn't—and wouldn't—have that.

The only problem was that Kerry scarcely went to campus functions, hadn't pledged the sorority—though she was a legacy, she seemed to have an aversion to any specimen that lived across the street from her sacred Spelman. She was about her books and her future. No man needed.

But, since Tyrian had been born and was here beating Millicent at Marco Polo in the pool, obviously Kerry had agreed, after much debating, to go to the Valentine's dance with Marcy senior year. There, as usual, the Spelman girl who'd been given the moniker "Black Barbie" by other coeds due to her long black hair and toasty brown skin, broke the hearts of any man who dared approach her. But then there was Jamison. And a spot of luck. A smile from a frozen heart. A spark. New love.

Marcy got her man and the machine moved forward to bind Kerry and Jamison. Marcy got pregnant before she got her ring (or got pregnant to get her ring—it depended on who told the story). Jamison popped the question to Kerry before a serenade compliments of his suited fraternity brothers and happily ever after was planned.

But "ever after" is a long time for two people from different worlds. And in ten years, "ever after" ended.

"Did you ask him about Val?" Marcy asked, turning to Kerry beside the pool. "Like ask him if they were dating?"

"There was no need, Marce. It was obvious. The girl couldn't write a decent sentence and she was making seventy-five-K a year? Where does that happen?"

"Fucking shame! Tax dollars at work!"

Kerry laughed with Marcy.

"But still, it's none of my business. You know? Who he's dating? I don't really care. Our shit is beyond in the past. I dealt with his bullshit for too many years."

"Well, I'm glad you feel that way now," Marcy said, "because that shit you had going on last year with that detective following him around everywhere was beyond crazy."

"I told you, I was just doing that to make sure he was handling the business correctly."

"And I told you, Miss Black Barbie, you can go and tell that lie to someone else. I'm your best friend and I know better. I'm just happy you stopped paying that man."

There was a telling silence.

Marcy looked at Kerry. "You did stop paying that man? Right? Please tell me you don't have a detective following your ex-husband around."

"Yes. I did," Kerry whispered unconvincingly.

"Paying that man $5K a week! I don't care if he was in the FBI. Ain't no fuzzy pictures from the Ramada worth that much money."

"Now you know that wasn't what I was looking for."

"Whatever, Kerry. Just tell me you stopped paying that man." Marcy locked her eyes on Kerry.

"I stopped paying him," Kerry said.

"Good."

"And, for the record, I repeat: I was just doing that to make sure he was handling his business correctly. We both had a lot of money wrapped up in his campaign. Those were funds from the business."

"Yeah, girl, I hear you," Marcy agreed comically before laughing with Kerry.

"And I don't care a thing about the new Mrs. Jamison Taylor," Kerry said. "I just need to know who's going to be around my son. And I don't see why he didn't tell me he was going to marry her."

"I agree. Your son's father getting married is your business. He should've told you something, Kerry." Marcy crossed her arms and scrunched up her face at the sun. "All that shit he put you through—please. He owes you."

A reel of dark images from the past played out in Kerry's head as she pretended to watch Tyrian play—Jamison leaving her twice for the same woman with red hair, coming back to Atlanta on his knees, her trying one last time and realizing there was no candle Jamison could light to resurrect her dead heart.

"Where's that crazy girl, anyway?"

"Coreen? In Los Angeles where Jamison left her, I guess," Kerry revealed. "I haven't heard anything else about her. His story was that she claimed she was pregnant, but when he told her he was coming back home to me, she went and got an abortion. He said it was over. But he still goes back and forth to LA. Claims it's for business."

The women fell silent.

"All that shit stirred up—courtesy of Jamison's silly-ass mother, Mrs. Taylor. All because she couldn't stand the idea of you two being together," Marcy remembered. "I'm like, did she really think her little plot to ruin your marriage would work? Set her married son up with some widow from her church?"

"Actually, if you really think about it, her plan did work. We're not together anymore."

"Old battle-axe! I sure hope she's getting what's coming to her."

"Don't say that, Marce. That woman is very sick," Kerry reminded her friend, and Marcy sobered up fast. Jamison's mother had had a stroke at Tyrian's birthday party a year back. Everyone, including a tear-soaked Tyrian, had thought she was dead. She'd been in and out of the hospital ever since.

"I just want to know how Jamison is going to explain all of this to his son. I mean, how could he get married without even having his son there?" Kerry said. Marcy sucked her teeth at Millicent climbing out of the pool with a head of wet hair.

"I guess we need to get going," she said. "It's going to take me all night to dry this girl's hair. And she's tender headed. What time is Jamison supposed to be here to get Tyrian?"

Kerry looked at the time on her cell phone and peeped Millicent counting as Tyrian went under water to hold his breath. "He's supposed to be here at five, but that'll be six. Maybe seven. Always late."

"Maybe I should stay. Be right here and go in on that motherfucker for you!" Marcy joked.

"Um, no! We saw that last time you all were here when he came to get Tyrian for his weekend visit. Horror!"

"I just asked him what life was like after losing the best thing that ever happened to him," Marcy said, laughing as they remembered her wine-influenced diatribe in which she promised Jamison nothing but ruin would befall him for all the days of what was left of his meager existence—she'd actually used those words.

"I'm not going through that again," Kerry said. "Plus, I have to get out of here as soon as they leave. I'm volunteering at Hell Hath No Fury tonight."

"You and that divorced women's center," Marcy said snidely. "Isn't it time for you to move on? You're pretty far from your divorce now."

"I know, but I can still help other women like me. And I enjoy it. Gets me out of the house, keeps me sane," Kerry said.

"Hanging with me doesn't keep you sane?" Marcy rolled her eyes.

"No. It doesn't."

After Marcy and Millicent had left and Tyrian was dry, fed, and sitting in the living room beside his overnight bag awaiting his father's arrival, Kerry sat across from her son wondering if she should say something. Try to prepare him. It was only months ago that Tyrian had stopped asking for his father in the middle of the night. His therapist said it was his way of asking why his parents weren't together anymore. Why Daddy was no longer available for post-bath back rides and pre-bedtime stories. They lived in separate places, and Daddy was only seen every fourteen days and sometimes further apart than that. His little heart was breaking, and nighttime tantrums were all he could do to express the pain. The therapist had said it would stop and it had. But that was no consolation for Kerry's own heartache, the incessant motherly pangs she felt right at her center anytime anything with the boy seemed out of place. This was motherhood.

She looked at Tyrian's lanky arms and brown skin as he tapped away at something on his iPad. He looked just like his father. A curse her own mother had promised.

"Things might be different at Daddy's house this weekend," Kerry started, careful not to speak with too much purpose.

Tyrian didn't look up. He kept tapping on the iPad. Then, just as Kerry was about to come up with some other way to say what she was meaning, he asked, "How?"

Somehow, Kerry wasn't ready for this prompt. She'd already decided that she wasn't telling Tyrian about Val or the wedding. That was Jamison's job.

"Well," she started. "Well . . ."

Tyrian looked up at her with Jamison's eyes.

"Just different. I just don't want you to be surprised."

"Why would I be surprised?"

Tyrian hadn't seen any of the news footage from the court-house. There was only one television in the entire house and it was in Kerry's bedroom.

"Just by anything new. I want you to keep an open mind. Okay?"

Tyrian shrugged and disappeared into the iPad again.

"And remember that Mommy and Daddy love you and we will always be here for you." This last line was stated only so Kerry could hear it. Tyrian was no longer listening, and if he was, he'd probably wonder why it was the hundredth time he'd heard his mother say this. Since the divorce, the boy associated the string of words with loss and preparation for something horrible. Kerry was about to repeat herself, but luckily for both of them, the doorbell rang.

Tyrian was at the front door pulling it open before his father could respond to Kerry's rigid, unneeded request of identification: "Who is it?"

"Daddy!" he squealed in a way that diminished the actuality of each of the twenty-four-hour periods in the fourteen days since he'd last seen his father and Kerry had been left with the duty of caring for him on her own. Somehow, it always seemed she was greeted less cheerfully when Tyrian returned home.

The boy was fast in his father's arms, his face buried in his great chest. Jamison looked at Kerry, surprised. He was the superhero. Again. Just for showing up. And this was fatherhood.

Kerry looked at the clock. He was two hours late. She wouldn't mention it again.

"Hey, lil man!" Jamison laughed, returning Tyrian's hug. "You got bigger!"

"Bigger? Really, Daddy!"

"Yeah, I'm sure of it. Heavier, too!" Jamison lifted Tyrian's skinny little body higher in a pretend struggle that made Kerry laugh with him. "What you feeding this boy, Kerry?"

"No pork!" Tyrian affirmed.

"That's right," Jamison said. "The black man doesn't eat the white man's pork!"

"Don't tell him that," Kerry insisted with a scowl.

"Why? It's the truth! Ask Brother Farrakhan!"

"Because he goes to camp and says these crazy things and I have to explain it to his teachers."

"All right! Fine, Mommy," Jamison drawled and rolled his eyes with Tyrian. "Well, whatever it is, keep it up. You're about to be a bodybuilder with all of these muscles, man!"

Jamison rolled Tyrian's arm up and pinched the peak of a budding prepubescent bicep. He growled and grimaced at Tyrian, who immediately repeated the wild gesture.

"You ready to go?" Jamison asked as he put Tyrian down.

"Yes!" Tyrian ran into the living room to get his bag and iPad.

"Jamison, I wanted to talk to you before you two left," Kerry whispered.

Jamison just looked at her blankly, though he knew what all she had to say. He'd been putting out the Forsyth County courthouse reporter fires for days. He had no reason to believe the embers hadn't drifted through Kerry's television set, as well.

"About the weekend . . . and your house," Kerry added quickly before Tyrian returned with his things and an eager smile.

Jamison put his hand on the boy's shoulder and thought of how easily he could slip out of the house without saying a thing about Val to Kerry. He'd avoided the conversation for this long and he knew Kerry wouldn't say anything in front of their son.

Tyrian looked up at him.

"You ready, Daddy?" he asked.

"Hey, why don't you go to your room and get some more of your books, so we can read them this weekend," he said.

"Really?" Tyrian dropped his bag and darted up the stairs.

"And get only the best ones," Jamison added. "The ones I haven't read yet."

"Okay!" Tyrian agreed, though he was already long gone.

"What do you want to talk about?" Jamison asked.

"Your new wife. Val."

"What about her?"

As she'd imagined herself doing so many times in the past, Kerry thought of slapping Jamison just then. His answers, always so light and breezy, mocked any attention she gave to any matter. He almost never seemed present with her. And it wasn't that she was asking him to make amends or kiss her ass. Just a simple honest conversation would do.

"Well, she's your former assistant."

"Okay. Half of the world knows that now. What else?"

"And a stripper."

"Something else that's been widely broadcasted. Anything else?"

"Yes, Jamison," Kerry said, filling her voice with a building annoyance at how cavalier Jamison was being. Again, she imagined her open hand slamming against his cheek. "There is more. I don't want her around my son."

Jamison exhaled and stepped back from Kerry, leaning against the front door.

"That's impossible. You know that—"

"No, I don't know anything, because you don't tell me anything."

"Tell you what?" Jamison asked.

"That you were getting married. Was I supposed to find out by seeing it on TMZ like the rest of the world?"

"Yes. I got married," Jamison admitted. "I'm sorry I didn't tell you beforehand. But it wasn't exactly planned."

"I'm coming, Daddy," Tyrian hollered from upstairs.

"Slow down, son," Jamison replied. "Go back and get three more books. We're going to be doing a lot of reading."

"Uggh!" Tyrian pouted at his father's stalling. "Okay."

"Look, Val and I didn't want to do anything big. We were going to make an official announcement yesterday. And I would've told you before that."

"I should've known sooner," Kerry scolded.

"Why? I don't ask you who you're dating." Jamison held up his hands. "We don't play that game. Right?"

"But I have a right to know who's around my son. And I don't like her or want her around my son."

"She wouldn't do anything to Tyrian and you know that."

"No, I don't." Kerry retorted.

"Yes, you do. You're just being—" Jamison knew better than to finish his statement. Any way he could conclude his idea would lead to an argument. And there were only so many books Tyrian could fit into his backpack before the child realized something was up.

"I'm being what?" Kerry pushed.

"Just being difficult—that's all I was going to say," Jamison settled on.

"I'm being responsible. I'm being a parent." This was a jab right in the jaw—a slap in the face that needed no hand.

"So, now you're calling me a bad father?"

"Two days twice a month and I'm supposed to call you a good father? What happened to you taking him to karate on Wednesdays? Coming to tuck him in on Mondays? I give you the opportunity to see your son and you just can't make any—"

"My time is just limited. You know I love my son!" Jamison stopped and lowered his voice. "Don't go there."

"Love and time are two different things. And soon, just saying you love him won't be enough to show up and be a superhero every time."

The words crashed into Jamison's face a little harder than Kerry had intended. Later, she'd remind herself that outcome was the problem with slapping someone with words—you never knew how hard it would hurt.

"Daddy, come pick out a book with me. I can't decide between *Brothers of the Knight* or *Joshua's Masai Mask!*" Tyrian called down to his father at such a time that it seemed he could feel his father's pain from upstairs.

Jamison bit his lip and looked at Kerry hard before heading up to their son's room. He'd deserved that hit. He'd expected it. But that didn't mean it hadn't hurt.

Al Green was talking about something when he sang "Love and Happiness." It can make you do wrong and make you do right. He should've followed up with "Pain and Regret" though, for a little bit of irony, because they seemed to have the same effect. And most assuredly, pain and regret will follow Al Green's love and happiness. They devour them. Eat them whole and spit them out on a war field where there are no rules of battle. Pain and regret make everything ugly. Made me ugly. Made Jamison ugly. Two people who had been dancing to Al Green what seemed like minutes before were now ugly and raw and vengeful like the devil himself . . . and all over one thing . . . a divorce.

Anyone who's been there knows. It's like an endless night that drags you into darkness, and all over a simple piece of paper that signifies the dissolution of something you ought to have known would end—love and happiness. Marriage.

And who were we then? I was new. Unarmed. Blissfully naïve. Open and available.

Jamison was the same. An empty cup. An unlit candle.

We ignored everything anyone had to say. His own mother. My own mother.

We created our love and happiness on top of sand. And when the tide water came in to claim our fickle ground, we emerged from either side of what was left of our marriage with hearts wrapped in alligator skin and fish scales covering our eyes.

He cheated. I took him back. He cheated again. I wished him dead and took half of everything he owned. It was mine too. I'd helped him build it.

I left the battlefield and tried to rebuild again.

But now I don't believe in love and happiness anymore, I don't think.

I don't go to weddings. I gave myself permission to stay at home and watch television. Maybe go to the yoga studio. I just couldn't resist the urge anymore to run up to the bride and groom and warn them of the war coming in the wind. How pain and regret would outplay Al Green. And love and happiness would become a shadow.

I first met Val one rainy Monday morning when I stopped by Jamison's office downtown. Tyrian had promised his teacher his father, the mayor of Atlanta, would come speak at their school's town hall meeting. The only problem was the mayor had no idea about the meeting and though he agreed to do it at the last minute, I was left doing all the running around to make sure things went smoothly and Tyrian got to be proud of his dad again—plus he hadn't seen Jamison in three weeks.

I stopped by the office to pick up a letter from Jamison stating any security details or program desires he needed for the town hall meeting. Val was sitting at a desk looking at her fingernails when I walked in.

She smiled weakly. Asked my name, though I was sure from her glance that she knew exactly who I was. She didn't have to lean over in her seat for me to see the thin strip of flesh that trailed the part between her fake breasts. She was wearing a red dress with red nails and red lipstick. So obvious. Her computer screen was off. Her cell phone was on her desk. A blue screen let me know she was on Facebook.

"He didn't leave anything for you," she said with pretend urgency after I explained that I was there to pick up a letter. "But you can run along and I'll make sure he gets back to you when he returns to the office. I'll email the letter myself."

"It's for his son's school," I said.

"Oh, Tyrian?" She smiled and I just knew. Just knew.

"You know my son?"

"Yes. I met that sweet boy at the house. So cute. Looks just like his father. You think?"

Val was telling me everything I needed to know in her way. The way women shared secrets. She weighted the words "house" and "cute" and "father" with a taunt that said, "I'm fucking your ex-husband."

And I didn't care. After our divorce, Jamison had been spotted in strip clubs and was being courted by half of the social-climbing single sisters in Atlanta. I knew he wouldn't be on the market for long. But there was something about Val that made me . . . just interested. She was so much younger than me. Maybe ten years. Had a skinny neck and skin that might've looked like butter even if she wasn't wearing makeup. She was the kind of woman most black men would stop and look at—ask out on a date just because they had to try. But something about her was dark, angry, and I thought that was probably what attracted most men to her. Attracted Jamison to her. She seemed complicated. Like a trip. A wild ride.

Her cell phone rang. A picture of Jamison was on the screen. I looked at her clear, chunky high heels as she spoke to him softly. Laughing. Twirling around in her seat.

Then I heard my name—mentioned from her lips like she'd said it before.

"Kerry, he wants to talk to you," Val said, looking up at me like I was her mother about to speak to her boyfriend. She held the little cell phone out to me. I almost didn't want to touch it, but knocking it out of her hand like I wanted to would reveal too easily my emotions. I decided to talk to Jamison instead.

"I told you I'd email the list to you, Kerry," Jamison hammered in without saying hello.

"I said I would come get it," I answered. Both he and I knew this was just nonsense—my stopping by the office for a document that I probably hardly needed. But in the face of my desire to see where he was working, I had to rest my wants on a visit. During the divorce I'd assumed fifty percent of the current and future profits of a lawn care business Jamison had started when we got married. Rake It Up was the Southeast's most profitable black-owned manicuring corporation. Jamison made more than five million dollars a year and he wasn't happy about giving me a dime associated with what he'd called his success, but a judge wasn't convinced that my connections and assistance early on in the business hadn't contributed to its success. So after months in battle, I got half. When Jamison decided to run for mayor, he needed capital, so I bought him out for another ten percent and loaned him ten percent. I then had the lion's share of the power over a self-sufficient business that had a CEO and needed little more from me than a signature here and there. I was rich. I didn't have to work another day in my life. And so was Jamison. Rich and free. And when he won the election, he became rich and free and powerful.

"Fine, then," Jamison said on the phone. "I'll just have Val give you a list. Can you wait?"

"I'll wait," I said.

Jamison said something to Val and she powered up her computer like it was the "flux capacitor" in Back to the Future. The thing struggled to attention like it hadn't been turned on in days.

I sat down and watched her type out the letter with one finger. I took a picture and texted it to Marcy with a note: Jamison's new assistant.

She responded as only a best friend could: Assistant dick holder?

When I finally gave up and was about to leave the office without the letter, I heard the printer begin to churn out a page and Val turned to me announcing that she was "All done."

"Great," I said, standing up to get the letter.

She stood, gathering the letter from the printer, and I saw that her skirt barely covered her upper thigh and a large red butterfly that looked more like a bleeding bat was etched into the space just above her right knee.

She handed me the letter and I read quickly what sounded like something Tyrian had written a year ago when he was in kindergarten. There was no date, no address, she'd managed to misspell "Kerry," and her sentences sounded like she'd typed exactly what Jamison had said over the phone. She'd misspelled "sincerely" and had the nerve to try to take the paper back from me so she could sign Jamison's name.

"No need to sign it," I said. "I'll just take it like this." (I was going to toss the thing as soon as I walked out.)

"Okay." She rolled her eyes at my quick movement and went back to her seat.

"Hey, how long have you been working here? For Jamison?"

"Just a few weeks."

"And he's paying you?"

Val must've caught onto my tone because her next response was tampered with a mix of braggadocio and defensiveness.

"Yes, seventy-five-K. You looking for a job or something?"

"No. My days of working for Jamison are long gone," I said. I folded the letter and was about to walk out, but I saw in Val's eyes that she was about to say something.

"You ain't better than me," she said.

"I didn't—"

"No, you didn't, but I know what you're thinking. I saw you take a picture of me when you were waiting. What, you into girls now?"

"I didn't take a picture. I was just—"

"It's fine. I know what you were doing. Because I know what women like you do. But remember that you ain't better than me. We want the same things. We just go about getting them a little differently," Val said. "And you don't have to worry about my job, or how much I make. I'm Jamison's assistant, and trust me, he's well taken care of. I earn every dime of that salary."

"Allies and Alpha Males"

For a politician, the media machine is a gift and curse. A complex casino where a loser can come out a winner or a winner could emerge a pauper or champion of the world. Interestingly (or ironically—depending on how things turned out), one just never knew how things might end up from one day to the next. The media machine is a ferocious eater and a man who looked lucky at 9 AM might be pulse-free by noon . . . and then resurrected like Jesus Christ by seven that night. It all depended on the spin. How the chips fell on the green craps table that looked like life. How the pundits polled. How the little grandmas who sat glued to their televisions from dusk to dawn clicking from CNN to FOX News felt the headline related to their church or their checks or to the mundane choices they made each day and felt some politicians were set to take control or take away a right they weren't even using.

The calamity outside the courthouse in Forsyth could've gone so many ways for Jamison. A new mayor in an old city like Atlanta is born with a mark on his back. There was too much money and too many powerbrokers in the city that housed the world's busiest airport for backstabbing and treachery not to be a factor at play for the man who was in charge of it all. It wasn't just par for the course. It was the religion of Atlanta politics. Polite smiles over mint juleps. Knives in necks over an unsigned contract. And one little pseudo stripper turned assistant turned wife made Jamison a next target. An easy mark. He quickly became a joke. Something no one needed to worry about.

But then . . . everything changed.

A baby was born at the Atlanta Zoo. No one even had known the mother was pregnant. But one morning a pink little miracle was screaming and hollering begging not to be crushed by his mother. The news vans that had been parked outside of the mayor's mansion got on the road and headed to I-20 to descend upon what seemed to make men and women and children gasp in amazement—a little furry baby bear. Polls went up on websites. What would they name the panda bear? How long would it be before he took his first steps?

The furry thing eclipsed the mangled mayor. New news was new news. And after a while, Jamison's old deed seemed less spectacular and shameful and more ordinary and predictable. Men in barber shops were saying things like, "Man, she probably pregnant. This stripper from Macon got my cousin caught up on some shit like that, too. I feel sorry for the brother." Women were saying things like, "A man is a man. Always gonna be a man. Wonder what kind of awful things his first wife did to him that he turned to some back-street trash like that." There were variations on these sentiments, of course, but the point was that in just one month, Jamison went from being a media loser to being a media winner. And his purse was filling up fast.

Apparently, the viral video had gotten him more attention both nationally and internationally. People laughed at him, yes. But after they laughed, they looked into Jamison's profile and it was what they found that ultimately endeared him to them. His life read like a comeback-kid novel. Born to loving parents in the poorest neighborhood in Atlanta. His father had died when he was a kid and Jamison's mother had been left to raise a man on her own. He had always been good in science. A mentor paid his way through Morehouse so long as he promised to go on to medical school upon graduation. But he was in love with a Spelman coed named Kerry and though he'd been accepted to Cornell medical school, he stayed in Atlanta to help her through a rough patch. He married her. He started Rake It Up with a cousin and a van and a lawn mower. In three years, he took over most of the commercial lawn care contracts in Atlanta. In three more years, he was opening offices in other states. Soon, he was a millionaire. He decided to run for mayor when the current mayor had shut down all of the midnight basketball programs in the city and used the money to build a new wing at the airport. Jamison's campaign slogan: "For every resident, a new promise."

Jamison walked into the back door of the Bill Campbell Community Center in Kirkwood just as the monthly fraternity meeting for his alumni chapter was concluding. He was wearing a deep black Italian suit and a lavender shirt. His fist-shaped fraternity pin was centered on his left lapel, right over his heart.

He seldom attended the fraternity meetings. It was something he just hadn't had time for since he started Rake It Up, but every now and again he used the meetings as an opportunity to be in an assembly of brothers who'd made a verbal vow to have his back and most of whom had actually followed through on that during his uphill battle of a campaign. And it didn't hurt that many of the men huddled in the forty-to-fifty-person meeting were major movers in the city. The president of the chapter was also chair of the board of trustees of Grady Hospital. The only black man on Georgia's Supreme Court was head of the mentoring program. The sergeant-at-arms was the chief of police. There were clinic-owning doctors. Practice-owning lawyers. Principals. Professors. Pastors. And professional athletes. And they were all connected to three Greek fraternity symbols and could be found in one place at the same time.

When Jamison walked in, there were hugs and whispers in his ear. Some brothers reminded him of promised lunch dates. Others just asked that he let them know if he needed anything at all. The other brothers fell into pairs and small groups to gossip and plan, project and remember. Barbershop talk in suits.

The meeting space at the back of the community center looked like a huge cafeteria. Many of the brothers had been vying to move the meeting to a more luxurious locale. They had connections to ballrooms in major hotels downtown. Boardrooms in Midtown. "Shouldn't the men of this frat have the best?" But the old guard, the men who'd made an Alpha male out of Jamison, reminded them of otherwise. The brothers were to be a beacon of manhood and prosperity within the community. If they were going to serve the people, they had to be with the people. And that included chapter meetings where the service was being organized. "If one young brother sees us with our pants up and our heads high and thinks, 'I want to be like that man when I grow up,' then our job is halfway done," one gray-haired brother once said. The meetings at the Bill Campbell Community Center were to continue.

"Mr. Mayor Taylor . . . in the flesh!" Judge Emmit Lindsey was a sometimes active member of the chapter who leveraged his power on the bench and lined pockets to become a political juggernaut and general back-page-news gossip churner. His arms were open toward Jamison, though Jamison never really knew where he stood with him. He was slim. In his late sixties, but obviously took good care of himself.

"Judge Lindsey!" Jamison fell into the man's embrace and gave him a tight fraternity grip only an old-timer like Emmit could appreciate. "Just the man I've been looking for. I thought I heard you retired and moved to Montego Bay!"

"That's a kind joke, son," Emmitt said laughing. "And if I had my way, it wouldn't be too far from the truth."

"I'm sure Judge Clara Neale Lindsey wouldn't mind making a move like that," Jamison added, making sure to say the woman's full name as she liked it called in her courtroom. Emmit's wife was also a judge and a member of Kerry's mother's sorority chapter.

"Yeah, that Clara likes to soak up the sun . . . yes, she does," Emmit countered solemnly.

"How's she been feeling, man?" Jamison asked, while embracing another brother who'd walked up to say hello.

"Feeling better. Not good. But better," Emmit said. Two years earlier, Clara had found a lump in her right breast. Being the fortuitous leader she was, she had taken the news that the lump was malignant as a call to act. She had a full mastectomy on both breasts and returned to work a month later with a pink ribbon on her shirt. Three months later the doctor found new sick cells in her spine. The answer to that battle wasn't as clear. She was still fighting. "Glad you asked."

"She's a good woman, you know? Just let me know if you two need anything."

Emmit grinned. "Don't you mean, let *us* know?"

"Us?"

"You speak for two now, Mayor Taylor."

After a pause and a thought, Jamison said jokingly, "Oh, you heard?"

"The whole fucking world heard!" Emmit blasted Jamison so hard the other brothers around them started laughing with him. "What the hell is wrong with you? On my flat-screen television looking confused as hell? Got that young Morehouse man all in your face? Don't you all have a code against that or something?" Emmit was an Emory University grad who loved picking on the Morehouse brothers in the chapter.

"I can't call it. You know?" Jamison laughed at the brother. People had been making fun of him for weeks, but there was something about the jokes from his brothers. It was coming from a place he knew. There was no disrespect or name calling going on. Just a little comical honesty.

"I do know. I just hope you know," Emmit said, winking at Jamison.

"Shut your old angry ass up!" an older man with a round belly that made him look thirteen months pregnant ordered, bumping into Emmit purposefully.

"Oh, Scoot, ain't nobody talking to your crusty ass," Emmit said as Jamison greeted the other man with a hug, as well.

"You fools should be. I say let the man make his own decisions. Live his life. Make mistakes." Scoot looked into Jamison's eyes with careful speculation. He was a retired detective who'd been serving as the chapter's historian for seventeen years.

"Oh, there's no mistake here, gentlemen," Jamison proclaimed. "I love my wife." He smiled as he had practiced in the mirror before the press conference he'd held with Val just three days after the wedding.

Emmitt and Scoot looked at each other with wide smiles and then, after a little straightening, back at Jamison. They knew what he was doing. They knew why he was doing it.

"Well, that's wonderful, young brother," Scoot said as earnestly as he could after having three shots of bourbon before coming to the meeting. He patted Jamison on the shoulder.

"Young love. Good as gold," Emmit added, patting Jamison's other shoulder.

"Good as gold," Scoot repeated. "And, on that note, I believe I have a date with my favorite friend—Jack Daniel's." He laughed a little and pointed both index fingers at Emmit before starting out the door.

"Oh, I'm coming," Emmit said. "Jamison, you coming out with the old men for drinks? It's fellowship time."

"Drinks? Where?"

"You know. The Rainforest," Emmit revealed, referring to the rainforest-themed basement bar of another brother.

"Oh, hell, last time I hung out there I almost lost my wallet," Jamison recalled.

"That's all?"

The two laughed, and Jamison quickly looked over both shoulders before he spoke again.

"Hey, I actually wasn't joking when I said I was coming in here to see you."

"What's going on?" Emmit's softened demeanor matched Jamison's new low tone.

"I need some information, and I know you're the guy to get it from."

"Oh, my ear hasn't been to the streets in a minute," Emmit said, using his normal bow-out in a routine that both parties knew would end with Jamison getting the information he needed—if he begged in the right way.

"Come on now, Judge. Everyone knows the streets don't move unless you allow the stop lights to change. I'm just the man in the pictures." When Jamison was running for mayor, Emmit became a kind of unofficial mentor to the new politician. He knew the right hands to shake. The right shoulders to rub. And the snares to avoid. His friendship promised Jamison reprieve from a testy old guard that Emmit knew well. All the old-timer sought in compensation was loyalty and privilege. Though Jamison wasn't always sure from which pocket Emmit was drawing, he knew he needed his insider knowledge and influence.

"Stop it, now," Emmit said. "I'm just an old judge on his way to retirement. You said it yourself." Emmit pushed his fingers into his pocket to begin to play with his car keys.

Jamison knew then that he was prepared to talk. "I need to know what's up with Ras. With his case." Jamison stepped back and put his hands up to show how serious he was about needing the information.

"Ras? Come on, man. Everybody knows that's a done deal. Eleven pounds of marijuana in his trunk? Easy felony. The judge will take a nap on that case. Bring the gavel down on the side of justice."

"It isn't that simple," Jamison said. "He's a Rastafarian. It was his weed."

"Well, he must be getting pretty fucking high."

"You know the particulars of the case, Emmit. It was for his brothers at his house."

"Brothers or no brothers, he's going to prison. Intent to distribute," Emmit pointed out. "And you know that. Makes me wonder why you're even asking."

"We went to school together. He's a good man."

"A good man who likes white girls and weed," Emmit laughed. "Now how's a Rastafarian going to get pulled over doing ninety-three in a BMW with a topless white girl in the passenger's seat and a trunk full of pot? If the court don't kill him, those nappy-headed Rasta women will."

Jamison nodded along with Emmit's equation for the perfect storm. But, really, the more he'd thought about it, the storm just seemed a little too perfect. Ras had been his roommate at Morehouse for one year. He knew the man was harmless.

"You stay away from that, son. You've got enough heat on you right now. Last thing you need is a white girl with her little pink titties out in the front seat of your car."

Jamison nodded again. What he wouldn't tell Emmit—or rather thought he couldn't tell him—was that just a week before Ras got caught doing ninety-three on 85N, his old roommate had agreed to close a major deal Jamison had been hoping to pull off with the starting five players of the Atlanta Hawks. Before the last mayor shut down the city's midnight basketball program, Ras had been the director, and for years he'd been talking about getting the NBA players together to sponsor his program. Once the program had been shut down, Ras had continued to finesse the relationships, and when Jamison got into office, he'd shown up at Jamison's door with his dreadlocks down to his waist and told the new mayor of his plan—the starting five players had committed to donating a million dollars per year each to a scholarship fund for as long as they were contracted with the Hawks. The kick was that the scholarships would pay full college tuition, room, and board for college-bound black males from Atlanta's poorest neighborhoods. When news of Ras's arrest got out, the players got skittish about the deal, considering their squeaky-clean NBA images. Jamison hadn't been able to connect with any of them since.

"That may have been your boy way back when," Emmit started, leaning into Jamison, "but this is me telling you to stand back. Don't go around here asking questions about that man."

"But he just had weed—"

"Eleven pounds. Listen to me, son," Emmit said. "Don't make that your cross to bear. Not because he's your old roommate—who gives a shit about that? And not because he's some drugged-up community organizer—more will come along. Let it go. That's for your own good." Emmit winked and clicked back on his heels. "Now, I believe my brothers are waiting on me at the Rainforest. You coming along?"

"Yeah, I'll stop by. Just give me a second," Jamison said.

"Suit yourself."

Jamison went to say hello and good-bye to a few more familiar faces, but through each of those conversations his mind was still on Ras and Emmit's advice to stand down for his "own good." He hadn't even mentioned to Emmit that he'd intended to do anything, but here the old brother was giving him such solid directives. That wasn't uncommon coming from Emmit's ilk. They were always doling out advice, and since Jamison had started out on his campaign trail they'd been whispering in his ear what he could and couldn't do. And Jamison was no fool. He knew he had to listen most times. Because those men talking to him were listening to someone else. But something about the situation with Ras was picking at his gut. So, with this on his mind, Jamison went along smiling and shaking more hands. He spoke to the chapter president about making an appearance at the fraternity's annual blood drive and promised to donate a thousand dollars in new furniture for a home they were building for a single father of three who'd lost his house to a fire that had claimed his wife and youngest child. After he had finally made a horseshoe shape through the crowd and had even stopped to take a few pictures with some of the younger brothers, he was heading to his car when he felt a light tap on his shoulder. He thought it was Emmit reminding him about the Rainforest and turned quickly to tell him that he was on his way right behind him, but it was one of the younger brothers he'd just taken a picture with inside the community center.

"I'm ssss-sorry to disturb you, Brother Taylor—I-I-I mean Mayor Taylor," he said nervously. Jamison noted that he had a slight stutter because he paused between many of his words to refocus his tongue.

"Brother, it's fine," Jamison allowed, smiling.

The man stood for a second and just looked Jamison over the way he always thought white people tended to do whenever he traveled to speak in areas outside of the city.

Jamison held his hand out to remind the man to introduce himself.

"Oh," he said excitedly, taking Jamison's hand. "I'm Keet Neales . . . Brother Keet Neales."

"Great to meet you, brother."

"I wanted—wanted to thank you for taking that picture with me."

"It's always an honor."

"And I wanted to just speak to you f-f-for a second. I'm a police officer," Keet revealed.

"Okay." This was no news to Jamison. Keet had been chatting with a group of five fellow officers who'd invited Jamison to join their mentoring program session before the next meeting.

"I've been on the force for a few years and I'm—I'm looking to get out." There was a pause. "I want to—want to go into politics."

Both Jamison and Keet seemed relieved that Keet had gotten this all out. The tension between his tongue and nerves had his doughy complexion turning a light rose from forehead to chin.

"That's great. We could always use a few more of our own out there," Jamison said in his public, media-friendly voice. Really, at that point, his words meant nothing. It was just about pleasantries. His mind was still on Ras. And most every day someone was cornering him to tell him about his or her new venture into politics. It was like writing a book—everyone wanted to do it and had the greatest ideas, but when it came time for the follow-through and people realized they'd have to roll up their nice shirts and get their hands bloody just to make an outline for the thing, they bowed out before they finished the first try.

"Really? You think so?" Keet was beaming like a little boy. His color returned. His eyes drank Jamison in.

"Sure. The more the merrier." Jamison patted Keet on the back the way the older brothers had done to him. It signified that the conversation was over. He smiled and started toward his car again.

After three steps, he heard, "So—so, can I come work for you, Mayor Taylor?"

Jamison didn't stop. "Get your resume to my assistant. Let him know you're my frat brother."

Keet watched Jamison walk all the way to his car before turning back to return to the community center.

In 1976, Brother Renaldo Lex showed up at his three-bedroom bungalow in East Atlanta with a five foot papier-mâché palm tree one of the students in his art class had made as a final project. His girlfriend, Pearl, with whom he'd had three children but had never married, stood out in the driveway looking confused as he pulled the palm tree out of the back of his van. Pearl didn't say anything though. Renaldo was a failed painter who'd missed out on so many opportunities to do what he'd loved; questioning him about just anything threatened to send him into a drunken rage. Still, Renaldo was a reasonable man and the house was actually Pearl's so he told her what the tree was for on his way into the house. "Building me a bar in the basement. A place where my frat brothers can come and drink." Pearl just smiled at the man she loved, and like most women in love with men like Renaldo, she secretly hoped his plan failed fast enough so that no one got hurt or killed—or hurt and then killed.

When Renaldo set the ugly palm tree in the middle of the floor in the unfinished basement, "Rainforest" was the first word that came to mind, so from there everything else he brought to go into what Pearl was calling his "little lair" had to match that "theme": the life-sized orangutan from a local arcade that had closed down, stringed lights decorated with miniature plastic bananas, dingy mosquito nets from the Salvation Army, and so on. Soon, lumpy green couches, hard brown chairs, and tables edged a tacky tiki bar that had WELCOME TO THE RAINFOREST etched into a wooden plate on the front of its overhead glass holder.

Thirty-six years later and no one was hurt or killed and Renaldo's old basement bar was still serving drinks to frat brothers. It was open twenty-four hours a day, three hundred and sixty-five days a year. No one worked there, but everyone got served, the bar was always stocked, and the little money the Rainforest made paid off Pearl's mortgage ten years before Renaldo died of a massive heart attack in his classroom, so she was still a happy woman.

While Jamison was sure the old dust that lined almost every surface in the Rainforest had been responsible for the little rash he'd gotten on his neck just three hours after he'd pledged and been invited to the Rainforest as a rite of passage, he still frequented the hideaway to reminisce about some romp he'd been pressured into there that had proved to him that he was still a boy or else make fun of its dated décor that hadn't changed one bit since 1976. The old joke was that the only thing that changed at the Rainforest was "the bottles and the brothers—due to those who'd passed on like Renaldo (and may God—who is frat—bless his soul)."

Emmit and Scoot were at the tiki bar in the Rainforest plenty drunk when Jamison walked in. They pointed at him and laughed, hollering something purely nasty that Jamison dared not commit to memory. As always following a chapter meeting, the bar was packed with brothers—well, as packed as a bar could be that was housed in the basement of a three-bedroom bungalow in East Atlanta. There were even a few women peppered here and there between brothers and on laps. No wives or girlfriends or longtime sweethearts or sorority sisters to worry about. Just women who knew what they were there for and abided to such planned and unplanned activities as they came.

One woman met Jamison midway through his entry with a beer in her hand.

"I heard you liked Golden Monkey," she said, her arm outstretched. She was much shorter than Jamison. Had a petite, hard body and a face that made him wonder how beautiful her mother must be. Soft lips. Colored pink.

Jamison took the beer and kissed the woman on the cheek.

She walked away. She'd come back to say hello later.

"You made it, young buck," Scoot said, watching Jamison as he took a seat on a stool at the bar beside the one that was no doubt struggling to support Scoot's jolly girth. "Thought you were going to stand us old ladies up."

"Never that. You two are my favorite sweethearts." Jamison clanked his beer against Scoot and Emmit's glasses of Jack Daniel's.

As usual, time was easy but ferocious in the dank, harshly decorated basement. There was an endless stream of jokes and laughter. Toasts. Women taking shots off of one another. Old stories. Card games. Brothers being carried out and in. And then the men were all four hours older. And then five. Six.

Jamison was on his third Golden Monkey. He knew better than to move off of his stool. The petite girl had returned and was standing beside him, laughing at Scoot's old-timer "Shine and the Titanic" jokes and rubbing Jamison's back like they'd known each other for a long time or not at all.

Emmit had gone outside to talk with another brother he'd been in business with for a while. They were silent owners of a massage parlor on Piedmont in Buckhead. It was crewed by dozens of non-English-speaking Vietnamese women who might be underage but were definitely illegal. The place catered to a stable list of regulars—cops and lawyers, businessmen who claimed to visit the Lotus Health Club because they liked the authentic Vietnamese food and cheap drinks. Emmit, who'd served in the Vietnam War for two weeks before it ended in 1975, had absolutely no visible ties to the parlor. According to business and tax records, the sole proprietor was a Vietnamese woman named Lang. Her daughter, Natalie, had finished at Spelman two years before Jamison. She was half black and had tiny elf-like ears like Emmit's, but she'd never met him.

"So, what's going on at de mayor's office," Scoot asked after he'd finished telling his jokes.

"Lots of paperwork and baby kissing," Jamison said.

"Ass kissing, too. I'm sure of it."

"Now that's always on the menu."

"I was playing golf with Governor Cade the other morning and he seemed pretty entertained by your recent headlines." Scoot chuckled.

"I'm sure he was," Jamison said, shaking his head disapprovingly. Governor Cade was a white-haired Republican who openly longed for the old South that had been dying since he was a boy. Not that he wanted segregation and for the world to be unkind to those who hadn't been lucky enough to be born in his world, white, and male, but he dreamed of a place where things could be less complicated, and there were clear lines he understood and he could move as he wished. Simple. Every man was responsible for his family. And how he fed them was his own making. He was one of the suburban business types who avoided "colorful" Atlanta and only mixed crowds when a deal was at stake. Since Jamison had been in office, he'd only seen the governor at press conferences and sometimes at events where they'd been forced to take pictures together. Jamison noticed that Cade hardly spoke to younger black men and mostly sent messages to him through the likes of Emmit and Scoot. "Don't take it too hard, young man," Scoot said. "We all get caught with our dicks in the sucker sometimes. You just have to get a better strategy next go round."

When Emmit walked back into the bar, he was following behind a woman in blue shorts, black fishnet tights, and stylish wire-rimmed glasses. Her hair was long and blond and messy. She kissed the woman beside Jamison on the lips and ordered a drink for Emmit.

Scoot and Emmit and half the other brothers their age in the bar watched the girl's soft buttocks move around in her shorts as she purposefully leaned over the bar. The woman beside Jamison stopped rubbing his back and started rubbing hers.

Scoot kept on joking like nothing was happening, but Jamison reminded himself that he'd need to leave soon. There was a time in any night like this in a place like that when men like Jamison had to be gone. The men were seven hours older, and the beer and liquor was setting in. Night was outside. Things could go any way from there. And though not one soul had any intention of remembering that Jamison was there, the potential for a snitch in the sacred space grew as he became more powerful.

He looked at the women. They were girls. If men ever thought like that, Jamison might discern that they were a little more than half his age. Just young enough to be Emmit's granddaughters. They were laughing.

"You okay, baby?" the petite girl named Iesha asked Jamison. "You want some more beer?"

She almost fell into Jamison, but Scoot caught her and all of her attention transferred to him then.

"He don't want no beer, girl. If you came here thinking you're just going to be serving up beer all night, you're mistaken," Scoot pointed out, but his voice was more playful than commanding.

The girl's answer wasn't: "I came here for more than that."

It seemed everyone in the bar heard this affirmation, and there was this invisible ear turning.

The girl in the fishnets was all the way up on Emmit's lap in the chair, whispering something in his ear. The way his muscled, gray-haired arms were wrapped around her waist made her look like a child about to be carried upstairs to bed. But then there were hands firmly placed on her butt.

Jamison turned to listen in on Iesha making promises to Scoot. He wondered if his beer had worn off yet. He tried to step down from the stool and realized it hadn't. It was 2 AM. Too late to drive home with even a little bit of alcohol in his system. No way any cop would miss that chance to get his name in the papers. He thought of calling Val to come and get him. Leaf. He sat up a little more and laughed at something stupid Scoot was saying to Iesha: "You can bounce up and down on my stomach for thirty minutes until this Viagra sets in."

Jamison glanced over at Emmit to avoid seeing Scoot pull his infamous bottle of Viagra from his shirt pocket. Awaiting his spectatorship was another vision he'd seen previously but was never quite prepared for—Emmit's whole tongue was caged in the mouth of the girl on his lap. She was gyrating over him to some song no one else heard, but they all, men and women, watched like they were privy to her tune. The bartender, a younger brother who volunteered at the Rainforest to get to know the older brothers, cleared a mess of empty glasses from behind Emmit as the girl pushed him back into the bar.

Jamison tried again to busy himself. He pulled out his phone and looked for something he wasn't really seeking. His last text message had been received at 10 PM. It was from Kerry: Are you coming to Tyrian's golf tee on Saturday morning? He keeps asking me about it.

Jamison heard the other brothers in the bar cheering. He responded yes to Kerry's message. He looked at her name for a few seconds. Looked at the talk button. Heard the cheering. Saw the girl's boots on the bar. He remembered Kerry's hair. How long it had been when they met. She'd always worn it out, too. He thought to press talk but knew it was the beer pushing him on. Then the phone rattled in his hand. It was a message from Kerry: You respond five hours later at 3 a.m.? Really? WTH?

The cheering stopped. Iesha had pulled the blonde off of Emmit, and the two girls, who Jamison had seen take on drink after drink, were stumbling to the back of the bar area, where there were two bedrooms and a bathroom.

"Young girls will kill you for sure," Emmit said, elbowing Scoot.

"Nah, they won't kill you until they get that money out of you," Scoot said. He got up and tucked his shirt into his pants in a way that was meant to make him look dignified. He grabbed another drink off the bar and gave a military salute to his comrades before waddling toward the back of the bar area.

Emmit made the sound of a plane taking off and moved his stool over closer to Jamison's. He was drunker than Jamison had ever seen him. His eyes were red and his breathing was so heavy his head tilted back and forward with each breath.

He seemed to notice how Jamison was looking at him and straightened up a little on the stool—as much as he could.

"So, tell me, what are you going to do about that Uncle Tom reporter?" Emmit asked.

"Guess I need to talk to him," Jamison said. "Have to. I have a long way to go in office and I can't have him sniffing around every time I fart. Got to find out what's got him up my ass."

"Fuck 'is ass!" Emmit declared harshly, and then he laughed at his outburst. "What the young people say—no homo?"

"I know what you meant."

"That fool ain't got no territory in this motherfucker. Just young and dumb. Thinking he can use his stories to make it to CNN. Take more than that."

Jamison watched a few brothers trail one another to the back of the bar with their hands moving in and out of their pockets.

"He's falling for that Obama post-racial America shit. We'll see who gets his ass when the white people are done with him."

"White people?" Jamison quizzed. The way Emmit said the words was so solid it sounded like he might have a clue who was behind Dax.

"Oh, no, man." Emmit seemed to straighten up as he read Jamison's interest. "I don't mean it like that. I mean in general. But we can find out. I can have him pumped." Emmit looked at Jamison hard. By pumped he meant he'd get a full folder of everything Dax had ever done in his life. Anything and everything. Deeds and dirt. If he loved his mama, Jamison would know. If he liked kiddie porn, Jamison would know. Politicians, bigwigs, and shakers used pumps to keep folks in line. None of the information was ever reported to the police—they were usually the ones who delivered the pump to the person being pumped. The person who requested the pump just used it to gain clout in the dispute, whatever it was.

"He's clean," Jamison said, even though he might not have revealed that much information to Emmit if he wasn't drunk. He'd already ordered one the night after the scene at the courthouse.

"Clean?" Emmit laughed as he got up from his stool. "Ain't nobody clean."

Though no one had left, the bar was half empty. The only people left were couples sprinkled around on the couches, leaning into one another.

"Ain't nobody clean. Ain't no old lady clean. The pope—that nigga ain't clean," Emmit went on.

"I checked, Emmit," Jamison repeated.

"No, you didn't."

"What are you saying?"

Emmit picked up a toothpick off the bar and pulled a little meat from his right front tooth that had been bothering him all night.

"I'm saying," he said while sucking the little piece of flesh back into his mouth, "let me order the pump. My man is good."

"Really? You'd have Dax pumped for me?" Jamison looked at Emmit crossly. This was the kind of exchange two men who liked each other or owed each other had. He was never really sure how much Emmit liked him, so he wondered what he owed him. What he'd want.

"Yes, young man, I would."

"For what? What will I owe? Or do I owe you already?"

Emmit stretched and turned in a way that let Jamison know he was heading to the back of the bar with everyone else.

"You leave the Ras situation alone . . . stop asking questions, and we'll call it even." Emmit grinned and waited a few seconds before turning away from Jamison. "I'll have the pump to you by the end of the week. I think my grandson has a golf tee with your son on Saturday. Be there and we'll talk."

Jamison didn't respond. It was customary that he not do so for so many reasons.

"You coming back here to see about these girls? Compliments of the house," Emmit asked as Jamison got up from his stool.

"No, big brother. I'm headed out to my car to sleep this off," Jamison said.

"Suit yourself," Emmit said. "And make sure you sleep in the passenger's seat."

"I got you."

"Desperate Housewives"

Jamison woke up to sedans rolling past him filled with people on their way to church. The sun was up and bright, making everything outside of the front window of his car carry a white light around its edges. The inside of his car was warm and the pool of sweat that had been gathering on the leather beneath where he'd rested his head on the passenger's seat would be dry in minutes once he was behind the wheel.

Most of the cars that had lined the street outside of Brother Renaldo's house were gone, but some still remained. He checked to see if he could spot Scoot's truck or Emmit's Porsche, but neither was in sight. After looking at the time, he knew he'd missed a meeting and two church appearances. He didn't have to look at his phone to see how many times Leaf and probably a few other people, including his mother, had called. He just turned on the car and drove home.

He walked into the kitchen, where Val was moving around trying hard not to look like she was waiting for him.

It was a little after 10 AM, but she was fully dressed. And not in church clothes. She'd started wearing these floral-print shorts and slacks with matching tank tops he'd seen some of the other women wearing in the neighborhood. Today the shorts were pink and white and green. The tank top was lime green. None of it looked good on Val. It was the kind of stuff Kerry might wear. Jamison figured Val was trying to fit in, maybe appear the way she thought she should look, being his wife—that's what his publicist, Muriel, had instructed Val to do after suggesting she get a stylist. Val, of course, took offense to this and went about doing the work herself. She'd asked about having her auburn hair weave removed: "It doesn't look like the mayor's wife. Does it?" Jamison had just shrugged. He agreed but didn't know what else she could do with her hair. If she even had any on her head. She was always wearing wigs and weaves.

"Leaf called you three times. He came by here like an hour ago," Val said, removing the hot water kettle from the stove. Lorna was off on weekends. "Your mother called twice, too. I didn't pick up though. Didn't think she was trying to hear my voice."

Jamison put his keys and cell phone on the counter where he always left them and continued walking toward the staircase to get upstairs.

"Jamison!" Val called, but it sounded more like shriek.

This little scene, short as it was, mirrored how most of their days had been together since the day at the courthouse a month ago. Val tried to pull Jamison into some exchange that was disguised as being casual, with no expectations. Jamison built an impenetrable fortress around himself that was meant to alienate, divide, evoke purposeful silence. The only time the husband and wife, mother and father, were engaged in anything that was decidedly communicative was when Val waved her white flag in the middle of the night and jumped on top of him to hear him breathe heavy sighs into her ear.

But more and more, Val was wondering why she was waving any flag. What she'd done to be losing so miserably at a war. Or what the war was. Well, she knew what the war was. But shouldn't he be over that by now?

Jamison heard his name, so he stopped walking. He turned around. He was unbuttoning his shirt. He looked at Val but never asked why she'd called him.

The silence nearly humiliated Val, standing there in her lime green tank top and floral print pants.

"Did you hear me?"

Jamison frowned before he was forced to speak. "About what?"

Val pondered before she answered. "About anything? I've been talking to you—I keep talking to you. It's like you don't hear me."

"About Leaf? My mother? I'll call them both back when I get out of the shower." Jamison was about to turn back around.

"It's not just about that," Val said. "It's everything. You don't hear me about anything."

Jamison's expression was as serious as a doctor's when giving a grim diagnosis. "I ignore you," he said.

Val wasn't ready to hear what she knew.

"Why?" she asked.

"I don't know. The sky is blue?" Jamison laughed wickedly.

"Don't do that."

"You won, Val. You got pregnant. You got married."

"And you?"

"Yeah, I don't know what I got." Jamison looked through Val.

"Oh," Val said, walking toward Jamison. "So you don't know me now? You used to."

"I used to know a lot of things."

Val stood in front of Jamison. Her stomach was getting larger, but still it was smaller than he thought it should be for a woman who was well into her second trimester—well, that was what Jamison's mother had said when she pressured Jamison to find out more information about the pregnancy.

"Tell me something I don't know, Val. How many months pregnant are you?" Jamison asked.

"What?"

"Just answer the question."

"Why?"

"Val!"

"Why?"

"I'm the father. I should know when the baby is coming. And you know what the publicist said, we need to make an announcement soon. What are we going to announce? Is the baby coming in January? February? March? July? When?"

"I don't remember the exact date," Val offered.

"Don't remember?" Jamison grinned like he was solving some mystery. "How don't you remember something like that? When your baby is due?"

"Well, if *you* were coming to any of the doctor's appointments with me, you'd know when *our* baby is due," Val said.

"Whatever." Jamison tried to turn again.

Val stopped him again. This time with her hand on his arm.

"Just talk to me. We have to talk to each other. Not this arguing all the time. That's not getting us anywhere." Val's every utterance sounded like groveling.

Jamison heard a disruption in her he wouldn't have thought could be there. Not the girl in the platform high-heeled stilettos. The girl with the fire in her voice. The attitude that always sounded like she was in charge, or thought she was. When they'd met that was what had kept Jamison watching her. She was beautiful. Had a body. But so did so many other women who were making themselves available at all hours since his divorce from Kerry was final. But there was something about Val. Her attitude. Even when she was serving him, she was a feisty bird. And here she was now sounding like her wings were clipped.

"Tell me what you said the day we met at the club," Val said softly, invoking an exchange they'd often reminisced about when times were easier and Val was wearing lingerie or making Jamison fried chicken in the middle of the night in her thong.

"I don't want to do that right now," Jamison said.

"Just do it. . . . Just say it. Say what you said to me. What you asked me. That's all I'm asking."

Jamison relaxed his jaw and tilted his forehead toward Val. "I asked what a beautiful girl like you was doing trying to get a job working in a strip joint."

"You followed me outside to my car. You opened the door for me. I told you I was about to get evicted. I needed someplace to stay. Or a way to pay my rent." Val looked at Jamison for the next line in the story. It was a smooth line she knew he liked repeating.

"I told you it was your man's job to make sure you had someplace to stay." Jamison's ice dissolved to the floor. He grinned in an honest way.

"And I said maybe you should be my man."

Jamison caught and held Val's stare. He stayed there with her in the memory for a few seconds and then tried to look away from her, but she caught his chin and turned his eyes right back to hers.

"And then you gave me money for my rent. And then you gave me a job," Val said. "All so I would promise you that I wouldn't be a stripper." Val pulled Jamison's body to hers by his chin and her voice went lower. "You were my hero. My knight in shining armor." The hand on Jamison's chin went to his belt buckle.

"What are you doing?"

"Thanking you."

Jamison's pants fell from his waist with a clank from his belt buckle as it hit the floor.

"Don't do that—don't—" he requested, but there was no real will in his words, no command. It was a soft whine that Val appreciated. It reminded her of where she might be in control.

Val squatted down and made an obtuse pyramid of her knees with Jamison's skinny naked legs in between.

Jamison looked up at the ceiling and slowly rolled his eyes closed as the warmth of Val's mouth made him erect. He held his hands at his waist like he was being fitted for a new suit.

He thought he was saying "don't" again, but the only sound in the room was coming from his cell phone ringing hysterically on the counter.

Val moved her hands in long strokes up the sides of Jamison's thighs and groaned like she stood to gain something of physical pleasure from the oral reward of a desperate new wife trying to make love *make* love.

As Jamison's breathing slowed, Val's movements became quicker, more sporadic.

He sighed and tried to back away. But then his heart quickened and suddenly his breath came harder and fuller. All ties to the world left his brain and the blood moved so quickly from his head he felt it zap at his heart. He nearly teetered onto Val but caught his balance and tried to steady himself by opening his eyes.

And there, standing on the other side of the closed kitchen door, looking through the glass window, was a pale face that at first glance looked like a ghost.

"Shit," Jamison yelled and he jerked back so quickly he almost fell over in the trap of his pants.

"What?" Val followed his eyes and turned to the door too as she got up. She wiped her mouth and squinted at the prying eyes before walking out of the kitchen.

"What the fuck?" Jamison wrestled his pants up on the way to open the door. "Man, what the fuck?"

Leaf walked in, holding his cell phone out. "I've been calling!"

"That doesn't give you the right to roll up on my house like that, man! Me and my—We—Man, what the fuck?"

"I couldn't reach you. We had a meeting scheduled with the Rizzolis and when you didn't show there, I figured you'd be at St. Philip or First Iconium in East Atlanta."

"I know. I know," Jamison admitted, letting Leaf inside the kitchen. "I was fucked up last night. Slept in my car. I was going to call you when I got back on my feet."

"No problem," Leaf said coolly. "You make messes; I clean them up. I told everyone you were ill but wanted to send me ahead to apologize for your absence in person. They ate it up."

"Good. Good."

"But that's nothing. Right? We have bigger trout in our pond right now," Leaf said excitedly.

"What do you mean?"

"What do you mean, 'What do you mean?'? I'm talking about Ras," Leaf said.

"Ras?" Val reentered the kitchen with her brown bob "mayor's wife" weave back in place and calmly joined Leaf and Jamison around the large island in the kitchen.

"Good morning, Mrs. Taylor," Leaf said formally with a hint of placation in his voice. "I certainly apologize for my intrusion."

"No problem, Leaf," Val said. "What about that skank Rasta?"

"Val, stop calling him a—" Jamison ordered.

"Wait, you two haven't heard about last night? You don't know?" Leaf looked from Jamison to Val and back.

"Know what?" Jamison asked.

"It's all over the news. It's everywhere," Leaf half-answered.

Val and Jamison reached for the little gray television remote at the same time. Val got it first and clicked on the forty-two-inch screen hanging beside the dishwasher. The television was parked on the cooking channel Lorna watched as she cleaned the kitchen. Jamison told Val to turn to Fox. As she clicked, Leaf started with pieces of the headline.

"They raided his house early this morning," Leaf reported, and then there was a picture of Ras on the screen. "They found guns. A lot of guns." Leaf looked at Jamison. "You know anything about that?"

Dax was standing in front of the little Old Fourth Ward house Ras had inherited from his grandmother when she died. Jamison knew the house well. He'd helped Ras install new hardwood floors for Ras's grandmother one summer.

"That's a reported seventy-nine semi-automatic rifles found in the basement of drug kingpin Glenn Roberson's—aka Ras Baruti's— home here on Boulevard," Dax said to the camera sternly. "Police have been clearing the place out since a bust that started at about three a.m. this morning."

"Drug kingpin? What the fuck?" Jamison said.

Val shook her head. "Crazy-ass motherfucker—"

Dax started speaking again and Jamison and Leaf quieted Val with annoyed hand signals. He was cradling an earpiece to his ear and speaking slowly to suggest he was giving the latest reports from the wire.

"This just in—Roberson's estranged wife, the mother of the two children he has custody of, was apparently the one who tipped police off to the arsenal found here in this small community," Dax added. "Karena, the wife, told officers, and I quote, 'He is a dangerous man.' " Dax grimaced gravely. "Such a shame. The people of this great city are truly better off now that this monster is off the street. Let's hope our mayor makes sure it's permanent." He snapped out of his mood quickly and pepped up. "Back to you in the studio, Bob."

Jamison grabbed the remote from Val as the image on the television shifted to the anchorman and pressed mute.

"I can't believe this shit," Jamison said. "A drug kingpin?"

"It's already all over the Internet," Leaf revealed. "There are even some pictures of Ras training boys with the guns at some militia camp on the coast. Have you been there?"

"It's not a *militia* camp," Jamison said. "And since when is owning guns illegal in Georgia?"

"It's not," Leaf said, "but it doesn't look too good for someone facing an intent-to-distribute charge. Jamison, they're trying to build a case against him. The feds want him."

"The feds?"

"Good, let them carry his ass off to prison, good riddance," Val said. She'd met Ras a few times at the office and had decided she didn't like the way he looked at her.

"Leave it alone, Val. You don't know him," Jamison said. "This isn't like him. None of this is."

"Won't matter much longer," Leaf interjected. "It won't matter at all."

"They're lynching him," Jamison said.

"What? Lynching him why? For what?" Val asked. "Please. Everyone's talking about what he does in the community. Weed and white girls? He ain't no Martin Luther King. Why would anyone want anything to do with him?"

Leaf looked at Jamison.

"Something has to be done," Jamison said.

"I know you have a lot riding on him, but I don't think you should get involved right now—not if you don't have anything to do with it," Leaf advised. "It's a watch-and-wait game right about now. You get in the rink and whoever's after him will come after you."

There was a sobering quiet as Jamison thought through everything Leaf had said.

And then Jamison's phone rang and clanked on the counter pulling all eyes to it suspiciously as if the "who" that Leaf had been talking about was about to teleport right through the little technological device. It rang in the silence two more times before Jamison looked at the screen to see the word MAMA and the little pudgy woman's face smiling in a picture she'd uploaded to the phone herself.

Jamison answered with the voice of someone who was relieved.

"I done called you five times. Called the house too. Bet that Val was there just looking at the phone ring." All this without saying hello.

"Mama, I was going to call you back when I got out of the shower."

Val quickly rolled her eyes and turned away from the conversation, busying herself with something on the kitchen counter.

"I don't hear no shower going right now," Mrs. Taylor said.

"That's because I'm not in the shower."

"I don't care if you're in the shower, boy!" This declaration was so loud Leaf could hear it.

"Mama, what do you want?" Jamison pushed.

"I'm in the hospital."

"What? Why are you at the hospital?" Jamison had already reached for his car keys. Val turned to him and asked what was going on.

"Don't go all crazy. I was just breathing heavy when I woke up this morning. Was about to go on out to the church, but my breathing wouldn't get right, so I came on to see my doctor."

"What did he say?"

"They're running tests. My pressure's high again."

"I'm on my way over there," Jamison said. "You stay right where you're at."

"What's wrong with her?" Val asked when Jamison hung up the phone. "Is everything okay?"

"Leaf, cancel everything for the rest of the day," Jamison said, walking toward the door. "I'll call you later."

"Jamison, what happened?" Val pushed. "Is everything okay?"

I damn near had to run Jamison down in the driveway to get in the car to go to the hospital to check on a woman who hated me and who I hated back—maybe more. But what I hated more than that was knowing that if I didn't get in that car, it would give that woman more ammunition to convince Jamison to hate me. Call it duty or defense, I wasn't letting my husband leave that house without me. I left Leaf standing right there in the kitchen.

I tried to calm Jamison on the way to the hospital, but there was something that just got into him wherever his mother was concerned. If she told him the sky was purple he'd believe it without concern. Like he owed her something. For a long time I kept telling myself it was just that I'd never seen the insides of a mother-son relationship—I only had sisters and for most of our lives we hadn't wanted anything to do with our mother. But the more Dorothy Taylor dug her nails into my back, the more I kept thinking there was more to it. She had it in for me and I knew she wasn't the type to stop things at "good enough." She was going to cat fight me into a corner and force me to claw my way out. And when I didn't, she'd look at her "baby boy" and say, "See, I told you so."

Jamison stopped the car in the front of the hospital and I had to park before walking over to find him and his mother.

When I walked inside and approached the nurses' station in the emergency room, I felt all eyes on me and my stomach and wished I'd taken my sweater out the backseat of the car. I asked a male nurse in a fuchsia smock for Mrs. Taylor and the other nurses all went to whispering about me.

"She's right down there, hunny," he said, smiling at me and pointing to the right of the desk as a nurse behind him pretended to be sending a text to a friend, but she was really taking a picture of me. A month before I would've snatched her skinny nurse ass up in that emergency room, but Leaf and Jamison's publicist Muriel kept talking to me about watching how I acted in public. That "everyone" was watching me and that I didn't need to give people more news than they already had. I funneled my hate through a smile before I walked to the room the other nurse had pointed toward.

Jamison looked like he was about to climb into the bed with his mother. They were whispering and huddled up so closely, I stood in the doorway for a second thinking they were praying.

When Jamison finally stepped back, there was Mrs. Taylor in a red jogging suit with her blond wig perfectly styled. Nothing about her looked sick. She looked like she could slide on a pair of sneakers and jog around the hospital a few times.

"Hey," I said, waving from the door.

"Oh, you came, too?" she said like I was some crackhead Jamison had to peel off of the floor of a crack house just before he pulled up.

"Yeah, we wanted to make sure you were okay," I said, making sure she heard "WE."

"Oh, I didn't mean to get you two all riled up. I just wanted to let my baby boy know I'm okay," Mrs. Taylor said.

"Any of the tests come back? What's your doctor saying? Where is he?" Jamison rattled off, sitting at his mother's side with his back to me. He was cradling her hand in his so desperately I wanted to walk out the room and vomit in a corner. There I was, pregnant with his child and running behind him to the hospital, and he hadn't even asked me one time how I was feeling or if I needed anything.

"They said I need to relax. Too much stress in my life. Got to stop getting my pressure all up like this," Mrs. Taylor said, and I was happy Jamison couldn't see me because I was mocking every ridiculous statement she made. What stress? She didn't work. Her only job was chasing Jamison around. That and fucking with me.

"See, Mama, I told you to take it easy. You get yourself too worked up."

"I know, baby boy, but it's just all this stuff with you and . . ." She looked over at me. ". . . and Val. I get so worried. Can't let nothing happen to my family."

"And we can't let anything happen to you," Jamison said, turning to me. "Right, Val?"

"That's right," I said, backing him.

"Oh, that makes me feel so good, ya'll. My family is all I have," Mrs. Taylor said so softly I could nearly smell the salt she was trying to toss into my ocean. And then Jamison opened up the flood gates.

"You know what, Mama, I can't have you alone like this anymore. Let's just do it," he said, looking back at his grinning mother. "Let's just move forward with our plan."

"Really?" she asked.

"What plan?" I asked.

"Yes," Jamison answered his mother. "It's settled. Let's do it."

"What? What's settled?" I asked.

Jamison turned back to me and said, "Mama's coming to live with us at the house."

"What? Who? Live?"

I swear I was either hearing Jamison wrong or I was in the middle of a nightmare that was about to end with Mrs. Taylor twenty feet tall and chasing me down a hallway.

"I'm moving in with you two," Mrs. Taylor said so happily it was a dare for me to oppose.

"But I—don't we need to—"

"Jamison and I already discussed it last week. He said that I should move in to help you two get ready for the baby, but I said, no, because I know you young people need your space," she said, cutting me off. "But now that I'm sick, I do agree with him that it's the best thing."

I looked at Jamison, but he'd turned back around.

"For how long?" I asked his back.

"Mama, the most important thing is that you get better. You can stay with me for as long as you need," Jamison said, answering my question to his mother.

By the time I really, really, really, really realized what was happening, Jamison was telling me to head home alone and get the guest room ready so he could drive his mother to her place in her car to get some of her things.

I wanted to scream. That or at least ask Jamison how he thought someone suffering from shortness of breath or whatever the hell was wrong with her could get into a car and drive herself to the hospital.

"What's going on?" I asked Jamison in the lobby. I insisted that he walk me outside of the room.

"My mother's just coming to stay with us," he said.

"You didn't even ask me. We never talked about this."

"That's because it just happened. What do you want me to do, Val? Let her die?"

"That's a bit much," I said. "Considering that we don't even know how sick she is. Did you speak to her doctor? I didn't see a triage bracelet around her wrist."

"Are you calling my mother a liar?" Jamison asked. "Be very careful."

"I'm not saying she's a liar. I'm saying you didn't discuss anything with me. She said you asked her to move in last week. I can't believe this."

"I was joking with her," Jamison said.

"Apparently, you weren't."

"Look, she's my mother and that's my house." Jamison threw up his hands. "And that's it."

"That's it? You say it and that's how it goes? What if I did something like that? Moved my mother in?"

"Go ahead. Do it." Jamison turned and walked back toward the room, and I saw the nurse pretending to check more text messages.

I gave her one solid middle finger to post to wherever she pleased. Fuck it. Fuck everyone.

"We're Still a Family"

Friday. Midnight. Friday night at midnight. Midnight on Friday night. It seemed like it was always that day and time. No matter how many times Jamison looked at his watch to keep track of time, somehow he'd forget to check and somehow when he finally did, it would be midnight and Friday.

That might have been okay for a young man who was trying to make it to the weekend to party until sunup and sleep until sundown. But Jamison was no young man anymore. He had the gray hairs sprouting on his temples and softening biceps to prove it. He wasn't trying to waste time; he was trying to slow it down. Savor it. Find more of it. Hold on and maybe just once look down at his watch to see that he had a little time. More time. Or extra time. And each Friday night when he looked down and saw that it was midnight, he knew his time was running out. Another week was done. Gone. And the clock was a terrible reminder. A loop of meetings, and meetings about meetings and meetings to set up meetings and trying to find time to work out to build his biceps again, and not working out, and eating in his car, and being late and getting four hours of sleep and arguing with Val or Kerry or missing Tyrian or whatever it was and there he was again—looking at his watch on Friday night at midnight.

Somehow Jamison had thought that being mayor might slow this tick to something more meaningful. Something that mattered. That he could take stock of. Make the blur of moments in his week seem so eloquent, so necessary like they did in all the black and white pictures he'd seen of Dr. Martin Luther King Jr. eating dinner with his family, or speaking at a church with brown babies in the front or meeting with Abernathy and Jackson, Hosea and Lewis in a dark back room clouded overhead with cigarette smoke and dim lighting.

But now he was thinking that maybe time had been the same way to Martin and maybe Malcolm, too. That their time was just them moving between here and there and those old black and whites that meant so much to any person who wanted to be as great as those men were just impressions of fast time caught standing still. If Martin was like him, when he was at dinner, he was already late for the speech at the church and when he was at the church, he was thinking about what the people in the back room would say afterwards.

Where was the time? Friday at midnight? What about all the things he wanted to do? Get that pothole fixed on Lee Street. Sit down and have the simple conversation he needed to have with Val. Visit his father's grave. Cut his own grass. Sleep. Make a change. Change himself. Time was up. Friday. Midnight.

Jamison went to sleep on Friday night at midnight and rose on Saturday morning having forgotten everything he promised himself he'd do as soon as he got up—all the things he hadn't done that week. Instead, he was rushing. There were reminders and text messages and missed calls on his phone. Everyone already had a plan for him.

Val was hiding in the bathroom. She'd started spending most of her time in there. Jamison pretended not to notice these extended visits to the boudoir, where he could hear her talking on the phone, clicking away on her laptop, or watching television. He told himself she'd be all right in there. The bathroom was nearly the same size as the bedroom. There was a couch and ottoman in the closet and even a refrigerator/microwave combo. Plus, he knew what Val was hiding from.

It had been just six days since his mother had moved into the guest room and as Jamison already knew, her presence was a cup of oil poured into a thimble of vinegar. In six days, his mother and Val hadn't had a single verbal altercation or physical fight—both of which seemed highly likely and overly imminent—but Jamison knew that wars between women were seldom fought that way. It was about what they weren't saying and weren't doing. When they didn't complain. When they did turn the other cheek. For women it could be World War II and most men would never know—not until the bomb was dropped and radioactive waste was seeping into the earth.

What Jamison could see was that the women were staying out of each other's way. His mother was in her room. His wife was in her condo/bathroom. Maybe it was peace-talks time and things could actually get better. He wanted to believe this, but each time he saw Lorna—the official secretary of state of the house who had to carry messages between the bedroom and bathroom as she cleaned the house—frowning at him, he knew the time of peace would soon blow over. And he had to do something. Lorna was sending him not so subtle signs of her limitations, letting him know she had signed up to clean up after one man and she wasn't a "carrier pigeon" or cook or best friend. But what was he supposed to do? Any talk about Val with his mother would lead to more questions about the baby and reminders about how that "Memphis trash" had trapped her baby boy. Talks about his mother with Val would lead to her hollering again about why he'd let his mother move in anyway when he knew his mother hated her and knew she hated his mother. And that was the one thing he could really care less about doing anything about.

Concerning his mother, Val was sounding more and more like Kerry. Resentful and suspicious. And maybe they had a point. His mother had put the first nail in the coffin of his first marriage by basically setting him up with Coreen, and every time he saw her eyes on Val, he knew she was trying to find the right nail for that situation, too.

He knew that everyone thought he was a mama's boy. And that his mother was a big, pecking hen. And, yes, he knew she was no sweet angel. But she was his mama. And just on that alone, she came before anyone. None of them had seen how life had pecked her. Neither Kerry nor Val had seen his mother wake up before the sun and get ready to take three buses just so she could go across the city to clean old white people's houses. Her feet so swollen she bought shoes two sizes too big. Her hands bleached so white from scrubbing floors he could barely see the cuts to pour the iodine on when she had passed out on the living room couch. None of them had heard her wails, so loud and sharp and mournful the morning his father died in their bedroom. She'd sounded like she'd found out everything in the world was a lie. And then she looked over at him and said, "You're my baby boy—all I got now." Almost everything he ever wanted to be, to do in his life, was to make up for what she had been forced to do, made to lose. What had pecked the hen.

So, so be it. And so be the silence.

Jamison knocked on the bathroom door and Val let him in to take a shower.

She sat on the side of the tub and watched him in the water.

"Where are you going?" she asked.

"What?"

"I asked where you're going," Val repeated, raising her voice so he could hear her over the water.

"To Yates," Jamison said. "Tyrian has a tee-off."

"Ohh." Val looked down to think before she would ask to go, knowing it would just lead to an argument about Kerry and then Jamison storming out of the house. He'd just started talking softly to her again and she didn't want to turn that fate. But she was bored and didn't want to be stuck in the house avoiding Mrs. Taylor for another day.

"That'll just be for a few hours though and then I'm meeting with the president of the Urban League," Jamison said, and then he remembered something he'd promised himself he'd do before he'd gone to bed at midnight. "Hey, you free for dinner?"

"Dinner?" Val repeated the noun like it was in another language. She and Jamison hadn't been out to dinner since—well, since she'd realized she was pregnant.

"Yes. I was thinking we could talk. Like you asked."

"Where? When?"

"I was thinking Paschal's. At like 8 or so. I'll have Leaf make the reservation."

"Paschal's?"

"Yes."

"But that's so . . . so, like public," Val said. The only time Jamison had ever taken her to a place like Paschal's, where Atlanta's own black heads of state gathered just to say they'd been there, was when she was still holding on as his assistant, and then she'd had to sit two chairs away from him and keep her legs uncrossed.

"We're married. We should be seen in public together. Why don't you put on something nice?"

This sounded like the tape-recorded voice of his publicist. Just an hour after Val had left Jamison at the hospital on Sunday, pictures of her stomach and middle finger had been all over the Internet and on the front page of the *Atlanta Journal Constitution*. Muriel went into full spin mode and had Jamison release a statement complaining about the nurses at the hospital not respecting his space as he was dealing with his sick mother and that his wife was so stressed out she'd had no choice but to act when she saw that the illegal pictures were being taken. She'd advised them not to fight back against the pictures of the baby bump and pregnancy rumors. They'd let it sink in, all the while acting like newlyweds that had each other's back, and then release their own statement. In the meantime, they had to be that perfect couple. Suddenly, Jamison's simple date idea sounded like a media move.

"Oh, I see," Val said, each single-syllable word loaded with a hidden response.

"So, no Paschal's?" Jamison went right for the easiest interpretation of her words.

"Paschal's is fine. But what are you going to do about your mother while we're out?"

As lackluster as Mrs. Taylor's "sick mother" performance at the hospital had been, her visit had turned out to be timely. The doctor, who actually hadn't noticed any true health-related symptoms other than the fact that Mrs. Taylor was talking so loudly he thought she was deaf, had only run basic tests for people with heart problems. He found that two of her arteries were basically closed. It was amazing that she was walking around and complaining and talking so loud. He ordered more tests and more medication. He talked in low tones with Jamison about a possible surgery. Said his mother was a very sick woman. Jamison thought it was a joke at first. His mother was just trying to get his attention. She was probably jealous of Val. But then he saw X-rays.

She went home with him and seemed to get sicker by the day. The doctor was looking at more aggressive treatment options. In the meantime, his mother needed someone to look out for her around the clock. She was still trying to move around like nothing was wrong with her, but Jamison didn't want to risk anything happening.

"I'll ask Lorna to stay here until we get back," Jamison answered Val. "Mama won't be a problem. Probably try to send Lorna to the store for some Boone's."

Val laughed and mentally planned out her outfit. "Okay," she said, forgetting all about her initial desire to join her husband at the golf course. She went to the closet to try on some of her shoes. Her feet were swelling. Then she heard the voice that was keeping her in the bathroom: "Jamison, baby boy, come in here and see about your mama."

Before Tiger Woods had been a success or a thought, black men had been spending early mornings in tiny carts, wheeling around grassy knolls until they absolutely had to go home. Golf wasn't just a sport or a hobby for these men. It was a conviction. A way of life. What united them and divided them. Kept them sane. Kept some of them alive.

Even before the white golf courses had been integrated (and that wasn't too long ago), the golf course had been the meantime matter of the country-club black man in Georgia. Where he made new connections and new deals. Somewhere at a hole on a quiet lawn was someone he needed to know or see. A business owner, pastor, or politician who was relaxed and open to talk. But there were janitors there, too. Hardworking blue-collar black men who saved and paid pretty pennies to go up against men who were their bosses or enemies in other settings. Here, they all dressed alike and had the same amount of information. Any man could make the shot as long as he had the skill. Not the money. Not the degree. Not the standing in the community or accolades of any kind. His fame came with his swing. Everyone cheered—but none too loudly.

When Jamison had gotten to Morehouse, his mentor had told him he needed to learn three things if he was going to make it: how to play chess, how to play tennis, and how to play golf. He explained that Jamison had to know those things if he was going to communicate with other men. Men who mattered. Jamison didn't understand that at the time, but he committed himself to the charge. Succeeded at all three. And like most things his mentor had told him to do, the payoff had been enormous—maybe even immeasurable.

"Hey there, my big man." Jamison took all of his son up in one arm. The little boy had run toward him after spotting Jamison heading down a brick walkway that cut through a pristine path of green that led to the practice holes at the Yates Country Club on the East Side of Atlanta.

"Da—Daddy! Daddy! You—you—you're here!" Tyrian was stuttering. He was past being beyond himself. His little body was shaking in Jamison's arms because he was so excited to see his father.

"I know I'm here. I had to be here," Jamison said, stroking Tyrian's back to calm him the way he had sometimes when the boy was just a baby and got so anxious about something he couldn't stand up straight or sit still. "I had to see my best guy practice his swing."

"Really? Really?" The pupils in Tyrian's eyes glittered as he waited for his father's confirmation. And it wasn't really a confirmation that he'd heard his father correctly, but that this was important to him. That it was special enough.

"Of course I had to come. You're the next Tiger Woods." Jamison placed his pointed index finger on Tyrian's heart as he said, "you're." He could feel the little gathered flesh thumping toward his fingerprint. Jumping toward the affirmation from his father.

Jamison put Tyrian down, and the boy merrily led him to the practice session he'd abruptly exited. It was a carefully selected group of five or six well-groomed, well-dressed little black boys and girls standing dutifully before their teacher, Sir Fently Adams, a svelte older gentleman in archaic golf attire that looked more comical than classical. For effect, Sir Fently Adams spoke with a deep British accent and carried a pipe that was never lit. Most of the parents and grandparents and godparents who surrounded the to-do in support chuckled lowly to one another in decided agreement that Sir Fently Adams was a joke.

Jamison spotted Kerry standing toward the back of the well-entertained group, holding a cup of coffee. She was talking to Clara Lindsey and her daughter. He knew Kerry had spotted him when Tyrian ran toward him on the pathway, but she wouldn't acknowledge him until he walked over to say hello and then she'd probably ask him how long he'd been there. During the separation and divorce, Jamison had thought this was a kind of "game" Kerry played to get his attention, gain some kind of point on the divorce champion scoreboard of mind manipulation, but more and more he was considering that this was just who she was—how she was. That was the woman he'd met. The woman of rules and order who claimed so much that that wasn't what she was about. But Kerry was really just her mother's daughter. A black socialite's progeny. And because of that, he knew, she'd always return to those games. Sometimes he'd play into it to keep things moving along and make peace so he didn't have to deal with the aftereffects of not playing the game. But today wouldn't be such a day, because of her company.

The daughter standing beside Emmit Lindsey's wife was Congresswoman Countess Lindsey. On a cloudy day, the loudmouth Countess was moderately attractive, but she had big breasts, loose morals, and a husband who'd only slept with her to produce his one son—and even that had been up for debate. A month after Kerry signed the divorce papers, Damien, Marcy's husband, invited him to a private swingers party at some plastic surgeon's estate in Alpharetta. "You need to get on with it now, Jamison. Move on. Let her go. Let your dick go," Damien joked on the way there in his charcoal Bentley coup. Though it wouldn't be Jamison's last time attending a party at that address during those murky months after the divorce, the first visit had been like a jolt to his every sense. He'd never been to a sex party or even really dedicated time to thinking about what one would be like and even if he had, there was no way he could imagine anything like what he saw that night. There were women and men he knew and respected walking around inside and outside with bare backsides. They were pinching and pulling, touching and sucking each other like the sun would never come up. Damien disappeared before Jamison made it to the bar to ask for a drink and shot to calm himself. Damien's assistant and her best friend were waiting for Damien there and they knew they had to handle their exploit expeditiously because Marcy was known to show up at the parties looking for her husband.

After downing enough shots that equated to a chaser fifth of alcohol, Jamison wasn't getting the desired effect of his alcoholic intake. He wanted to calm down. To accept everything going on around him and maybe see some action of his own. But instead he was feeling edgy, a little too alert and so nervous there was no way he'd be able to get his penis hard enough to even get close to any action. Enter Countess and her breasts. Jamison didn't remember how he'd ended up in the pool house with Countess's right nipple between his teeth, but there he was. And there she was.

Jamison could hardly look at her in public anymore, but as life would have it, she always seemed to be everywhere he went.

He decided to take the long way around the hole, so he'd walk past a few of the other divorced dads before making it to Kerry, in hopes that Countess would be gone or have dropped dead by that time.

The interesting thing about the old people who came out to see the new golf players was that most of them were there for business and networking connections. During his campaign, Jamison had raised more than fifty-five thousand dollars while chatting up other fathers at one of Tyrian's tee-offs. These were the sons and daughters of people who understood that it was worth paying five hundred dollars a month for their children to play golf for a total of ten hours with a man dressed up as Bagger Vance—all so they could meet others who could afford to do the same thing. And who might those people be?

"Christopher 'Ludacris' Bridges! What's up my man?"

"I can't call it, Mr. Mayor. Just out here watching my little girl beat the breaks off these young fellas."

Jamison laughed after hugging one of Atlanta's top rappers, who was enjoying a lengthy career and budding standing among the elite due to his many investments and community projects.

Beside him was AJ Holmes, a popular news anchor who'd had a show on CNN but quit and started his own Internet news network when he realized how much control the station had over his programming.

Jamison hugged him as well and then the three men stopped chatting for a minute to watch AJ's daughter, the youngest in the group, swing in the exact opposite direction of the ball.

"Ohh." They grimaced in unison with the other parents and kids.

AJ's wife, Dawn, who was devotedly standing behind the three-year-old, covered her face as if the hanging jaws around her were a judgment of her parenting skills. Her shame was only interrupted by little Zora, who turned around all cherry-eyed to her mother and cheered, "I swing, Mama! I swing!" To this, Dawn smiled weakly and looked back at AJ.

"Guess I'll have to take her to get ice cream after this to cheer her up," AJ said to Jamison.

"Zora looks fine," Jamison said. "She's handling it like a big girl."

"I'm not talking about Zora. I'm talking about my wife."

Luckily, by the time Jamison had pushed through a few more of these middling exchanges, Countess was nowhere to be found. Emmit had taken her place beside Clara and Kerry.

"Your boy's got a pretty good swing there," Emmit said as Jamison hugged Clara.

"We'll take all the compliments we can get," Jamison said. Tyrian's swings hadn't been any better than Zora's. Then, again, none of the children had really hit the ball just yet.

"Compliment? I was just pointing something out. My grandson's swing is better," Emmit added.

"By better, you mean Alexander came closer to hitting the ball?" Clara said, jumping in on the joke. She was thinner than Jamison remembered from the last time he'd hugged her. But her hair was coming back in and the summer sun had her skin less pale.

"Thank you, Mrs. Clara," Jamison said, adding an additional kiss to her cheek.

The couple waited in silence, looking away as if nothing was going on as Jamison greeted his ex-wife.

"Oh, you made it," Kerry acknowledged weakly, hoping Jamison couldn't read anything she was thinking behind her greeting. Her coffee had been replaced with a bottle of water.

"Yeah, I did," Jamison said. "Had to see my little man."

"Well, I'm glad you did. It's all Tyrian's been talking about for days."

There it was. She couldn't just say hello and leave it there. She had to add some kind of meaning. Something that was meant to diminish what was being done right by invoking the specter of what had been done wrong.

Slammed on top of an endless mountain of uninvited evaluation of his personal life from everyone from Internet-crazed nurses to blood-seeking reporters, this felt especially unwarranted. Jamison was about to react when Emmit knew he should step in with a lifeline for his fraternity brother.

"Jamison, you have a look at that WorkCorps city place proposal? The committee sent it to your office earlier this week."

"Yes. It looks good. Brother Perry Watson came to my open office hours with it. Training and jobs for young brothers who graduated from high school with no skills? I can't see why the city couldn't get behind it. We'll just have to figure out how much support we can give. The governor has my hands tied on some of these funding projects."

"Well, all we need from you guys is to push the contract through the public school system. We want to know that we have their commitment to passing these kids along to us. We can get them to work in the city where they live," Emmit said. "People want to know why crime is so bad in this city? I see it all the time in my courtroom. These young men don't have jobs. They have no way to make money. And no one to teach them how to do it."

"No fathers at home," Clara added.

"WorkCorps will bridge that gap," Emmit went on. "Get them off the streets and tracked to work."

"And speaking about getting them off the street, what's going on with that fella from the midnight basketball program?" Clara asked. "Drugs? Guns? White girls? Is that where our tax dollars were going? Hard to believe."

"No," Kerry said. "That's not Ras. He's a great guy."

"Well, he's a good guy with a long rap sheet right about now," Emmit reminded everyone after they stopped to clap for Alexander, the first to swing and hit the ball within feet of the hole.

"And I don't believe any of those charges against him," Kerry added passionately. "Not one of them."

"Do you believe it?" Clara asked Jamison.

Everyone, even inquiring ears in circles beside them, stopped to listen to Jamison's response.

"I can't say it sounds like something Ras would do," Jamison said, picking his words wisely.

"*Doesn't sound* like?" Kerry's face called the sincerity of Jamison's comment into question. "You lived with him for one year."

"Yes, and that was more than a decade ago," Jamison pointed out.

"So you're saying he is capable of being some kind of pimping, drug-dealing underlord who's planning to arm every little black boy in Atlanta? Is he capable of that, Jamison?" Kerry pushed.

Clara and Emmit traded stares. There was nothing they could do to stop Jamison and Kerry from sparring at that point. They were wise enough to know that maybe the little debacle was about Ras being in jail, but likely it wasn't. Conversations between divorcees were seldom that first level.

"I didn't say that either," Jamison said. "But people change."

"People don't change that much," Kerry retorted.

"People change enough."

"Jamison!" Countess appeared in the circle and immediately threw her breasts against Jamison's chest. "I thought I saw you walking up earlier."

"Hello, Countess," Jamison said, sounding as stiff as a British court guard.

"For some reason, I'm always so surprised to see you at these things," Countess said.

Kerry frowned at this a little, but Jamison decided that she hadn't really picked up on the meaning of Countess's bright stare set on him.

"So how are things?" Countess asked. "I hear you have a new wife and a baby—"

Clara grabbed Countess hard by the arm and shook her head for Countess to shut up, but the monkey wrench had already been thrown.

"Everything is great," Jamison said judiciously. "Thanks for asking."

Kerry crossed her arms and looked away.

"Wonderful," Countess said.

Tyrian and Alexander showed up at the circle to claim their parents.

Alexander had his chest poked out, but Tyrian was obviously crestfallen and ready to go.

"Alexander played better than me," Tyrian said when his parents knelt down beside either shoulder to comfort him.

"Ahh, he's a little older," Kerry lied to pull her son out of his rut.

"Just two months," Tyrian said.

"Don't worry. You'll do better next time," Jamison tried. "We'll get you some private lessons with old Bagger Vance over there."

"Don't make fun of Sir Adams," Kerry whispered. "The kids love him."

"I want you to teach me, Daddy," Tyrian requested softly. "Can you?"

"Yes. I can do that," Jamison said. "We'll start next weekend. All right?"

"Great!"

Emmit came over and tapped Jamison's shoulder.

"Hey, let me chat with you for a second before you all head out," Emmit said.

"Okay," Jamison agreed. He knew what Emmit wanted. "I'll meet you two by your car," he said to Kerry. "I wanted to talk to you about something."

Kerry nodded and walked off holding Tyrian's hand after saying good-bye to Emmit and Clara.

"Pump came through clean," Emmit said after looking around to make sure no one was in earshot.

"I told you—my guy did one and couldn't find anything on Dax. I guess—"

"Hold on—it came through clean, but then we got a break."

"You got something on him?"

"Humpf." Emmit looked around again and stepped in closer to Jamison. "Like I told you, we all have secrets."

"What did you get on him?"

"Dax Thomas has herpes." Emmit's index finger dug into Jamison's shoulder with each word.

"Herpes?" Jamison repeated as he drank in the information. He hadn't really decided yet what he'd do if something came out of Emmit's pump. If he really wanted to stop Dax or just get the kid to lay off. Pumps had a way of getting out of control. He'd seen people's lives ruined. Seemingly innocent front-page news stories about married Secret Service agents sleeping with under-age girls in Colombia looked like commonplace news stories to the public, but insiders knew it was just likely a caper consciously produced to collect damages for some intimate infraction that would likely never bubble to the surface. It was ugly.

"How'd you find out?"

"His ex-girlfriend came to my guy after he slipped her some pictures of Dax with some new girl he met online." Emmit laughed. "That'll do it."

"But I don't get it. Millions of people have herpes, Emmit," Jamison said. "How's that going to get him in the pocket?"

Emmit began to whisper. "Because the ex-girlfriend didn't know Dax had herpes until she got it from him. And the new girl-friend had no idea. The beauty of online dating."

"I don't know—"

"Look, Dax is young, single, he has a little bit of money and his face on television. There's no way he wants this to get out," Emmit pointed out as Jamison weighed the information. The dan-ger in pushing someone based upon this kind of information was that sometimes the person didn't care about the information being released. Sometimes they went ahead to their wives about their porn addictions and male mistresses. Checked into a sex clinic and then came out singing like a free bird. Singing loud and long notes.

"It's risky. You know it."

"No, what's risky, youngblood, is you letting this cat continue to keep his foot lodged in your ass. How's the baby?"

Jamison didn't respond. This was a jab about the pictures from the hospital. Dax had covered that too. He came to the office with a camera crew and hard questions. Made Jamison look like a fool.

"And that's just the small stuff, Jamison," Emmit said. "What do you think he'll do when he runs out of parlor shit?"

"What if we can't pin it on him? If this woman's just some angry ex?"

"We have pill bottles. Herpes medication with his name on it."
Jamison let out a deep breath.

"You're running with the big boys right now," Emmit said,
sensing Jamison's uneasiness. "This is what we do. You can't be
powerful if you don't know how to keep power, son."

Jamison nodded.

Emmit stepped back and searched Jamison's face for approval.

"I'll have my guy talk to him," Emmit said when he saw the
lines in Jamison's forehead soften. "Just a conversation. See where
he's coming from."

Jamison looked away. Buried his hands in his pockets. "I don't
know. Let's just wait on that."

Emmit looked unsurprised but still a little annoyed. "Suit
yourself," he said. "I'll be waiting."

And just like that the brothers departed like strangers. One
walked in one direction; the other in another.

Kerry was waiting for Jamison outside of her car. The motor
was running though. Tyrian was inside the backseat watching a
movie on his iPad.

"What did he want?" Kerry asked Jamison, nodding to the position on the knoll where he had been talking to Emmit.

"Just some frat stuff."

Kerry looked like she'd just smelled something rotten.

"Why are you always like that about Emmit?" Jamison asked.

"Come on, my mother's friends with his wife; I know who he
is," Kerry said. "And it's nothing to play with." She locked her
eyes on Jamison. "I keep trying to tell you."

"Well, there's nothing for you to worry about, so you can stop
with the ugly mug."

"I'm not worried about anything. You're not mine to worry
about," Kerry said coolly with just a hint of sarcasm.

"Okay. I'm glad you realize that," Jamison answered patronizingly to point out her unnecessary tone.

"So, what did you want to talk to me about?"

Jamison looked at Tyrian locked in the air-conditioned car with his movie. The sun was high and its heat seemed to be especially cruel on the treeless course.

"Well," he started and spoke slowly as if he was picking every word before he used it. "Val and I are holding a press conference this week."

"Another one? You guys are like celebrities," Kerry shot with a flat smile, though she was in a deep battle about what she knew was coming next. She'd seen the pictures from the hospital like everyone else. They confirmed what she'd already thought. She'd cried anyway. Cried hard into Marcy's chest. She kept repeating that she was over Jamison, so she didn't know why this was stinging so badly.

"Yes. Another one."

"Why?" Kerry asked this thinking maybe he'd say something other than what she knew was to come next.

"She's pregnant." Jamison actually felt a little relief letting that out. Maybe he was really hearing it for the first time. Sometimes people keep secrets from others because they really want to keep the secrets from themselves. Maybe this was one of those times.

Kerry leaned against the car. "So, you're having a baby," she said. "I knew it." Kerry looked up and set her eyes on a few clumps of clouds gathering over the parking lot. "So, what's this? Why are you telling me?"

"Well, I was thinking I should tell you before I told anyone else . . . myself."

"Why?" Kerry worked hard to see the clouds as she forced so many tears back down.

"Because you're the mother of my child and I want you to hear it from my mouth. I wanted to tell you earlier, but it didn't work out that way," Jamison said.

"You got married without telling me." Kerry looked at him.

"That was a mistake. I told you. You weren't supposed to—"

"But I did. So—"

"Kerry, stop trying to . . . hurt me."

"Trying to hurt you?" Kerry laughed a little. "You married your assistant and now you're having a baby and you say I'm trying to hurt you?"

"We're divorced," Jamison pointed out, though he'd regret it later.

"Exactly, so why are you telling me all of this? You're the one who told me it was your business and not mine."

"I want to take Tyrian out for ice cream tomorrow," Jamison said. "Talk to him. Let him know what's going on before he hears it from someone else."

"Okay."

"Okay?"

"Fine."

"So, I can take him?"

"He's your son," Kerry said. "You don't expect me to tell him, do you?"

The two stood there for a second and listened to the boom from the movie on the iPad vibrate through the car.

Jamison saw how red Kerry's eyes were getting. Now, his heart was stinging, too. Through all of their pain, their missed signals and misfires, he'd never wanted to see her cry. His best friend had told him it was because Kerry was his first love and his first wife.

"I didn't mean to hurt you."

A tear fell. Kerry made sure it was wiped away so quickly maybe even God hadn't noticed.

"It's not that," she said so faintly. "It's not what you're thinking. That I'm jeal—"

"No, I get it," Jamison said. "It's not about you wanting me or anything. I know you don't want me." He looked into her eyes. "Right?"

She didn't respond.

"It's about what I'd feel if my first wife got married. Had a baby. I'd be feeling like you were once mine," Jamison said.

They looked at each other and Jamison added, "And that would hurt me. So, I'm sorry."

Kerry wiped away a few more tears and then perked up to restore her composure.

"Well, okay," she said, reaching for her door handle in a quick decision that the conversation was over. "And can you bring him home from camp? I have some things to do at the center tomorrow."

"Yes," Jamison answered.

"Cool." She paused. "And, hey, I was also wondering what you were going to do about Ras."

"Do?"

"You're going to help him, right?"

"I don't know," Jamison said. "It's not looking too good for him."

"Exactly, and that's why he needs you. You have power. You have friends."

"Kerry, it's not that simple, and you know it. You know it better than anyone else."

"You got into politics because you wanted to make a change for people. A real change. Ras wants to do the same thing. And I know you both are capable of that. That's why people love you. That's why people voted for you."

"I know, but that's not what'll keep me in office."

"You can't serve two masters, Jamison. I know those guys like Emmit. I grew up around them. They're businessmen. Not community men. Don't get confused. What they give, they give because of what they can get from it. And when there's nothing to get, they'll crush you," Kerry said soberly. Her family had a long history of doing big business in Atlanta. Her granduncle helped start Atlanta Life, an African-American-owned insurance company that had dominated for decades and still remained the nation's most wealthy black-owned insurance company. Jamison had used her family's connections to get his lawn care business going. He'd done the work that made the money, but she'd done the networking that made the work. And in that network, loyalty was everything, but you had to know where the loyalty was.

"Nobody's trying to crush me," Jamison said.

"Not yet."

On his way back home, as Jamison rode with the top down and the radio off so he could think about what Kerry had said about Ras, he received a call from someone who's name on the caller ID on the dashboard in his car made him smile. It was Damien, Marcy's husband and his favorite fraternity brother from college. Like their wives, the men's differences in upbringing meant they were unlikely friends but their bond through the fraternity was so tight the two had been through enough together to really consider each other brothers. It was Damien who'd helped Jamison through his divorce from Kerry, his affair with Coreen and now it was Damien who came to lend honest words about the situation he saw unfolding online with Val. It had been his idea that Jamison take Val out of the house and try to actually sit and have a conversation with her that went beyond angry words and accusations. When he'd met up with Jamison for a drink after the pictures of Val from the hospital hit the local news stations, he had explained to his brother that he had to set his feelings aside and do what was right to keep some peace until his child was born.

"You must need some money," Jamison charged, answering the phone.

"I sure do. Like a million dollars," Damien joked. "I swear Marcy spends it like she's earning it."

"Oh, Doctor Damien, don't go getting cheap on the wife, as much as she puts up with. She deserves those red bottom shoes."

Damien laughed and added, "Yeah, I hope Payless comes out with some red bottoms, because this clinic money isn't Mayor Taylor money."

"Oh don't go wishing that on me," Jamison said. "I just left the one who took everything I owned. Has about 80 percent as we speak."

"You speak to her about Val?"

"Sure did."

"Good. What about Coreen? Did you tell her about Coreen?"

"No," Jamison said, pulling into his driveway. "I don't think she's ready for that. I don't think either of them are."

"Dog, I told you, the man who speaks first wins. That's the bottom line. You have to tell Kerry. You have to tell Val, too."

"I know, but there's too much shit going on right about now. You know?" Jamison looked up at the house.

"You're a married man—there's always shit going on," Damien said and Jamison laughed with him at the judgment of the institution that had become more of a game of risk for him than anything else. He knew Marcy had gotten pregnant by him so he'd marry her. He actually loved her and wanted to marry her whether she was pregnant or not. But she was coming from the wrong side of the tracks and he wasn't raised to be the kind of blue blood to cross over. But the baby coming meant he'd had to marry her to save his name from shame. And while sometimes he thought his daughter's birth was a blessing that allowed him to keep the only woman he'd ever really loved, other times he resented Marcy for what she'd done. He also resented the fact that he couldn't bring it up without sounding like he hated his daughter. His therapist had said that resentment was why Damien had slept with so many women outside of his marriage—to try to control a relationship he felt was set up to control him. And since Damien didn't see any way he'd ever stop self-medicating through random sexual exploits that most often resulted in his being caught and a physical altercation with Marcy, the therapist suggested the two get a divorce. That was the last time Damien went to therapy.

"Just talk to them, man," Damien advised before getting off the phone with Jamison. "You have to start the conversation. Man up."

"An Ode to Mercy"

Paschal's was an Atlanta tradition with a solid heart that just wouldn't stop ticking. The West End soul food citadel, which had seen its height when it was known as a social club and meeting place for civil rights activists and Atlanta's black who's who in the 1960s, had become a place where white tourists went for fried chicken and politicians held court to collect big checks from the old guard, but there was still a solid following that took pride in sitting in its history on a Saturday night or seeing church ladies in big pastel hats line up for the infamous buffet on Sunday afternoon.

When Jamison and Val walked in, eyes shifted toward and away from them like they did at family reunions when a beloved uncle walked in with his wretched wife. Some people smiled and nodded, but no one took pictures or walked over to them. That wasn't the style at Paschal's. To be there meant you were cool and just not surprised to see who the mayor walked in with on a Sunday night. Only the workers could demonstrate delight at the sight. And, of course, this meant Jamison was led right to the best seat in the house—a table the manager always kept open for such visits.

Val went with sky-blue kitten heels to play it safe, but her feet were already hurting and she kind of fell into her seat to get the pressure off her toes as soon as possible.

"You okay?" Jamison asked.

"It's my feet. They're just growing by the minute." Val wanted to remove the water from the carafe on the table and pour the ice all over the toes that were already nude under the table.

"Is this normal—you know—in the second trimester?" Jamison asked. He didn't remember Kerry's feet getting swollen until the very end of her pregnancy with Tyrian.

"The doctor said everyone is different. It could actually go away. Just depends."

Jamison watched as Val picked up the menu and went straight to the dessert page as she always did. She loved cake and ice cream, just anything sweet. When they'd first started fooling around he'd noticed she would go entire days eating nothing but sugary sides that indulged her sweet tooth. So often that he wondered how she wasn't five hundred pounds and being rolled around on a stretcher. She never exercised or even tried to walk from here to there. But still she had a solid body that curved magnificently wherever any man thought it should.

"Can you feel the baby? Like really feel it moving?" Jamison asked.

It was the first time anyone had asked Val anything about the baby. Well, aside from her doctor, whose eyes always seemed just as judgmental as everyone else's as they rolled over her stomach.

"Yes," Val said so efficiently. "I mostly feel the baby move when you're around," she said, looking into Jamison's eyes. And he didn't shift either.

Jamison looked at Val's belly and another first came—he wanted to touch her stomach. He did. One arm outstretched, he laid his hand atop her stomach. And closed his eyes. And waited.

It was the first time he considered that there was a human inside of Val. A little human that was a part of him. Just like Tyrian.

Just like the baby Coreen had carried in her stomach so many miles away from home in Los Angeles.

Just then, some sharp and rude emotion kicked through Jamison's quiet darkness and he awoke from his listening. He snatched his hand away from Val's womb and opened his eyes as if his hand had been on a tomb.

"What?" Val responded to the sudden movement. "What happened?"

"Val, I need to tell you something," Jamison said, looking at Val.

"What? What is it?"

"It's about the woman I told you about—the one in—"

Jamison's words stopped when he saw a man approaching the table from behind Val.

"Jamison?" Val called, trying to get him to focus on her again, but his entire countenance was already changing, causing her to turn around to see what had his attention at her back.

As she turned, Jamison was standing and smiling, extending his hand past her breasts.

"Ma-mayor Ta-Taylor, I-I thought that was you wa-wa-walking in."

Smiling, Jamison shook hands with a face that froze away the feeling from every extremity on Val's body.

"Brother—" Jamison scrunched his face in a way that let the person shaking his hand know he needed reminding as to who he was.

He started, "Keet—"

But then Jamison recalled his last name and added, "Neales—Brother Keet Neales."

"Y-yes. Th-that's me," he said. "You—you remember." There was a big smile, almost childlike. Grateful.

"Of course. The brother from the last chapter meeting. You approached me in the parking lot about a job," Jamison recalled.

"Did you get my-my resume?" Keet asked.

"Actually, I did," Jamison said. "Very impressive. Howard Law? Three years working for the DA. Makes me wonder what you're doing working for the police department."

"We-well, I'm n-not one to sii-iit behind a desk all day. I-I-I prefer a hands on approach to ju-ustice," Keet got out.

"Good thinking," Jamison said. "Smart."

There was an awkward extended pause after Jamison spoke and so he felt a need to fill the space.

"I'm sorry, man," he went on. "We've been talking and I forgot to introduce you to my wife. Keet, this is Val."

Keet extended his hand with a smile that went from soft to sly, but Jamison didn't see this. His eyes were on Val's icy face.

"Oh, the first lady," Keet proclaimed without stuttering on one syllable.

Val offered her hand for a shake, but Keet turned it palm down and kissed the soft spot on top of her wrist.

"Hello," Val said.

"It's wonderful to meet you," Keet added.

"Same here."

Keet released Val's hand and looked back at Mayor Taylor.

"You're a lucky man—the mayor, married to a beautiful woman, and expecting a child," Keet listed admiringly.

"Well, my father once told me that luck is just preparation meeting opportunity," Jamison said, his unwavering pride eclipsing concern for Val's silence and full detachment. "Nothing can quite prepare a man for every opportunity, but if he's lucky, worlds collide."

"I can only imagine," Keet said, looking at Val.

Then there was that pause again; as some eyes went darting around, others seemed determined to not move at all.

"Well, let me leave you two to dinner," Keet finally said as the waiter arrived at the table. "I'mmmm sure Mr. Mayor and Mrs. First Lady ha-a-ave a lot to discuss."

"Thank you," Jamison said. "And look, brother, my office will be contacting you this week. I think we can find something for you."

"Re-really?" Keet's tone regressed.

"Yes. Nothing big, but something to get your foot in the door," Jamison said.

Keet nodded at Jamison and nearly bowed to Val before backing away into the crowd.

After Jamison and Val ordered their food, Jamison noticed that Val was hardly speaking or looking at him.

"Are you okay?" he asked in the middle of a review of all the things he'd seen on Keet's resume. "You're starting to look sick."

"I just feel a little nauseous," Val said, before taking a sip of her water.

"Do you want to leave?"

"No," she said, "I just think I need some air or something. I'm going to walk to the bathroom."

"Want me to walk with you?"

"No. I'm fine. Just need a minute."

"Okay."

Jamison stood and helped Val out of her seat.

I almost forgot to put my shoes back on before I left the table. And if Jamison wasn't looking at me so crazy like he was, I might have run away without them. Run far away from that fucking restaurant. And Keet.

But I couldn't. I knew he was coming for me soon and I'd promised myself I wouldn't run when he did. But how he came— that wasn't something I could have expected. Not from him. Or could I?

I closed the bathroom door and went into a stall. I locked it. Sat on the seat without pulling my dress up and lifted my feet as high as my baby would let me. I needed to be alone for just one minute to think. To plan.

Some woman who was standing in the bathroom talking too loud on her cell phone to some dude about nothing flushed the toilet in the stall next to mine and walked right out of the bathroom without washing her hands.

The door swung open again. I heard a click. Someone was locking the door. I didn't have to look down to see that the shoes clacking against the floor in the small bathroom weren't heels.

They stopped. I looked down. They were in front of my locked stall.

"Keet. What do you want?"

"Madam First Motherfucking Lady." He laughed. "Well, ain't you gonna come outside and holler at me? I know you ain't taking a shit in here."

I let my feet down.

"What do you want?" I asked again.

"Man, stop all this bullshit. In there acting like you done got all soft on a motherfucker," Keet said. "Bring your ass out here."

I put my hand on the lock. There was no other way out of that bathroom. And even if there was, I knew there was no other way out of this.

"That's right. Open the door. I ain't gonna hurt you. What, you think I'm gonna hurt you?" Keet laughed in a way that reminded me of how his breath smelled like cigar smoke and cognac. Of nights when I felt so wild and free but not safe.

I undid the lock and opened the door.

He was looking at me with a smile that said I owed him something.

"What do you want?"

"That's all you have to say to me? After all this time?" Keet held his arms out to me. "Don't you miss me?"

I sighed and struggled to stand my ground.

Keet was my ex-boyfriend. I was dating him when I met Jamison. He was a cop. A small beat cop, who was too smart to want to get off the streets. He liked fucking with people's heads too much. He mind fucked me for the longest time. Had me thinking he was some kind of prince charming coming to save me on his white horse, but all the time I knew something was off. There was something about how his eyes moved when I was speaking. How he could be so cold so quickly. One night we had been walking down Peachtree after dinner and one of those fat palmetto bugs had run across our path. I'd screamed or something, and Keet had stomped the thing so hard the insides had squirted out from under his shoe like shrapnel. Something about the sudden death had made me sad, but Keet had laughed like he'd enjoyed it and hadn't cleaned the bottom of his shoe.

He kissed me on the cheek and I smelled the cigar smoke.

"Come on. For real. I just want to say hello. See how my baby is doing. Got married. Expecting a baby. I see you're moving on up. Mr. Mayor himself."

"Why are you talking to Jamison?" I pushed Keet out of my way and walked out of the stall.

"No. Why are you talking to Jamison?" Keet grinned. "I guess I know that—onward and upward. Right?"

"Whatever you're planning, just stop it, Keet. What happened between you and me is in the past. Move on."

"I would. I should. But I can't," Keet said, coming up close to me. "See, my heart is broken. My baby left me and I can't seem to get over her."

"I never was your baby. You're your only baby."

Keet looked down at my stomach. "Am I my only baby?"

"Don't do that," I said. "This has nothing to do with you."

"I don't know," he said. "I'm thinking, if we do that math, we might be able to add old Keet's name to the equation. Should we call Maury?"

"We broke up a long time before I got pregnant," I said. "This is Jamison's baby, so let go of whatever shit you're trying to cook up."

"Wrong. We never broke up. You disappeared. And even then, we weren't through." Keet's eyes moved from my eyes to my lips and then peeled my shirt open. I felt him ingest me. Learn something I knew but didn't want him to know. "Were we?" he whispered.

I'd been dating Keet for three months before I'd realized who he really was. There were always girls around him. Calling. Stopping by his place. He claimed they were just friends. But they weren't just any girls. I knew some of them. Faces from night clubs. Bars. Double dates with basketball players. I started thinking he was a player. Was cheating on me probably. Just like all the other men. But Keet kept trying to reassure me. Telling me I was his only woman and every dime he had, even from his low-paying job, was going to keep me happy. And that money seemed to go far. Too far. He had a fifteenth-floor three-bedroom apartment in Brookhaven Square and a garage full of cars he switched in and out of weekly, though his primary car was a silver Maserati. It was unreal. And it was obvious something wasn't adding up. But I wanted to believe my dream was coming true. I didn't have to work. I had all the money I needed. He was talking about knocking me up. Then a little girl, she looked like seventeen years old, was Asian, Filipino or something, showed up at the apartment one night with no shoes on. Blood was running down the inside of one leg from underneath a royal blue miniskirt. She was crying hysterically. No purse. No keys. She was looking for someone she kept calling, "Daddy!" Saying she didn't know where else to go. Someone had taken everything she had. Raped her. She needed "Daddy." I was telling her I didn't know what she was talking about when Keet came charging down the hallway. He grabbed the girl by her hair and dragged her toward the elevator. "Close the fucking door," he'd yelled at me. "Don't let anybody in my spot." I didn't have to ask Keet what I was seeing. I'd been out there in the streets long enough to know.

"What do you want from me?" I asked in the bathroom. We'd been in there more than ten minutes and I knew Jamison was wondering what was taking me so long at that point.

"There you go with that same question again. Let me ask you this: what do you think I want?"

"I'm not giving you any money."

Keet laughed so loud I was sure anyone standing outside the bathroom could hear him.

"Money? You think I want money? From you? Nah, baby, you got Daddy all wrong." His voice was slithering then, and I remembered everything I'd felt that day when I'd met Jamison at the strip club. For a long time I'd pretended that I didn't know what was happening. How a cop could have so much money. So much control over so many people in the street. But you can only play dumb for so long. Soon, Keet had me in the middle of everything. I was meeting his girls. Taking them shopping. Making them feel good before he put them out on the street. It made me feel powerful. Like one of those mob wives on television. It was stupid, but I was falling for it. Our lovemaking became so intense. I convinced myself that we were our own mafia. All we had was each other and a whole bunch of clichés that went against whatever little piece of self I had left. But then Keet showed me what that really meant. The next time a girl showed up at our front door, this time asking for me, he stomped her into the ground and when she cried for someone to call the police, he laughed and dialed 911 himself. I realized then that I had to get out. It was only a matter of time before I'd be the girl on the floor. But I had nowhere to go. No money. Nothing. That was how I'd ended up at Magic City looking for a job. That was when I'd met Jamison.

"So, if you don't want money, what is it?" I asked Keet. "Why are you here? What's up with you lying to Jamison? Pretending you stutter?"

"You li-li-like that right?" Keet snickered. "That's my acting

skill. I took an improv class at Dad's Garage. You'd be surprised how a simple stutter disarms people. Learned that in my class."

"And I must've missed that you went to Howard Law," I said when someone knocked on the door. We stood there quiet for a second, but then we heard the person sigh and then walk away.

"There's a lot about me you missed. So much that it had me thinking, maybe I misrepresented myself. Maybe I didn't show you who I am," he said. "How does a man like Jamison—and not to take anything away from Mr. Mayor—take a woman away from a man like me? Like from right underneath me."

"He didn't steal me. I left."

"And I just kept thinking about it, and thinking about it," Keet went on as if I hadn't said anything. "And I realized that if that brother got what I had, then I want what he has. Everything."

"That's crazy. What you want to be mayor?"

"Yes. And I don't think that's crazy at all. You heard Jessie Jackson and Obama and all those other motherfuckers. All I have to do is dream. Believe and I can achieve. Right?"

"You're a pimp, Keet."

"People change." Keet smirked. "No, really. Look, it's simple. I don't want to hurt you. And I ain't trying to be nobody's baby daddy. I just need you to keep an eye on things for me."

"An eye?"

"Yeah. Let old Keet know what's going on in the mayor's head. If you hear some things. Some information . . ."

"What kind of information?"

There was another knock at the door.

"Val, you in there?" Jamison called from outside the bathroom.

"Yes," I said in a stare-off with Keet.

"Everything all right?"

"I'm coming out. Just finished cleaning up. I threw up, but I'm fine."

"Okay." Jamison stood there for a second. Keet turned one of the faucets on at the sink and let the water run loudly to make him

think I was washing my hands or something. He turned off the water and we heard Jamison walk away.

"Isn't that sweet? Mr. Mayor coming to see about his wifey," Keet teased. "If he only knew."

"I'm not doing anything for you, Keet," I said.

"Yes, you are."

"Jamison will figure out who you are. He's not stupid."

Keet laughed and walked to the door. He unlocked it and looked at me.

"If he's so smart, don't you think he'll figure out who you are, too?" he said harshly. "That is, unless he doesn't have to figure it out at all. Like if someone tells him first." He smiled like a used-car salesman. "I'll be in touch."

I walked back to the table with what sounded like police sirens blaring in my brain. When I sat down and fumbled through dinner, from a distant place in my mind, I watched Jamison eating and talking to me through my eyes like he was on television and so far away from everything that was happening in the world. Behind him, Keet was at the bar laughing with some of his other fraternity brothers. He'd turn and look at me and smile. I felt dizzy. Like someone was sitting right on top of my chest, bouncing up and down.

I'm sure it didn't look quite like that to Jamison. I laughed when he laughed. Answered his questions. Asked some of my own. I pretended for the rest of the night to be present for a conversation I knew I needed to have.

Jamison touched my stomach again. Put his hand on top of mine. He softened. Spoke about us needing to get along. To make it work for the baby. He wanted to try. He had to.

With the blaring sirens in my mind and the man sitting in front of me, I wondered which world was real. Which one would survive what was coming.

PART II

". . . for better, for worse, for richer, for poorer, in sickness and in health . . ."

"Old Acquaintances"

In the capital of the New South, for as long as time could remember, the heat of the summer meant more shootings. Random
gun violence. A robbery gone bad. Street crimes. Gang tiffs.
Scores to be settled. There was something about the months of
June, July, and August that made the city become a wild world
where white women with baby strollers jogging along dark streets
or black boys walking to the corner store to buy a bag of potato
chips fell victim to a bullet that could've been meant for someone
else.

For Jamison, the heat in the streets meant heat on him. He'd
have to go around to make speeches, declarations to stop the violence, make the streets safe, and save everyone from themselves.
He'd attend funerals where the caskets were so small they'd
looked like they'd been made to contain kittens and not humans.
Hold a mother's hand and say what he really believed—someday
things would be better. Sadly, the longer he was in office, the less
he actually believed that.

Just when the headlines seemed to need a break from Jamison
and his personal life and Ras and his white girl, weed, and guns, a
home invasion that had left two Mexican men dead from gunshot
wounds on the Southside of the city became the bloody steak the

media could sink its teeth into. Jamison, of course, felt the pain any young leader would feel for his people, and he made a few phone calls from his office and then saw the situation for something else it could be: a distraction. With eyes off of him and his old roommate, he could do what had been on his heart to do for days since Kerry had implored him at the golf course.

He didn't tell anyone on his staff that he was going to the jail. He didn't want opinions or projections, a script of what to say and do. This wasn't about politics. This was about what he had to confirm he knew—his friend.

When Ras walked into the visitation room, his long locks braided tight to the back of his head and his orange jumpsuit barely holding on to a slender frame, Jamison did exactly the opposite of what he'd thought he was going to do. He stood up and smiled, clasped hands with his friend, and hugged him.

"Taylor! Word!" Ras said, smiling back at Jamison.

"Ras!"

The guard at the door signaled for the men to sit at the only table in the small room that was actually reserved for prisoners meeting with their attorneys. Jamison had pulled a few strings so he didn't have to talk to Ras through a Plexiglas wall and old phone that was attached to a tape recorder. Jamison thought maybe when Ras walked in he'd look worn down, beat up, and starved near death—the way prisoners looked in movies when friends and family came to claim them. That there'd be feces on the wall and the stench of loss in the room so wicked it would bring tears to his eyes. But there was none of that. The room looked like some space in a community center and Ras looked as scruffy as any Rastafarian who didn't believe in touching a comb or cutting his hair. If it wasn't for the guard, orange jumpsuit, and silver cuffs, it might look like the two old friends were on their way to have a beer.

"How are you?" Jamison asked and immediately thought it was an odd question.

"Been better, man," Ras answered. "I could use a beach in Montego Bay and a spliff right about now, but it ain't so bad. We're all brothers in here."

"That's good to hear. But you know I'm not just talking about your current living situation."

"I know. I know." Ras kind of looked over his shoulder at the guard by the door, who was looking back at him.

Jamison and the guard exchanged glances and the guard nodded before stepping outside the room and closing the door behind him.

Ras's eyes were big on Jamison when he turned back around. "Wow, Mr. Mayor has it like that? Got the guards moving out the way?" He laughed a little.

"No, those Benjamin Franklins have it like that," Jamison explained.

"Money, power—" Ras started.

"And respect," Jamison finished. After a short pause, he added, "So, what's really going on?"

Ras sat back in his seat. "I don't know, J. One moment I'm out there. Next moment I'm in here."

"But how'd all that happen?" Jamison pushed. He noticed how vague and detached Ras was being. Almost avoiding his eyes. Any notions he'd had of Ras's guilt or innocence were being weighed through this unclear communication. He needed more.

"How? Man, I don't know." Ras seemed to slip even farther down in his seat. The distance between the former roommates was growing.

"Come on, Ras. You know something. What's up?"

Ras looked around the room, from corner to corner, ceiling to floor.

"What? You think the room is bugged?" Jamison asked. "You think *I'm* here to record you? Me?"

"Again, I don't know. I don't know anything anymore. Know anybody."

"You know me, man," Jamison. "We go way back. Way back."

Ras just looked at Jamison.

"I helped you install those hardwood floors at your grandmother's house that summer," Jamison said.

Ras gave a weak grin.

"It was hot as hell in that house. No air-conditioning. In the middle of the A," Jamison recollected for Ras. "And she wouldn't pay us."

"Wouldn't even give us any sweet tea," Ras added.

"Just water," Jamison continued. "But I showed up to help you. Three hot summer days in a row."

Jamison fought with Ras's eyes to get his attention.

"What's up, Glenn?" Jamison said, calling Ras by his birth name. "Talk to me. No one else in this room but me and you."

"I didn't do this shit, J. They're setting me up," Ras spat.

Jamison let the words settle in the room before he decided what to say next.

"Weed?" Jamison laughed in a tone appropriate to mentioning marijuana in front of his friend who'd once attempted to cure himself of the flu by smoking pot for two hours straight. When the experiment was done, neither had been sure if it had worked. But they had been sure they were high.

Ras laughed before explaining, "I had a few ounces. Nothing big." Ras leaned into Jamison. "Nothing unlike what I normally roll with. You know."

"So, it was your weed?"

"I had nine bricks. Maybe. I ain't fucking with no cops. I got kids. You know the black man knows the law."

"So, the cops planted extra weed on you?" Jamison concluded.

"More weed, more charges. Less weed, I go home."

"Why wouldn't they want you to go home?"

Ras sat back again and looked into Jamison's eyes. "What are you here for?"

"What?"

"You ain't been to see me in all the weeks I been locked up. Suddenly, you show up. Just today? Why?"

"Kerry was saying . . . I mean, I was thinking . . . I just wanted to hear the truth." Jamison saw the distance in Ras's eyes again.

"What, you don't believe me?"

"I don't know who the real people are and who the agents are."

"An agent? Of what? And what would make you think I'm one of them?" Jamison asked.

"Because they mentioned you."

"Me?"

To get an answer, Jamison had to soften Ras again. He'd called him Glenn. Reminded him of the time they'd broken into their professor's office together the night before the midterm exam and stolen answers. They'd gotten all the way back to their dorm with the answers to the chemistry exam, but then Ras had started feeling so bad, remembering something his grandmother had told him about cheaters, that he'd convinced Jamison not to use the answers. They'd stayed up all night studying, quizzing each other. By morning they had been chemistry gurus. But they'd both failed the exam anyway.

"I got this call two weeks before I got pulled over," Ras told Jamison. "Some man was talking about how he knew I was dating this white girl from the Highlands and wouldn't it be a big blemish on my record if everyone in the community knew I was running around with a white girl."

"So, the white girl wasn't a plant?"

"Nah. Nora's a little something I got on the side. You know. She likes to smoke and shit. Just a little something, something. Anyway, I was high as shit when the call came, so I was laughing. I was like, 'Fuck is this? I don't care who knows.' Then he said he had pictures."

"Pictures?"

"Yes. Told me to look at my phone and I did and there was a bunch texts from an anonymous number. Pictures. Nora and me . . . you know." Ras ran his fingers through his locks nervously. "I got kids, man."

"What did they want?"

"For me to stay away from you."

Jamison listened as Ras told a story about a whisper through the wire that told him to stop the negotiations between the Hawks players and the city. If he didn't, the pictures would go out everywhere—his kids' school, the community center. Ras said he wouldn't comply. Two weeks later, he was riding in the car with Nora. There were blue sirens behind them. Two officers got out of the squad car. Two more men, dressed in black suits, got out of a black Impala trailing the squad car.

"One had on your ring," Ras revealed.

"What ring?"

"The black fist on top of the phoenix. Greek symbol in the middle. I know that ring. You wore it every day after you pledged," Ras said.

"That doesn't make any sense. You have to be mistaken. There are plenty of rings out there just like my fraternity ring," Jamison said. "I mean, even if some crazy cops tried to plant weed on you and catch you out there with some white girl from the Highlands, what does that have to do with what we're doing with the Hawks? With us getting scholarships for kids? Why would they care? And why would anyone in my fraternity be involved?"

"I was hoping you could tell me."

"No reason—that's all. And that's why this sounds crazy." Jamison was the one who sat back that time. "That's why you have to be mistaken."

Ras took notice and asked, "So, you don't believe me?"

"How high were you that night when you got that phone call? You sure it wasn't me on the phone?"

"Jamison, I've been smoking for over twenty years. Weed is like water for me," Ras said. "I actually think more clearly when I'm high."

"Okay. I'll give you that. But what about the ring? Every fraternity, social club, college, and sports team has a ring. Maybe you thought you were seeing something you weren't. Got confused."

"I've gone through this in my mind a million times."

"So you think the call and the bust are connected?" Jamison asked.

"No doubt in my mind, brother. I told those motherfuckers no, and now they're setting me up," Ras said.

Jamison searched and saw nothing but truth in Ras's eyes. While he couldn't confirm everything his old friend was saying, he knew Ras believed it.

After giving the guard ten one-hundred-dollar bills, Jamison walked out of the jail feeling like his world had just gotten a little smaller and more complicated. With every question he couldn't answer, he thought of a new question. Kerry was right. Ras wasn't a liar. He wasn't a criminal. He wasn't crazy. He wasn't stupid. But if all those things were true, everything he was saying must be true. And if those things were true, many things Jamison thought he knew were false.

His phone rang. He looked down to see Leaf's name. His world fell into itself more. Felt more complicated. He didn't take the call. Stuffed the phone into his pocket and descended the steps to make it to the parking lot. Then the small world crashed in some more.

Lights. Cameras. Dax.

"Mayor Taylor," Dax called, rushing up on Jamison with his microphone extended. The common company of cameras and men were behind him. "Can I ask you a couple of questions?"

"Not today," Jamison said, avoiding the urge to put his hands up to the cameras and grab one that was in his face with a bright light hanging over it.

"But we see you're leaving the jailhouse and we know your former roommate, alleged militia drug lord, Ras Baruti is inside.

Were you here to see him today?" Dax and his crew were following closely behind a briskly walking Jamison.

"No comment." Jamison felt his phone vibrating in his pocket.

"Are you here to support him?"

"No comment."

"Are you a part of his movement?"

"No comment."

"Come on, Mayor Taylor, give us something. The people of Atlanta deserve to know what their mayor is up to. They put you in office. They can take you out."

Jamison stopped walking and looked at the man holding the microphone to his face like he was an insect on a wall.

"No comment, Dax."

Dax pulled the microphone back.

"So, you remember my name *now*?" Dax was wearing a nasty grin. The kind that started fights. That made grown men spit on one another.

It took a few quick reminders for Jamison not to jump on Dax. He reminded himself of who he was and where he was and who was watching. He looked into the camera and saw so many layers of mirrored glass.

Dax just kept on pushing. That was his plan.

"Is it true that this drug dealer is your friend and you two were doing business together? Working on a contract with the city?" Dax asked with hints of his grin still tugging at the sides of his lips.

"He's not a drug dealer," Jamison said, feeling his pocket vibrate again.

"So, you did see him in the jail?" Dax's voice went lower. Became more intense. Accusatory. "He is your friend. You are working with him."

"What do you want from me?" Jamison couldn't really say whom he was asking. His little world was eating itself. He was forgetting to breathe.

"This interview isn't about what I want," Dax said. "It's about what the people want to know about you. About your activities."

"Interview? Activities?" Everything was spinning. Jamison was sinking in now, too. He knew what he was supposed to say; his publicist had trained him for moments like this: no comment. No comment. But where was that? His pocket was vibrating. "What are you talking about? What do you want?"

"The people are beginning to question your judgment, Mayor Taylor. The headlines. Corruption in City Hall." Dax held the microphone to Jamison again.

"There's no corruption."

"With Ras Baruti on your staff, I'm sure you know we know that's a lie," Dax claimed. He was pushing his microphone back to Jamison again when a white Mercedes turned sharply around the corner and stopped just short of where Jamison was standing. All eyes turned to the screeching tires. The blackened window came down, and Jamison saw Leaf in the driver's seat.

"Get in," Leaf said to his boss.

"What? What are you doing here? How'd you know I was here?" Jamison asked, still dizzy from Dax's interrogation and confusing the men for maybe being two in the same.

"Come on!" Leaf pointed at the cameras that were still rolling.

Jamison got into the car, and Leaf pressed the gas pedal like he'd been waiting for such an incident all his life or maybe he'd done it before.

Jamison turned to look out the window and watched Dax watch him ride away.

"You got something against answering your phone?" Leaf asked.

Jamison ignored the question, but when they were out of the lot and driving up Peachtree, he turned to Leaf with his own question.

"How did you know I was there?"

"I've been calling you. I'm always calling you. You don't answer."

"Leaf!"

"I got a tip."

"On me being at the jail? From who?"

"No, my tip was about Dax. I've had a tail on him since the courthouse thing. My tip said Dax had a tip about you. I just followed the cheese," Leaf explained.

"The cheese?" Jamison looked out the window once more, remembered everything Dax had said. The smug look on his face. "Fuck! That motherfucker!"

"I told you to stay away from the jail," Leaf said rather authoritatively, but Jamison was too busy hearing Dax in his brain to discern this. "Why did you go there?"

Jamison's anger had him pulling out his phone, dialing a number.

"Send your guy in," Jamison ordered into his phone to a voice that sounded garbled to Leaf. "Get Dax."

"Who is that? Who is on the phone?" Leaf asked.

Jamison clicked the phone off and sat back in his seat stone-faced. "Just drive," he said. "Drive."

Kerry had rung the doorbell three times, knocked more than that. Now she was banging. When she was about to pull out her cell phone and call to reconfirm her reason for being at Jamison's front door, the big block of wood opened just a few inches and the former secretary with poor letter-writing skills was on the other side with sleepy eyes.

"Yes?"

"I'm here to get Tyrian," Kerry barked. She wasn't the kind of woman who'd put her hand on her hip, but there it was. And her eyes were rolling, too. She had reason to be annoyed. She'd called ahead to let Jamison know she was on her way to retrieve her child after he'd picked him up from camp. She'd expected the boy to be waiting on the steps with his book bag dangling at his feet. That's how they always did it. Then she wouldn't have to speak to anyone in the house. Not Val, of course.

"Tyrian?"

Kerry's eyes widened. Also out of character for the Southern belle was saying something nasty . . . but there the words were, right in her throat. Still, she decided not to let the situation pull her away from who she thought she was.

"He is here, right? Jamison picked him up from summer camp today. I just spoke to him. Told him I was on my way," Kerry said.

"Oh, I didn't know. I've been asleep," Val said, stepping back and rubbing her stomach a little. "Our baby keeps me up all night."

"Sure. So . . . Tyrian?" Kerry kind of shifted her eyes into the house.

"Well, Jamison left out a little while ago, but let me check to see if Tyrian is still here. He's probably upstairs with Mrs. Taylor."

Val was about to go into the house and close the door in Kerry's face, but then she came up with a better way to put Kerry in her place.

"Come in and have a seat." She opened the door and led Kerry into the living room.

They could hear Tyrian upstairs giggling.

"Oh, there he is," Val said, acknowledging his laughter as if Jamison hadn't told her Tyrian was in the room with his mother and asked her to have him ready to go when Kerry got there.

Kerry was steadily biting her lips and considering all the ways she'd talk about Val to Marcy later. And there would be much to say. In the living room, where Val was leading Kerry for no reason other than a show, there was a brand new fresco over the fireplace. It was a swirling mass of primary colors uniting separate images of Val and Jamison; she'd commissioned a painter to make it look like a professional portrait. Val had ordered it at the mall before the wedding. It looked like it.

"Mommy!" Tyrian hollered from the top of the steps, his head bobbing over a banister that was almost as big as he was.

"Hey, sugar bump!" Kerry called to her son, forgetting all about the garish painting and Val and her stomach.

Tyrian began to climb down the steps, but he didn't have his backpack or the Braves baseball cap he'd been wearing when Kerry dropped him off that morning.

"Wait, honey, get your things," Kerry said.

"I got 'em! I got 'em," called a familiar voice.

Kerry and Val looked behind Tyrian at the top of the stairs and saw a face that served to unite them.

In a hot-pink silk muumuu with shiny silver jewelry and a brand-new jet-black wig was the mother-in-law.

A frown was too low of a calling to describe the look on Kerry and Val's faces. Even a scowl was a slight. It was the countenance of hidden rage.

Tyrian was smiling.

"I don't want to go home, Mama," he pleaded, climbing down the steps with Mrs. Taylor holding his hand.

"But you have to. There's camp tomorrow."

"I don't want to go to camp. I want to stay here with Grandma T! We were having fun. Weren't we, Grandma T?"

"Yes, we were, sweet baby boy! Grandma always has fun with her precious grandbaby. Because he's the most special little boy in the world."

Tyrian beamed, standing next to his grandmother at the bottom of the steps. When she'd gotten sick at his birthday party, Tyrian had been beside himself. He didn't understand the possibility of death, but the idea of his grandmother feeling any pain was pain enough for him.

"No camp, no allowance. No allowance, no more apps for your iPad," Kerry listed her common sanctions.

Tyrian pouted audibly just so his grandmother could hear him and respond, which she did.

"Don't worry, Ty-baby. If your mama won't give you any money for apps, G-ma T will do it," Mrs. Taylor oozed, rubbing Tyrian's head.

Kerry took note of the clear infraction and simply added it to her list of reasons she hated this woman and was glad she no longer had to pretend she had any value to her. The woman next to her was still in that position though. And at that moment, Val didn't know if she should continue her unspoken war with Kerry or unite with her in a stare-off against the woman who'd had her locking herself up in her bathroom each day.

"Come on, Tyrian," Kerry said, holding her hand out for his.

The little boy trudged over to his mother, pouting the entire way.

"Poor thing," Mrs. Taylor said, pouting too. "Makes me sad to see him sad. I don't see why he can't just live here with me and his daddy anyway. Wouldn't that be nice? That way you and G-ma T can watch our *General Hospital* reruns together all night."

"Yay!" Tyrian cheered.

"You watch *General Hospital* with him?" Val asked.

"Yes," Mrs. Taylor confirmed. "Watched it with Jamison, too. It's good for them. Shows the boys how to love. And Jamison loved that wedding scene—when Luke and Laura got married. That boy watched it a million times. I always imagined he'd have a huge wedding—just like the one Luke and Laura had." She cut her eyes at Val first and Kerry second. "When he finds the right woman."

"Well, that's enough," Kerry announced abruptly.

"Oh, Ty, come give your gammy kisses." Mrs. Taylor stooped down to stall the departure.

Kerry was running out of space on the insides of her lips to bite.

And then—as Tyrian gave "Gammy" her kisses, Mrs. Taylor repeated, "Maybe you could come live with us. Stay with Gammy and Daddy."

Kerry let go of the inside of her lip. "Well, no, he can't live with his daddy because he lives with his mommy. And he sees his daddy on weekends—when his daddy is free."

Mrs. Taylor walked over and placed her body right in front of Kerry's.

Val might have considered getting between them if a to-the-death fight wouldn't lead to the total elimination of at least one person she no longer wanted to see on earth. Due to the current situation, she found herself on Kerry's side.

"Are you saying my son is never around his son?" Mrs. Taylor pushed.

"Actually I didn't say anything like that," Kerry backed up—she had meant this but hadn't expected Mrs. Taylor to repeat it in such a way that Tyrian would hear and understand. She decided that it would be best to cut the conversation short to avoid more consternation. She grabbed Tyrian's hand and pulled him to her side.

But, Mrs. Taylor pulled him back.

"A boy needs his father," she quipped.

"I'm not going to argue about that," Kerry said, and then she added as if it was a new epiphany, "because I don't have to. I'm not doing this with you." She pulled Tyrian back to her side and started heading toward the door.

Mrs. Taylor laughed a laugh so deep at Kerry's back it was more of a wicked cackle.

"So sensitive," she said to Kerry. "That was always your problem. No backbone."

Kerry stopped in her tracks and considered a few lines she could share that might defend her strength—the pool of power that had been but a dithering puddle when she'd first met this woman talking behind her back. It had since grown into an abyss that had given her so many options of defense against the powers of evil—one being walking away. She looked down at Tyrian's eyes, saw them drinking in every one of her actions, and decided on a course: one foot in front of the other.

Mrs. Taylor was still cackling at her victory when Kerry was out the door and in her car.

Val was silent. Standing in front of the fresco like a pregnant paper doll.

"Thank God my son ain't married to the stuck-up one anymore," Mrs. Taylor said, really to no one, but it just so happened that Val was in the room. She sucked her teeth and let out a loud sigh like Kerry had been the aggressor in the exchange. "Straight-up simple. Like she has any business raising that boy. She needs to be somewhere figuring out what she's going to do with her life. Can't mooch off my boy forever." She snapped her fingers in the shape of a Z at that last point and started toward the steps to head back to the refuge of her bedroom.

But something was going on downstairs still. The outburst or random conflict or foolery—whatever anyone would call it—had led Kerry to walk away (an action Mrs. Taylor had predicted), but Val was a different creature. She wasn't a Southern belle, she was a Southern gal, and though she'd been playing it safe to stay in the good grace of Mrs. Taylor and her not-so-obliging husband, any wise person could say of the situation, "It's only a matter of time." Now was said time.

"You didn't have to say all that," Val shot back, not in Kerry's defense, but speaking in a way for a circumstance she could predict in her future. "Not in front of that boy."

Mrs. Taylor stopped the same way Kerry had. "What?"

"That wasn't right. You shouldn't have spoken like that in front of that boy." Val's conviction didn't waver. She was getting louder.

Mrs. Taylor, who'd made it a few steps up the staircase, turned around and headed back to Val ready for combat. "That *boy* is Tyrian. My grandson. I know what he can and can't take. So you don't need to add any amount of change to this conversation."

"I don't care who he is to you or anybody else; you don't speak crazy in front of a kid," Val snapped. "Who doesn't know that?"

"I know one thing, and it's that you have a whole lot of damn nerve if you think you're just going to walk up in my son's house talking about what I can and can't say in front of my own damn grandson."

"Wrong," Val started, her voice confident she was about to one-up her opponent. "I didn't just walk up into anyone's house. I live here. This is my house. I'm the woman of this house."

"Hell you are!"

"Hell I ain't!" Val pointed to her face in the fresco.

Mrs. Taylor felt the jab, but it only made her more defensive. "What's that cheap shit supposed to mean?" she asked after a pause. "You ain't on the mortgage. The deed. The taxes. You're just visiting."

Val felt so small then. She could run right toward Mrs. Taylor's stomach and tackle her to the floor.

"I mean, as smart as you were to get pregnant by my son—if that's the case—you seem pretty light-headed to move into a house you don't own fifty percent of. That's rule number one."

"Fuck you!" was all Val could say.

"I'm glad you said that," Mrs. Taylor said coolly. "Get used to it. You'll be saying that a lot. Stick around. You'll see. I got rid of that Kerry. You think you're safe?" Mrs. Taylor laughed like a heavyweight and started back up to her room. "Mama's always on the job. Out the house, on the job"—she made it halfway up the steps and looked down at Val fuming—"in the house, on the job. Always on the job."

Seemingly building upon a new talent, Jamison walked into the house after all of the fighters were back in their respective corners—Kerry at home serving Tyrian dinner, Mrs. Taylor in her bed, Val in her bathroom. He was still surprised by the silence that met him at the front door. He ignored the fresco in the living room and climbed the steps lightly so his mother wouldn't hear him and request a visit to sit by her bed and watch *General Hospital*. He was waiting to hear back from Emmit's guy with a response from Dax, and he couldn't wrap his mind around the mental gymnastics that would be required of him to sit and pretend he enjoyed anything about watching television with his mother.

When he got to the top of the steps and saw both his mother's open bedroom door and his closed bedroom door, he considered getting down on all fours to lighten the impact his body made against the wood as he passed his mother's room to get to his. It seemed foolish, but it would be more foolish to get caught up in a verbal siege with his mother. Kerry had already texted him to say they needed to talk about his mother. He decided to try to make it to his bedroom on his tiptoes. But a few tips in, her television, which had been blasting so loud he was sure the neighbors could hear it, went to mute. He stopped in his tracks, frozen in fear like one of those fainting billy goats. He listened for her. She listened for him. Seconds passed. She gave up. Turned the television sound back up sure Jamison hadn't come home yet.

"I want your mother out of this house!"

Jamison cursed himself once he'd made it to the bedroom and heard this. Escape one bullet to catch another.

"She is driving me crazy. She is just . . . you know what she is!"

Val was shouting these accusations from the bathroom just loud enough so Mrs. Taylor could hear her down the hall.

Jamison started on a softer note, "She's in her room."

Val came barreling out of the bathroom ready for a fight. "Yeah, right now."

"And you're in your room."

"Right now!"

"You only have to deal with her a little while longer. I'm getting a nurse and—"

"That's not enough," Val charged. "She'll still be here. And if she's here, I can't be."

Jamison sat down on his bed and remembered how many times he'd had this same conversation with Kerry.

"She's my mother."

"You keep saying that. But I'm your wife," Val said before pointing to her stomach. "And this is your child. I thought you said you wanted to work on things. For it to get better."

"I did," Jamison agreed.

"Well, this ain't better. Not for me. Maybe for you, because you're never here anymore."

"Oh, don't start with that, Val," Jamison ordered.

"It's the truth. You're not here. And I have to deal with her constantly threatening me all the time."

"Threatening? Really?" Jamison grinned.

"Yes. *Really.* Everything she says to me has some kind of threat in it. And there's only so much of that shit I'm going to take." This last line had a little back-street Memphis in it.

"Please stop." Jamison got up and walked toward the television to get the remote control.

"You need to deal with her before I do."

Val kept talking, but it was only a soft echo of syllables in Jamison's ear. He'd turned on the news and was watching to see if the clip Dax took of him at the prison was airing. Dax wasn't live in the parking lot at the jail, so his story would likely run on the evening news—if Emmit's guy didn't get to him in time.

Val was still talking while walking around the bed where Jamison was sitting, watching each story like he expected to see his face pop up.

Val exhausted all of her claims and subclaims and threats and promises and sequestered herself in the bathroom again by slamming the door.

Jamison didn't budge. He was a man involved in a fight with a monster who was bigger than two women fighting over his affections. He wasn't sure who that monster was, but every day he was seeing its big footprints spread out more clearly over his. It was trying to crush him. It was everywhere in his life. But invisible in his world. As he watched, waiting to see his face, he thought, what if what Ras had said was true? All of it. That meant the monster was close. Right up on him. Breathing in his face.

As Val came out of the bathroom to add a few more charges to her list of demands, Jamison's phone started ringing again. He held up his hand to stop her from talking.

"Get down here. We're at the Rainforest. Come alone," a nondescript voice ordered before clicking off.

Jamison felt a hit in his gut that would later haunt him as he tried to recall why he'd gone to the Rainforest that night. A second-guessing he'd only felt three other times in his entire life.

"What? What is it?" Val asked. In the months they'd been together, she'd memorized about six of his expressions. One was fear—she'd seen it when she'd told him she was pregnant. She was seeing it right now.

Jamison said nothing.

"What's going on?" Val pressed.

Jamison got up from the bed and started for the door. He grabbed a black hoodie from a chair beside the bed.

It was then that she noticed he'd never taken off his shoes or opened his jacket.

"Jamison?" Val called to his back. "Jamison?" But he kept walking after mumbling something about being home later.

Val turned to the television in time to see the same man who was walking out of her bedroom, walking out of the county jail downtown, in the same suit.

⚜

Lairs. Caves. Cabins. Clubhouses. Tree houses. Bars. And boats. Places where men's worlds collide in a mishmash of bad ideas and testosterone-laced dreams come to life. Sometimes this meant a good time. Beer pong and toga parties. Game night. Truth telling. Sometimes this meant a bad time. Fights to the death. War. Rape.

Rebellion. The Rainforest had seen both. Sometimes all in one night. Men called brothers would start the night smiling, shoulder to shoulder congratulating one another, toasting to a life that exceeded their parents' dreams. Hours later and a few drinks in, these same brothers could be tussling over a wife, a car, a drug deal or a loan gone bad. By sun-up, there could be blood on the floor. But then, someone would mop it up and start it all again.

When Jamison got to the Rainforest, he knew not to expect the early-night feeling. The sun was just going down, but he knew none of his brothers inside were hugging or toasting. There would be the late-night feeling. The bad time.

As Jamison walked up the driveway in a hooded black sweat suit he'd purchased on his way to the Rainforest, he noticed Emmit and Scoot's cars parked beside each other. A silver Maserati was behind Scoot's car. The lights upstairs in the house were dark and Jamison realized he hadn't seen the old woman who lived upstairs in months, maybe years. Aside from what people told him, he couldn't really confirm that anyone lived upstairs.

Inside the basement, the only person in the front room was a boy in a fraternity shirt standing guard over the liquor and set to eye heavily anyone who dared walk in. When he saw Jamison's black hood, the frail, inexperienced thing, whose first sexual encounter had been right there in that bar room, stepped out from behind the bar with intention.

His heart thumped in pitiful fear of the possibility of action. He heard his mother's voice: "I didn't send you down there to Atlanta to be running the streets with no fraternity." He could hear those words but not feel them. His heart was with his big brothers then. Mother's love and direction would have to wait. So, the boy was about to scream out for his big brothers when Jamison pulled his hood down and shined familiar eyes on him.

"Oh," the boy uttered with his fear dissipating so quickly he suddenly had to urinate. "Brother—everyone's in the back." He pointed to the back room. He knew not to say Jamison's name. Not that night.

Jamison nodded and returned the hood to his head before padding slowly across the sticky bar room floor toward the hallway to the back room. Brother Renaldo's old papier-mâché palm tree had dust balls dripping from its fading green leaves, making them appear heavy and sleepy like the Spanish moss growing on a swamp cypress tree.

Emmit was standing in the hallway talking to another brother, Sampson Davis. They were speaking in low voices, and were also dressed in black.

Emmit stopped talking when he saw Jamison. He reached out to him like he was a father or a priest about to bless someone.

"Brother, you're here," he said.

"Yeah," Jamison answered. He hugged Emmit and then Sampson, who was saying something about the water being turned off. "What's going on? Did your guy speak to Dax?"

"Yeah, he's here," Emmit said.

"Who?"

"Dax."

"Dax is here?"

"Well, some things happened and—"

"What *things* happened?" Jamison cut Emmit off with his eyes broadening and his voice louder. "Why is Dax here?"

"Calm down." Emmit held his hands up to stop Jamison this time.

Jamison noticed that his sleeves were rolled up.

"Why is he here? That doesn't make any sense," Jamison said.

"Brother Sampson, give us a minute," Emmit said.

"Fine, but ya'll need to decide what to do about getting this water back on. Ya'll will need to clean things up tonight before you leave," Sampson said before walking off.

"Clean up?" Jamison repeated to Emmit. "What's going on?"

"Look, Dax wouldn't cooperate," Emmit started to explain.

"I predicted that. Fine, we move on," Jamison said. "Where is he?" Jamison tried to get past Emmit, into the back room where the guys usually took the girls and pledges.

"Stop!" Emmit warned. "It wasn't that simple. He threatened my guy. Said he'd seen him before. Said he knew who he was."

Jamison fell into the wall. His heart ran hot. He felt like he was underwater.

There was a scream from the back room. Both men turned to look. There was threatening silence.

"I said this was a bad idea. I knew this was a bad idea," Jamison said. He'd made the phone call to Emmit in the car out of fury, out of anger. He'd wanted Dax stopped and he'd known he could do it. That was the power he had. The power Emmit had told him he'd have to fight to keep at some point. Getting power. Keeping power. Maintaining it. Wasn't the way it looked in movies. It wasn't about handshakes and cutting scholarship checks. Votes. It was about striking. Cutting off. Hoarding. Being hard. He couldn't be afraid. This was how it was done.

"Don't be a pussy," Emmit spat. "You knew what this was. What it is."

"No! No!" Jamison tried to catch breaths he didn't know he was losing.

They stood there for a while listening to whimpers. The sounds of men's feet moving around on a concrete floor.

"He's in the room?" Jamison asked.

"Been in there about an hour."

"Any information?"

The tone of the exchange at this point had lowered to sober revelation, the sound of a doctor revealing a prognosis of cancer. The patient wanted to know how long; the doctor said two months. The patient didn't cry; he asked what his odds were of survival.

"Nothing from him yet," Emmit answered Jamison. "We're working on him."

"Can I see him?"

"Not a good idea. He's beat up pretty bad."

"What?" Jamison tried to push past Emmit again.

This time, Emmit stopped him with his whole body.

"Don't be stupid. He'll see your face."

Jamison tried again, but Emmit pushed him back into the wall.

"Wait! Wait!" Emmit held Jamison back. He could feel his muscles tighten. "I'll be right back." He made sure Jamison wouldn't move and went into the room of whispers and whimpers.

Alone in the hallway, Jamison was still trying to keep up with his breath, with his reality. Most people couldn't imagine what it would be like to be in a place like that, at a time like that, but there he was, body shaking to numbness, so many questions he couldn't keep up. Somehow, his thoughts kept going back to Tyrian. He'd see his face and then Dax's. Tyrian had a red ball. Dax had a microphone. Both were smiling.

Emmit came out of the room in a rush.

"He's blindfolded," he said. "You come in and go right into the corner. Don't say a word."

Jamison was still. He looked at Emmit like he was a character on a life-sized television screen. Not real. Pixels come together to express some alternate existence.

"You hear me?" Emmit asked. He grabbed Jamison's arms and pulled him into the dark place.

There were four brothers in the room. All were in black. Jamison knew two of them—Scoot and Emmit. Dax was sitting in a chair beside a king-sized waterbed with dirty crumpled sheets all a mess in the middle. He was falling over in the seat. A rope held his back in place. His head was hanging to the side. A black slither of fabric covered his eyes, but Jamison could see a gash on the side of his face, blood dripping from his mouth.

Emmit pushed Jamison into the corner farthest from the bed where darkness fell over him like a solid form.

The brothers nodded at him and turned back to their business with Dax.

One of the brothers Jamison didn't know was sitting in a chair in front of Dax. The chair was turned backward and he was sitting casually with his legs wide on the back of the seat. The other one was standing over Dax with his fists balled for action.

The brother in the chair continued what had been an ongoing exchange of questions and no answers.

"So no one's giving you any information? We're supposed to believe a low man like you, fresh out the gate, just has all the right moves? Just knows where to be and when?" The brother laughed.

"I told you already. I'm not working for anyone," Dax cried defiantly.

"Lie." The brother in the chair nodded to the brother standing over Dax, and he hit him so hard a tooth flew out of his mouth to the floor.

"See, that's what happens. You lie to me, you get hurt."

Dax coughed up blood and spit it out.

"Tell him something, man. You ain't looking too good," Scoot said, laughing. "Don't know how long you're going to last."

"Fucking faggot," the brother in the chair said before slapping Scoot five.

"Is that what you are?" Scoot asked. "You dress up in a skirt and blouse? Yeah, that's you."

"Who you dressing up for, Morehouse *man*?" the brother in the chair asked as the other brothers laughed.

"Fuck you!" Dax barked, and his mouth met two more jabs from his captor.

The brother in the chair sighed mockingly. "I hate to see this. A brother going out like this on some bullshit." He paused for a second. "Look, you're going to have to give us something. If you want to make it out of here alive."

"I told you, I don't know anything. I'm just a journalist."

Emmit jumped in growling then. "Stop lying, motherfucker. We know you're with the FBI. That they're feeding you this information to take down Mayor Taylor."

"What? The FBI? No. No?" Dax struggled.

Emmit went close in on Dax, and grabbed his throat. "We

know they contacted you, boy. Stop bullshitting. Tell us what we need to know or you won't walk out of here."

"No—no—please don't—" Dax cried after Emmit kicked him and his seat to the floor and Dax could feel him hovering over him. "I don't know who he is. He just tells me where I need to be. What the stories are."

Jamison unknowingly stepped out of the dark place.

"He said there was corruption in the mayor's office and that he was about to go down," Dax added fretfully. "Said it was in my best interest to follow the stories. That's the truth. I swear it. That's all. I don't who he is. I swear I don't."

Emmit stepped back from Dax and looked at Jamison.

Another brother stepped to Dax, who was crying and repeating his claim as if it were a plea for his life. The brother reached for black gloves in his pocket.

Scoot nodded to him.

Everyone stood in place as Emmit walked to Jamison and grabbed him to drag him out of the room.

At 2 AM, Val woke to the sound of water running. She rolled over to see the light on in the bathroom and was about to roll back over, but then she heard a voice.

It was Jamison's, as she expected, but there was something about the sound. It was cracked and weak like Tyrian's after a fall. And where there might have been pauses for a response, she heard an ongoing lost nervous chatter that made her call out to her husband.

"Jamison?" Val was already getting out of the bed to see what the matter was in the bathroom.

Jamison was standing at the sink, bent over with his hands in a pool of water he kept splashing in his face.

Val stood in the doorway and watched this cycle repeat itself between bits of conversation Jamison was having with his reflection.

"What the fuck! Fuck! Fuck!" Jamison would bring his soaking hands to his face and rinse. He'd stand and look at his face in the mirror. "Fuck! What the fuck!"

"You okay?" Val whispered, almost afraid to interrupt him.

"Fuck, man! What the fuck!" Jamison's washing became more intense. As he brought the water to his face, drops went splashing to the floor.

"You need anything?" Val knew not to touch him. Not to try to intervene between him and whatever he was in the mirror. She'd never seen Jamison like that, but she just knew to step back, keep her distance.

Jamison stopped washing and stood and looked at himself. When Emmit had walked him to the car, his arm over Jamison's shoulder, he'd revealed Dax's fate.

"You get home, son. You stay there," Emmit had said.

"What about him? What's going to happen?" Jamison had asked.

"He knows who we are. He's not going to cooperate. We have no choice."

"Jamison?" Val called sympathetically.

Jamison looked at his eyes. His chest. His heart beating so fast through the black hoodie. He began to fight with the hoodie, trying to get it off, cursing "fuck" the whole time.

Val came into the bathroom to try to help him, but he pushed her away and pulled the hoodie off, throwing it to the floor.

"What's wrong, baby?" Val was crying then. "Tell me what's wrong. What happened? Where were you?" Val was thinking there was something with Keet. He'd promised he'd be back.

Jamison was facing his nude chest in the mirror now. He was shaking uncontrollably. Spit and tears were mixing at his chin.

"I didn't want this. None of this. I didn't want this," he cried to the mirror. He remembered Emmit's face as he'd stuffed Jamison into the car to send him home. "And I told you to stay away from the jail, didn't I, son?" Emmit had brought up. "Told you it wouldn't be no good. See what happens when people do what they're not supposed to do? Keep your promises." Emmit had closed the car door, and as he pulled his hand away, Jamison noticed the ring. The fraternity ring. Right on his pinky finger. A black fist on top of a phoenix. Their symbol in the middle. The vision burned through his brain. Screamed at him. Hollered like a drum in the middle of a desert. Everything was dead.

"Shit is crazy. He's just a kid. A fucking kid," Jamison contemplated with himself.

"Who, baby? Who is it?" Val pleaded. "You're scaring me."

"No, this isn't happening. Can't be happening. Not me!" Jamison turned from his face and bolted out of the bathroom to the bedroom. "It can't be. It's not real! No!"

"What is it?" Val asked on his heels.

Jamison got the remote control and turned the television back onto the news.

"Oh, you mean the story about you at the jail? Is that it? What's got you so upset?" Val asked.

The light from the television poured into the dark bedroom, demanding silence.

A reporter was standing in front of Grady Memorial Hospital with tears in her eyes.

"I apologize for the tears, but this really hits us hard here at Fox Five News," the woman said into the camera. "Reporter Dax Thomas was a rising star whose potential was without measure. His future was quite bright. But as reported at the top of the hour, tonight that light has been snuffed out. Dax was the victim of a violent home invasion. He fought for his life. He lost that battle just a few minutes ago here after being rushed to Grady Memorial Hospital."

Jamison and Val stood in the middle of the bedroom floor watching the television.

The reporter turned to a police officer in full uniform. It was the brother Jamison had seen standing over Dax's body, reaching for the black gloves.

"Officer Webb here is a spokesman for the Atlanta Police Department. He's been on the scene all night. What information can you share with us about this tragic loss?"

"Well, all we can confirm now is that Dax Thomas was involved in an apparent home invasion. There are signs of a struggle in the home. Some bullet holes in the walls. We can't confirm who was shooting just yet. But we do know Mr. Thomas died from a fatal gunshot wound to the head."

"Any suspects?"

"No comment. We'll be sure to inform the people of Atlanta of any progress when we can."

"A Mother's Love"

One man was dead. One man was dying. Inside. Inside of his house. On the couch. In the den. Lights off. Television on. For days. For nights. Two weeks passed. A mother was growing worried.

Mrs. Taylor was that mother, and one dewy late summer morning, she returned to her son's doorstep to terminate the matter of her worry after a morning walk she begrudgingly took with her doctor's orders.

Her daughter-in-law had come to her room the night Dax Thomas had been murdered. Val was hysterical, pointing down the hallway to her bedroom, crying that Jamison was going crazy. With her bedroom door open, Mrs. Taylor could hear cracking and breaking, trashing and thrashing about in the room down the hall. She hopped out of her bed like any mother would if she heard such a thing coming from her child's room at 3 in the morning. No robe on. No slippers. Her sagging breasts dented the fabric of her nightgown just above her navel. Her wig was off. Two gray plaits flanked her shoulders. In her son's bedroom, she found Jamison in the middle of a tirade. He was throwing anything he could get in his hands. Crying. Sobbing. Hollering about a boy being dead. "Just a boy. Just a boy."

A clock barely missed Mrs. Taylor's head at the door. She hardly moved. With the fortitude of a sergeant sent thrice into combat, she stood at attention and held her hand up to keep Val out of the room.

"Stay out here," she'd ordered the woman before stepping into the room and closing Val out. Mrs. Taylor moved into a corner and let Jamison wreck his world until he was exhausted. Soon, her little boy was sitting on the floor at the foot of his bed crying into his knees. Funny how he looked so small to her. How every man could always look like a little helpless, grinning baby boy to his mother. She was the only person who could never be surprised by his tears. She'd seen them first. Nursed most of them herself. Mrs. Taylor sat on the bed and moved Jamison's head to rest it against her knee. "Tell Mama," she urged with a stern voice black mothers reserved for business they knew their sons would bring in from the street. "You tell your mama everything." And Jamison told. Everything. About the phone call he'd made. About how his fraternity brothers had killed that reporter, put the body in that house, and planted their own evidence. About how he was responsible. Back straight up, eyes dry as egg shells, Mrs. Taylor held her son's head tight to her knee and let his tears run down her leg. He said how he'd never wanted this. How he wanted it all to stop. To go back. To stop everything.

"Shhhh," she began to quiet him as he got louder. "Shhh." She rocked and rocked. "Shhhh." Soon Jamison was quiet and a mother was giving orders. The first thing she told him was to never repeat what he'd said to her to anyone else in the world ever again. Not to Val. Not to Leaf. Not to Jesus Christ if he came down to earth himself. Never. Second, she said, "Let this shit go." There wasn't anything he could do about a dead reporter. Third: "Watch your back. Never stop watching your back. I don't care what you thought this was going to be. I don't care what it is. You watch your back like I told you to do. You never stop. We may not be in the West End anymore, baby. But the trick is that the West End don't stop when you get on the highway."

Two weeks later when Mrs. Taylor stepped into the house after her walk, she was sure Jamison had followed two of those points, but the lasting evidence of the mayor being holed up in the dark den watching television meant he wasn't exactly letting it go. She vowed to put that motion in order right then. And she knew she could do it. If she had to lift Jamison off the couch herself and carry him on her back out of that house and down to city hall to work, she would. It was just a matter of positioning.

But there was more than that to her matter of worry. There was the silver Maserati she'd seen parked around the corner. A man sitting inside. Her daughter-in-law sitting beside him, shaking her head like she was arguing with him. Mrs. Taylor had been approaching the car from behind, but she knew Val's facial silhouette. She'd studied it the way a lion memorizes the angles of the lock keeping his cage closed. She'd stopped in her tracks. Watched for a few seconds and turned around to return to her son dying of a dream deferred.

"Get up! Get your ass up!"—there was tough love when Mrs. Taylor walked into the den in her orange velour sweat suit and brunette walking wig. She left the light off, and went right for the window curtains—the shock of daylight would be far more of a threat to dilated eyes.

Jamison moaned like a sleeping giant at the white light. A thin beard was growing in from ear to ear. He had on glasses with one arm missing, boxers, and flip-flops. A bag of apples he'd been eating since the day before was on the floor beside the couch where he was lying. "Close that. I can't see." His hand was shielding his eyes from the light.

"Good. Now, get up. Tired of you laid up in here on this damn couch." Mrs. Taylor went for Jamison's feet first.

He pulled away from her and huddled in annoyance into the corner of the sofa. "Mama, stop!"

She continued to prod, standing over him. "Get up! Get out of this house!"

"I can't. I'm sick!"

"Sick? Well, what's wrong with you? How are you sick? What's aching you?" She shoved her hand through his force field of flailing hands to pat his forehead and feel the lymph nodes beneath his chin. "And don't tell me what you told that white boy, because I been your mama since you been on this earth and ain't not one of those summers found you with a flu. Not under my watch, they ain't!" Mrs. Taylor continued her fake health inspection as they tussled, and gave up with, "Ain't nothing wrong with you, boy!" She walked to the television and turned it off after an elongated search for the hidden power switch. "Now, get up!"

"You're killing me!"

"No, you're killing you!"

The word "kill" sat in the air for a second.

"I can't go outside." Jamison looked at the window.

"Sure you can. One foot in front of the other. How long you think that white boy can run city hall? Cover for you? Before he starts thinking he is you? Before other people start thinking he is you?"

"That's not how it works."

"You tell me how it works then. You going to quit at being mayor because things are getting hard?"

"This ain't hard," Jamison said, looking at his mother. "This is—this is bad. It's crazy. Out of control."

"Then get control. Take control."

"I don't know if I want to. If I can."

"You have to. Too many things out of order around here. Everywhere."

Mrs. Taylor sat beside Jamison and told him about Val parked around the corner in the gray Maserati.

"It could be anything. Don't jump to conclusions," Jamison

said, trying to consider why the color and the make of the car sounded so familiar to him "You sure it was her?"

Mrs. Taylor ignored this. "What kind of married woman sits in a car around the corner from her house arguing with another man? Wasn't nothing right about it."

"Maybe it was nothing," Jamison said.

"And maybe pigs shit potato salad. And maybe the Easter bunny is real. You know I don't make mistakes like that. Do I?"

"No, Mama. You don't."

"Exactly. Now, something ain't right with that girl. I been telling you that from the door. She ain't good enough for you and she's trifling. Now, beauty fades, son."

"Please don't give me a lecture. I'll get up. I'll leave the house. Just don't lecture me."

"No, you listen to me." Mrs. Taylor stopped Jamison from leaving her side. "Apples don't fall far from the tree. What you see in her mama is what you'll be looking at in ten years. I told you that about that Kerry and her mama. And when Val's mother left this house, what did your maid tell you?"

"What?"

"Don't play stupid with me."

"What? About the picture frame missing?"

"Yes," Mrs. Taylor said. "That and that silver candelabra from the dining room. And the little card holder from your office. Now, what does that tell you?"

"That Tyrian probably took all of that stuff and hid it somewhere in this house."

"And you're a damn fool if you believe that. Her mama stole that stuff. Probably pawned your stuff as soon as she got off the bus in Tennessee. Worse, she took it to the geechie man and got a voodoo rook on you. Ever think of that?"

Jamison rolled his eyes and finally broke free of the hold he let his mother have on him. He promised to do anything she wanted, only so he could escape her mouth.

⁓ ● ⁓

After I saw Keet at Paschal's that night, he started calling me every day, at every hour. I had Leaf change my phone number twice complaining some crazy person must've gotten my number, but when Leaf mentioned that he could stop the crazy person by having the calls traced, I knew I couldn't go back to him again. I had to answer the phone.

Keet wanted to meet. He wanted information. I told him I didn't know anything and he just laughed. He reminded me about some naked pictures I took for him in Negril. Said he was looking at them on his phone. Then he reminded me how often people lost their cell phones. I knew what he meant. And I knew Keet wasn't one to place idle threats. He was more than serious, so when he called from outside the house one morning when the sun was really low, I got my ass out of bed and went right to the window. He was standing beside his car in the driveway. Waving at me.

"You always look beautiful in the morning," he said when I got in the car.

I ignored him and insisted that he pull out of the driveway and drive around the corner so Jamison didn't happen to come to the window and see us sitting there. I had no intention of telling him anything—I didn't know anything. I just wanted him to go away.

"What's going on with my mayor? How's he doing?"

"He's fine," I said.

"No one's seen him around. I keep calling the office about my new job and everyone's quiet."

"He's sick."

"Sick or fine?" Keet looked at me, and I felt as fragile and breakable as that girl in the blue skirt outside his apartment that night. He looked at my stomach. "How's my baby?"

"Stop." I looked around the car to see if there was anything I could grab.

"I was thinking the other night about the last time we had sex."

Keet relaxed himself dramatically and cradled his head in his headrest. "I know we slept together last year. But that was eleven months ago, so if that was my baby you'd have had it by now."

"This is not your baby," I said, but he kept talking right over me.

"But there was also that other time," he went on. "You know when you came crying to me about how your new boyfriend and his mama were so mean to you. You remember that?"

"This is not your baby."

"Now, that couldn't have been more than six months ago, First Lady." Keet laughed. "You're about six months pregnant right? Isn't that what you told that reporter during the press conference you had with Mr. Mayor?"

"This is not your baby."

He looked at me. "But that'd be nice. Right?" He ran his finger along the side of my face. "So fucking pretty. Make a brother lose his mind, fucking with you. Got the mayor whipped—don't you?"

"What do you want to know?" I asked, remembering that Keet kept a loaded .38 in the glove compartment and probably had another gun under his seat and behind his back. "Just tell me."

"What's he been saying about Dax Thomas?"

"That reporter?"

"Yeah. Jamison been saying anything about him?"

"What about him? What would he say about him?"

"Everyone's seen the news," Keet said. "You know. Has he mentioned who killed him?"

"Do you know who killed him?" I asked.

"Don't play with me, bitch! What did he say?" Keet's eyes cut my face cold to let me know what was at stake. It was the look he'd give one of his girls on the street. I looked at the glove compartment without moving one of my pupils from his eyes.

"He didn't say anything! Didn't tell me anything."

"You sure?"

"I don't know anything," I said again.

Keet cut and cut and cut with his eyes.

I took every slice hard, but I didn't let on that I knew anything because I didn't know anything. Since that night Dax died, every inch of rope Jamison had given me had burned to nothing. He'd told me nothing. He was moving around like I wasn't even there. Looking around me. Past me. Through me. In his empty eyes I almost saw Keet. Keet in Jamison. It was like I'd left one gangster to be with another gangster, only the second gangster didn't even know that he was gangster. Or did he?

When Val entered the back door of the house, Jamison was washed, shaved, and standing in the kitchen drinking a cup of freshly squeezed orange juice that had come compliments of his mother. He hadn't yet decided what he was going to say to Val, but he started anyway.

"My mother saw you."

Val hadn't expected that Jamison would be out of bed. She tried to rush past him to get upstairs, but he kept talking.

"You were in a car around the corner?" he added.

"No." This flimsy answer was all she could divine in response to the direct accusation in her new husband's tone.

"So, she didn't see you in a car?" Jamison formed his question in a new way that gave Val little extra time to come up with something more explanatory.

"No. It wasn't me. I was walking."

"Walking?" Jamison looked Val over—she was wearing jogging pants, a tank top and flip-flops. Her darkening nipples were pressing through her shirt.

Val looked down at her flip-flops and nipples, too. She needed something better to say.

"It was just an old friend," she offered. "I was walking and I saw him and we talked for a second."

"Really?"

"Really. Is that a problem?"

"Well, a friend comes to knock on your door, not sit around the corner in a car," Jamison said, sounding like a father who'd caught his teenage daughter sneaking into her window after a night out partying.

"It was too early for him to come in," Val said, and she, too, was beginning to sound as if she was caught in the father/teenage-daughter scenario. Somehow that stung her nerves like a whip against her back. She felt she could hear Mrs. Taylor upstairs in her room laughing.

"Too early?" Jamison repeated the response as weakly as it had come off. "Do I look like a fool to you?"

"Well, do I look like a kid to you? Have to answer to you when I'm coming and going?" Val asked.

"Yes, I guess you do. Running around here with your breasts out, pregnant, jumping in cars with other niggas. Yes, you do," Jamison said.

"So, now I was with another *nigga*? You don't even sound right saying that word."

"You said you were with someone. I'm just going by what you told me. By who you are."

"Who I am?" Val stepped toward Jamison.

"I'm just saying, you know what they say about taking a girl out the projects," Jamison said. "Kerry never did anything like that."

"Fuck you, Jamison!" Val said, backing off from Jamison. She felt a little kick at her bladder as she hurried out of the room.

"Yes, fuck me," Jamison hollered at her. "Fuck me! Fuck me in my fucking house!"

Jamison threw his empty glass into the sink, where it shattered. He cursed to himself a few more times without looking at the tiny glass shards scattered around the drain.

He thought to follow Val up the stairs, continue the fight and put out the flames of a fire that would burn the backside of any man. But, somehow, the situation hadn't made that strong of an impression on him as he'd thought, as it maybe should've. The fire was competing on a long to-do list of situations that had higher flames scorching his rear. Flames that had him lying in bed pretending to be asleep when Val's phone had rung early that morning.

"Just send her the money. Call right now to say you're sending the money," Jamison said after calling Leaf to catch him up on a list of things he wanted done before they met at a lunch date with the chief of police. Leaf already had rescheduled twice after Jamison had come down with his summer flu.

"It's 7 AM in L.A. right now," Leaf pointed out.

"I don't care. Get it done," Jamison said.

"Okay. But you know we already sent something. I'm thinking we could just—how long do you think you can keep this up?"

"I didn't ask what you think," Jamison said. "Just do it."

"Okay . . . and what about the meeting? You need me to pick you up?"

"No, I'm fine. I'll get over there myself. And, look, get together all the information you can about Ras's case and the Hawks' starting-five program."

"For the meeting with Chief York?" Leaf asked.

"Yes. I want everything at the meeting."

"Why?" Leaf pushed. The meeting was supposed to be a short political photo-op where Chief York and Mayor Taylor were to be strategically spotted in deep discussion to put a stop to the media's hype about a new spike in violence in the city. Since Dax's death, a bunch of city-dwelling yuppies and buppies had reported to the letter any social infractions that would make headlines: rapes and bar fights, muggings and murders. Bad press about Atlanta was making its way around the country, and that bad press meant bad news for both the mayor and his chief. For the former, it meant a shortening list of new investors to the city; for the latter, it meant a longer list of new criminals to the city.

"Why? Because I told you to do it," Jamison said to Leaf while remembering his mother's charge about the younger man trying to take the older man's seat at the big table. He was sure this probably wasn't the case, but then there was also the matter of how many times his mother had been wrong about such things. If he was taking tally, she was right about Leaf getting cozy in his chair.

"Mayor Taylor, I'm not trying to step on your shoes, but I don't think it's a good time to bring that up. This is just a short meeting, and I'm not sure Chief York would be keen on hearing anything about Ras right now—not the way he's been talking about it with reporters."

Chief York had been using Ras as a poster child for his mission to clean up the filth on the dirtiest streets in the city, but during his sorrowful slumber, Jamison had determined that his first order of business would be to find any justice he could for his friend. Wallowing in his sadness about seeking revenge against Dax, he'd decided to avenge Ras. Well, maybe not "avenge," not "save" in the way superheroes swoop down from the clouds to capture a little boy who's about to be flattened by a train. And maybe not even find "justice" in a way that would make someone envision him going before a grand jury, putting his right hand on a Bible, and vowing that he'd never known his friend to be a lover of marijuana, white girls, and guns. But he was going to get rid of the questions picking at him. The old ones he'd had and the new one Ras had brought to his attention at the prison. He didn't intend to unfold his laundry list before the chief like a pop quiz or make a bunch of accusations and demands. He still wasn't even sure what he was dealing with, what he was thinking. But he'd try something anyway. He had to. If what the chief wanted was a photo-op with the makings of a marketing campaign that could save both of them, Jamison would give it to him. In the face of bad press, he'd bring up the possibility of more good press in the gold mine of promises from the basketball players.

"Don't worry about timing," Jamison said to Leaf before hanging up the phone. "Just have the paperwork."

A husband gone to a meeting meant a wife left home alone—a wife and a mother. And not just any wife. And not just any mother. One who was angry. One who was furious. Both who believed the other was the source of the overwhelming emotion.

And while the husband was away having barbeque chicken with specialty white sauce and macaroni and cheese with the chief of police, who also happened to be his fraternity brother, before cameramen miles away in Candler Park at Fox Brothers BBQ, these two women, who were actually more alike than different, stayed in their separate corners of a mini-mansion that might seem more like a castle to people with smaller personalities. But these two had big personalities, and as one might imagine even in the biggest space, two bigger things will eventually cross paths.

So, when the sun went down, the big personalities found themselves moving from their separate corners in the shrinking mansion, one from her bedroom with soap opera reruns playing on the television and one from her bathroom, where the cold tile was no longer useful to soothe her swollen feet. Both wandered somewhere neither could really avoid for long: the kitchen.

The mother was at the stove, in front of a boiling pot, stirring and singing and smiling and maybe whistling in between.

The wife was walking in, rolling her eyes, wondering what in the hell her mother-in-law had to sing and smile and whistle about. She went to the refrigerator and opened it, looked around for whatever compelled her to the kitchen. As usual, Lorna had packed the chrome subzero with all of Jamison's favorites, although Val had repeatedly emailed Lorna her list of items.

Val eased back on her swollen feet and considered calling Jamison to have him bring her back a plate from Fox Brothers when she heard a pleasant greeting from a familiar voice that wasn't ever pleasant.

"Baby, you hungry?"

Val couldn't see Mrs. Taylor. The open refrigerator door separated them like a partition between work cubicles. Val frowned and looked in Mrs. Taylor's direction suspiciously. She was sure Mrs. Taylor knew her son wasn't in the house, so she wondered who Mrs. Taylor thought could be on the other side of the refrigerator door who wanted to be called her "baby." Maybe Mrs. Taylor was sinking into senility, too?

"Well, I'm cooking over here if you're hungry. Making some soup. Got me some okra and chicken breasts and truffle salt and cayenne pepper in it. Just the way I like it." Mrs. Taylor droned on with Val still on the other side of the refrigerator. "A lot of people don't like it like this, but I do. *Nutritious and delicious!* That's what I like to say. What Jamison likes to say, too." She laughed some more.

Val was trying hard to keep her eyes rolling in steady rotation, but the list of select, otherwise odd ingredients in the peppered pot had her ears at attention. Those were the things on the list she'd emailed the maid. The things her belly bump had her craving. She closed the refrigerator door slowly, like a cat climbing out of a corner.

"You put a lot of pepper in it?" Val asked without realizing she'd said a word.

"Hell yeah! I like my food Cajun style! Hot and sassy—like me. Why—you don't like it like that?" Mrs. Taylor frowned regretfully.

"No, I do! I love spicy food!" Val's eyes and heart and gut softened at the idea of the boiling matter on the stove finding its way into a bowl for her. For the last three days she'd been craving the kinds of spices Mama Fee cooked in her big pot in Memphis. A soup of okra and cayenne might make her forget an old enemy. Might. But old habits seldom die in a kitchen. And when Val looked from the pot to the pot stirrer, her little phony smile hiding beneath a black wig, Val remembered everything Jamison told her about his mother's little spy job outside that morning and the frown returned to her face.

"I ain't hungry," Val said suddenly.

"What? Not hungry? But you just—"

"I ain't hungry!" Val set her eyeballs back into circular motion and turned to walk out of the room with a still empty belly that was now hollering out for food in audible ways. But when she reached the threshold, the fiery child who could tongue lash her own mother to tears realized she'd been walking away and turning her back from trouble all day and she was just plain tired of the action. Tired of all of the acting.

"And, so you know, you need to mind your business," she said, with her rolling eyes back on Mrs. Taylor. "What I was doing outside didn't have nothing to do with you. And if you had a question, you needed to come to me first. Because I don't have nothing to hide from you. Everybody else, including your son, might be scared of you, but I'm not." Val snapped back, crossed her arms over her chest, and waited for a return jab, but Mrs. Taylor just kept smiling and stirring at her pot. After a long time waiting, she had no choice but to ask the smiling woman, "What?"

Mrs. Taylor looked at Val with her purest smile. "I'm sorry," she offered meekly.

"What?"

"I'm sorry for what I did." She placed the long wooden spoon she'd been stirring with on the counter beside her brew and walked over to Val. "I was upstairs listening to you two argue and"—she extended a hand to place it on Val's shoulder in a tender way—"I felt bad. I *feel* bad."

Val snatched away from a touch that felt cold. "You should feel bad."

"You're mad. I get that, but I was just looking out for my son's best interests," Mrs. Taylor said. "You're not a mother yet, so you don't know, but you will soon. Being a mother is hard. You're always looking out for your kids—sometimes you can be blinded by it."

"Whatever. Look, I'm not about to take parenting advice from you."

"Okay. You don't have to, darling." Mrs. Taylor reached for Val's shoulder again and this time she did not move. "But I am asking that you accept my apology. Just for right now. We both want what's best for Jamison. Right? To make him happy?"

Val nodded.

"And that's only going to happen if we're getting along."

"You've said this before," Val said, remembering the little chat Mrs. Taylor had initiated at the courthouse.

"I know. I know." Mrs. Taylor laughed a little at her obvious backtrack. "But I really mean it this time. I heard Jamison's voice today, and I realized something—I don't want to hear him sad or upset. And I know he can't handle this situation, so I have to. I need to step up."

"Step up?"

"Yes. Look, I realized that after I get things in order here in this house between me and you and that baby, I can go. Jamison can handle the rest on his own. He'll know what to do," Mrs. Taylor explained.

"So, now you're moving out?" Val worked hard to temper her voice to hide jubilant emotions concerning that revelation. Still, her excitement gleamed through unsophisticated eyes that led Mrs. Taylor back to her pot.

"Yes, I am!" Mrs. Taylor claimed, walking over to the pot as she wiped her hands on an old Christmas-themed apron she'd found tucked deep in the back of a cabinet beside the stove. "And to celebrate, I decided to make some of my famous soup"—she looked back at Val when she made it to the pot—"for my daughter-in-law."

"You made that soup for me?" Val took two steps to the pot. Her hands were fidgeting behind her back like a little girl who'd just come in from playing in the snow to discover a cup of real cocoa simmering just for her on the stove. The unconscious emotion, a fuzzy memory of things Val had seen children expect and receive on television shows and in movies was something she'd hardly had in her life or appreciated enough to acknowledge as it was happening. It was mother love. Or mother comfort. Or something that was made to look like it.

Mrs. Taylor went to the cupboard and pulled out a huge sable bowl. "You sit down, baby. Get off those swollen feet and let me take care of you. I know you're hungry. I heard your stomach growling."

Val laughed and rubbed her stomach. "You sure?" she asked.

"Sure? I'm obliged. Go'on and sit down." Mrs. Taylor was filling the bowl with a healthy serving of the stew. She grabbed a spoon as she told Val about Jamison's love of summer soup and placed the bowl on the kitchen table.

Val was still standing. Looking at the chair and the bowl. The woman standing beside the seated meal.

"Sit down, baby. Eat!" Mrs. Taylor beckoned Val to the seat.

Something in the expectant mother's toes felt numb or cold or reluctant. She considered moving her feet, but with even the thought of progress, there was a little sting, preventing any movement. It wasn't sharp or painful. More like a pulse of a vibrating alarm set to low.

"Sit down," Mrs. Taylor urged more directly this time. "The soup is for you." She smiled when Val looked at her. "Come on. Sit and eat."

Mrs. Thirjane Jackson had never been the kind of mother to make a meal for her child. She never expected that from herself, so no one else ever expected that from her. She was better at other things—writing checks in support of sorority fundraisers, ordering furniture for furnished bedrooms, predicting if the sun was too high in the sky for a disinterested person of any hue to go outside expecting acceptable results. With this in mind, when Kerry called her mother to set up taco night at Grandma's for Thirjane's only grandchild, Tyrian, it went without saying who would do the cooking . . . and cleaning.

When Kerry had pulled up in her mother's driveway in a more dated section of Cascade where first-generation Cascadians whose parents had moved them to the Westside upper-class black utopia when they were just children still ruled the roost, she had brown paper bags in her backseat.

"No, you can't sell your sneakers on eBay. I don't care what Spenser's mother let him do," Kerry said to Tyrian in her mother's kitchen. She was standing by the stove, tossing softening onions and green peppers in a skillet.

Tyrian was sitting at the kitchen table beside his grandmother, showing her how to buy a Herman Miller Eames chair off of eBay on his iPad.

"But I can make money," Tyrian said. "A lot of money."

"What do you need with money?" Kerry asked. "I give you money. You don't need anything extra than what I give you. And I don't give you sneakers to sell on eBay."

Thirjane was struggling to keep up with Tyrian's finger moving so swiftly over the screen. She squinted in her glasses and thought maybe she should've just bought the Herman Miller in the showroom like she'd planned in the first place. She was redecorating her fourth bedroom for the third time. The saleswoman at the showroom, who was actually just tired of trying to satisfy Thirjane, had suggested the old woman search for the perfect chair on eBay. The items were shipped straight from their warehouse and for half the price.

"Slow down, Ty," Thirjane ordered her grandson. She'd refused to call the boy by his name or bother committing the jumble of syllables to memory. When Tyrian had been small and couldn't talk to tell his mother, Thirjane would take him to tea parties with her and lie and tell people her grandson's name was Thomas. Sometimes Thurgood. Depended on the crowd.

"Sorry, Grandma," Tyrian said, backing his hands up off of the screen to let Thirjane get a peek through her silver wired Laurent glasses. He clicked on a chair and handed her the iPad, so she could zoom in closer herself. "What about Daddy? Can he do it?"

"Do what?" Kerry asked. Hearing "daddy" had sent a little tingle up her spine.

"Sell my sneakers on eBay."

"No one is selling anything on eBay," Kerry ordered finally. "Not you or your father. No one."

"Maybe I should sell my old furniture on eBay," Thirjane said, making it clear she was half listening to the conversation.

Kerry sighed and turned the fire off on the skillet. She took a sip from a glass of Coke she'd managed to spike with rum from her mother's old mirrored bar in the living room. Her little rum nips were the only way she was guaranteed to make it through taco night with Tyrian and Thirjane a sane woman. Family dinner always seemed like a good idea in theory, but up close and personal, it was more like a country song that had death in the chorus.

It couldn't be said that Kerry had a strained relationship with her mother. It was simply appropriate for its place and time. Southern stalwarts like Thirjane with her real diamonds and real pearls and classic St. John sweater at the dinner table didn't have children to love and protect them. It was more of a mission of communal continuance. A new generation to continue a legacy of comeuppance. A tradition to ensure that a talented ten percent would carry on. And Kerry had been born into this world. She had been raised by a list of traditions relegated through Jack and Jill, sorority cotillions, prep school, summers at Hilton Head, and a list of acceptable HBCUs, sororities, neighborhoods, dates, and mates. And, for sure, the promise that eventually she'd meet a young man who'd been pushed through the same muck and birthed anew, fit to marry her to continue the tale. But Kerry had met Jamison at that Spelman/Morehouse Valentine's Day ball. And, well, that had broken her mother's heart. And when the new husband had danced with his new mother-in-law at his wedding, she'd whispered in his ear, "You'll be her *first* husband."

"So, how's old Jamison?" Thirjane asked her daughter after they'd argued about eBay through dinner and Tyrian had happily excused himself to the den, where he'd sneak to watch music videos. She'd finished watching Kerry clean the kitchen and they'd moved to the sofa in the living room.

"Who?" Another little tingle went up Kerry's back and kind of tickled the hairs at the nape of her neck, so she moved her hand to scratch there.

"Jamison, I asked about Jamison," Thirjane repeated, slapping her daughter's hand away from her neck. "And stop scratching your neck. You've been doing that all night."

Kerry moved away from her mother in annoyance. "So, how is Jamison."

There was the tingle again.

"Fine. I guess." Kerry sighed and promised not to bother with the tickle at her neck. She'd been trying to ignore it for days. Since she'd seen Jamison at the golf course there were all of these dreams she kept having of him. The two of them together. Sometimes in a pool. Sometimes in his old dorm room. Sometimes in his office. Always naked. Always panting hard. She'd told Marcy about the dreams and her friend just laughed. She said it was because Kerry hadn't gotten "laid in like a year" and that it was probably just a little internal fight she was having about Val and the baby. She'd get over it . . . after she finally got laid. Kerry had no sexual prospects—she spent all of her free time at the divorced women's group therapy house—so she found herself at a sex shop buying a vibrator in hopes of getting rid of her fantasies about her ex-husband. When she returned home, she loaded the pair of triple A batteries into the back of the skin-like plastic penis that had come in three color choices—knight black, brother brown, and mellow yellow (she'd gone with brother brown)—in the middle of the night for fear Tyrian would hear the noise and come rushing into her bedroom. She locked her bedroom door, turned off the lights and the volume on the television up to drown out the incessant sound of the vibrator. She initially found a little reprieve from her agony and was gaining confidence in her best friend's advice. But then, when desire pulled the lids over her eyes and she found herself floating in the oasis of blackness in her mind, she found Jamison waiting for her. He was in the pool again. It was dark outside, but the lights shining from the bottom of the pool met the moon in a spectacular light show on the surface of the water. Kerry was standing on the side of the pool watching Jamison float naked on his back through the lights, his brown skin floating under and over the waves as they lapped against his back. "Come in," he called to her. And suddenly she was in the pool beside him and he was undoing her bikini top. "I've missed you," he whispered in her ear before kissing her there and then licking her earlobe. As they floated along, legs intertwined, he continued to caress her as he stroked her nipples and promised to be so gentle. Kerry's bikini bottom was off then, sinking or floating away. His hands were between her legs and his tongue was in her mouth. There was silence but she felt him say, "I love you" as he slid his penis into her vagina and pulled her on top of him. He kept them afloat until he made it to the side of the pool where a Romanesque fountain sent trickles of cool water between them. Their bodies moved with the water pushed by the moon. Slow and ethereal. They moaned into each other and their human sounds became a vibration that united their sensations. Kerry thrust her legs up and down over Jamison's waist, wrapped her arms tight over his head and felt them move against the waves. Hard and harder. She was about to forget where she was, but then, Jamison looked into her eyes and she saw that he was feeling the same thundering palpitation. She widened her legs and squeezed her middle, pulling him into her. Their moans became an animalistic crescendo into the open sky, chins facing the moon, they bayed and bayed and bayed. . . . and bayed.

"Girl, are you listening to me?" Thirjane plucked her child in the forehead. "Sitting there like you're a zombie or something. Hello?" She plucked Kerry again and again until Kerry came out of the memory of the pool.

"What?" Kerry queried distantly.

"Finally," Thirjane said. "If I wasn't mistaken, I'd think you were fantasizing about something." She cut her eyes.

"What? No. What are you talking about?"

"No, what are *you* talking about?"

"What?"

"About Jamison. You were about to tell me about Jamison."

"He's fine, Mama," Kerry almost growled. She knew her mother really didn't care about how Jamison was doing—unless he was doing poorly. It was no secret how Thirjane felt about Jamison and Mrs. Taylor. She'd held a dinner party the night Kerry's divorce had been finalized.

"Fine, my ass," Thirjane said. (She'd also sipped some of the rum—it was the only way she could make it through taco night too.)

"Mama, watch your mouth," Kerry said, playing mother. "What if Tyrian hears you?"

"Listen, my mama, daddy, and husband are all dead; I speak as I please now," Thirjane said. "Yes, Lord!"

"Fine, Mama."

"So, how's he doing?"

"I said he's fine."

"No, he isn't. I saw him on the news."

"Well, if you know he isn't fine, then why did you ask?" Kerry looked at her mother.

"Lord, sometimes talking to you is like talking to an inmate," Thirjane said. "You're so defensive. Act like you're still married to him."

"I know I'm not married to him anymore. I'm the one who filed for the divorce. Remember?"

"Yeah, after he came back here with his tail between his legs after running off with that redhead gal to Los Angeles." The rum made Thirjane shake her index finger in Kerry's face. "I told you. I always told you. No class amounts to *no class*. Can't change that. It's just the way it is. Him and that mama of his. Lord Jesus, I saw that circus a mile away."

"Well, thank you for all of your advice and support," Kerry snapped, remembering how her mother had left her sitting in a jail cell after she'd been arrested for fighting with Jamison in front of police officers when she'd found his truck parked outside the redhead's house. Kerry had been eight months pregnant.

"There you go again. What's gotten into you? Why are you so touchy about this, dear?"

"I'm not touchy," Kerry said. "It's just that there's a lot going on. And Jamison is Tyrian's father, so . . ."

"So?"

"So, I care." Kerry looked at her nude ring finger. For months after she'd removed her wedding band, she had been sure the sliver of blond skin would never darken, but soon it had. "It's like everyone is trying to make it sound like he's so horrible. Like he's bad. All in the news. You know, a listener called into the radio today and said Jamison was a drug dealer? That he was leading a cartel?" Kerry laughed. "It's like he's down and everyone's trying to kick."

"So?" Thirjane flashed a sarcastic frown. This was reason to celebrate—not gain an attitude. While she was no Mrs. Taylor, her love for her daughter was as fierce as that of any mother who could produce a child imbued with such careful attention to others. And like any mother who'd seen her daughter through a painful divorce, she forever hated those she blamed for it all. So, if people were kicking Jamison while he was down, she'd volunteer to get right in line.

"So . . . it's not right. He's not a drug dealer. And he's not a bad person. You know that, Mama," Kerry said. "Come on, you may not like Jamison, but you know he'd never do anything to purposefully hurt anyone. His heart isn't like that."

"*His* heart? Kerry, that man broke *your* heart."

"No, once upon a time, that man tried to mend my heart. You know what he did for me. What he did for us. For Daddy," Kerry replied, bringing up the reason Thirjane couldn't seem to get the decorations right in the fourth bedroom. After her husband had come home from the hospital after being in a coma for so many years, his ribs looking like they'd poke through his skin, Thirjane had moved him and his hospital bed into the room and painted it blue. The miracle of his recovery, which had given his wife two more years with him, was due to the stories Jamison whispered into his ear while he was still in his long sleep. While Thirjane and Kerry had long stopped going to visit their husband and father hooked up to machines and wasting away in a bed, Jamison had visited his father-in-law in secret.

"You feel sorry for him now?" Thirjane said as if that was ridiculous.

"I just want everyone to give him a chance to do what I know he can do. To stop this lying."

"Nothing you can do about that now," Thirjane said. "This is about old Atlanta. That old wall. I told you that when he was running for office. They may take him in, but he's never going to be one of them. One of us."

"That world is over, Mama," Kerry defended, though she knew her mother wasn't wrong.

"It's never over. Can't be. Not in a city like this. Been here all my life and one thing I know is that history moves Atlanta—from Peachtree down here, to Peachtree up there," Thirjane said.

"And class moves history. You add that up and you know what I'm saying is true. Jamison may have the money to play, but they're only letting him play because they need him right now because of his position. Need him for contracts, signatures, deals. That's it. Money. Then he's out. Atlanta. I've seen it too many times." Thirjane laughed. "I told you first."

"I know. But there has to be something I can do."

"No. Better you sit aside. Keep your own name intact for when it all comes down. My name."

Kerry looked down at her glass nervously and said lowly, almost as if she didn't want her mother to hear, "I called someone."

"Come again?" Thirjane leaned over.

"I called someone to, you know, to get some information for me," Kerry revealed. She hadn't told her mother about the detective she'd hired to follow Jamison after the divorce.

"Someone like who?" Thirjane leaned into Kerry and whispered, "Like a detective?" She backed up. "For what?"

"I can't tell you now, Mama. It's just a lot going on. I feel like I need to talk to him . . . but I promised some people I wouldn't say anything. Do anything." Kerry looked down into her empty glass. It was times like this when she missed her old aunt Luchie, Thirjane's sister, who had worn heels with sweat suits and had run off to Paris with the love of her life when she was what most people called a senior citizen. Aunt Luchie had taken Kerry in when she first walked out on Jamison. She would've understood about the detective. Told Kerry to follow her heart and back it up with her brain. She'd died a month after Kerry's father. Kerry had flown to Paris alone and sprinkled her ashes into the sea in Cannes. "But I need to protect my family. I have to say something. That's my son's father."

Thirjane was shaking her index finger again. "No-no-no. You stop yourself right there. You have to let this go. To let him go. He's not yours to protect. That man has a wife and a child on the way. You let them handle his mess."

"I can't."

"Why?"

"Because of my child—because of Tyr—"

"No, that's where you're confused. You need to let him go for Tyrian. Not hold onto him," Thirjane said. "You move on for him. So he can move on too. You got that boy thinking his parents can still get together, because you won't move on. You don't think he knows his mama has one foot still in the water? I think both of you do."

"One foot in the water? No, I don't," Kerry said. "And he doesn't either. We've moved on. Both of us."

Thirjane grinned like a wise woman. "I know what you're doing. I know how you feel. I'm your mother. You can't hide anything from me. Not even what you hide from yourself. You still love that man."

"No, I don—"

"All that schooling you have. Talking about how you're getting back on your feet. Went and cut off all your pretty hair. Joined that yoga studio. The divorce group. And no man in your life yet?"

"So?"

Thirjane laughed. "So? That's not moving on. You're still young. Still beautiful. You should be remarried already. Dawn, Ethel's daughter, found someone after her divorce. Married that news anchor. Had two more babies. That's moving on."

"That's different," Kerry said. "And I'm not competing with Dawn. I'm living my life how I choose."

"I guess you *choose* to live it alone then," Thirjane pointed out. "But Jamison sure isn't. Heard he even slept with that tart Countess Lindsey. And now he's put a ring on a stripper. Got her pregnant."

"You already said that," Kerry said.

"And I'll say it again soon. As many times as my heart pleases. I'm hoping you'll hear it. Someone needs to." Thirjane got up from the couch and went to the bar to make herself another drink—without the Coke.

So many years later, when recalling this night with a friend at a bar in Memphis, Val would remember that the pain started in her right side. It was nine o'clock at night. She was lying in bed and she felt the pain, clear and sharp like a razor blade over her thumb; it flashed through the right side of her body, from back to navel. She rolled over and called Jamison immediately. She just knew to do that. Told him to get in the car and get home faster than he could.

Jamison would never tell anyone that he didn't do that. He told Val he was right on his way, but he wasn't. It actually took him ten more minutes to leave the bar where he was having scotch with the chief. And this was for nothing but a hunch. The cameras were gone. The chief wasn't talking, agreeing, planning. Jamison kept thinking if he could say the same thing in a new way, maybe, just maybe, he'd get somewhere with the person he'd put in office. But there seemed to be some closed door between them.

The chief, whose sheer size, both physically and mentally, was bigger than that of any man Jamison had ever known, was talking about wanting to stick to protocol where Ras and his dying project to get scholarships for boys in the hood was concerned. So, Jamison said it in a new way: "What if they took Ras's name off the project?" It could be the chief's project. He could be the one to get all the hugs and shine from connecting the feathers of hawks with the earthly beings who watched them fly. Then the giant man who led a force of giant men mentioned not wanting to ruffle someone's feathers. So, Jamison asked, "Whose feathers?"

To that, the chief said the kind of thing that ensured little boys outgrew their belief in giants: "I can't do it. My hands are tied on this." He jumped up from his half-finished scotch and put the straw fedora he was wearing back over his massive head.

Jamison simply asked, "Why?"

The chief, a man Jamison knew had a good heart, smiled and said something that would prove to be the mayor's greatest teacher: "When you're in the police academy, you're taught that the truth you're seeking is right in front of you. It's seldom as mysterious as you believe." He held out one arm to hug Jamison but used his other hand to give him the fraternity handshake. In the embrace, Jamison felt the chief's fraternity ring stabbing into his gut.

Val was sitting on the bathroom floor. Shaking. The white sides of her hands were turning blue. Her pink nightgown was warm and sticky and crimson at the bottom. She was saying something to no one. Not even herself. Just a litany of sorrowful syllables that might sound like a cry to someone listening on the other side of the wall.

Jamison found the bed empty. The sheets stained. He called Val's name as he stepped into the bathroom. Looked from her sitting there shaking to a mess in the toilet no person should see or recall.

Val pointed to the toilet. And then there was a mother's wail. It commanded every sense. Shook the very walls of the house, sent ripples along the concrete sidewalks, set a fire in a forest someplace far away.

"Oh my God!" Jamison fell to his knees where he was. His tears erupted from someplace old. Erupted from someplace tired. From someplace where nothing was going right. Where an ending could overtake a possibility. A beginning. He cried out in his solitary space in the bathroom beside his wife.

He didn't notice that the blue in her palms had overtaken her face until her back was on the tile and a seizure made her head thump against the floor.

"Val!" Jamison went to her. Gathered her up into his arms like a rag doll and tried to shake her awake from the tossing. "Mama! Mama!" He cried for help, but these echoes were more helpless than the lips that had produced them.

The doctor on the right side of the hospital bed made a pyramid of Val and Jamison. Val in the bed, her empty stomach covered by cold, crisp white sheets, Jamison on her left side, his head in his hands, his eyes swollen to lemons.

The doctor was talking like this ending was a beginning. Moving on. Saying something about how this just happens to some people. No one knew why. It just happens. They could try again. There was no harm in trying again. There was no guarantee there'd be another miscarriage. The odds were in their favor.

"I was fine," Val said, her eyes fixed on the white sheets. "I felt my baby. My baby was inside of me. My baby was fine."

"That's what I'm telling you," the doctor said as delicately as he could. He'd seen things before. Women who never came back from this. Men who left. People who died for the dead. The unborn dead. "There is nothing wrong with you. Nothing wrong with your baby. We've run tests. Everything was fine. It just happens sometimes." This was one of those moments when life made a pupil of science. When men were powerless to protect a woman from her pain.

Outside, the sun was coming up. New nurses were walking the hallways. New cases. New tears.

The doctor stood, nodded sympathetically at Jamison and promised he'd return. A nurse would be by shortly. Val needed to get some rest. She'd lost a lot of blood.

When the doctor was gone, a hand Val had been using to wipe her tears fell against the sheet, palm up, fingers curled.

Jamison looked at the hand and then at Val.

She was looking back at him.

He looked back at the hand. At his hands, wrapped into one another, balled up in anger or fear or sadness. A tear fell and landed on his thumb. He closed his eyes to trim the torrent. He hadn't stopped crying since the red lights came flashing in front of the house. Every new tear had a different altar, a different reason for gathering. And last was Val.

Almost as if reaching for a ring buoy while sinking into a sea, Jamison crept his fingers over the bleached fabric and made a tight knot with Val's hand. He didn't look at her or say a word. The tears continued to fall.

With the sun came the press. The hospital was filled with suspicious characters with hidden cameras. Men with tape recorders were asking nurses questions. Why was the mayor there? Why was his wife there? Was the baby okay?

The mayor's personal security staff cleared the hallways, briefed and required a confidentiality statement from every medical professional who'd been on the third floor since 11 PM.

"You should've called me. I should've been the first person you called," Leaf advised Jamison in the hallway outside the room where Val was lying still with her eyes closed.

"My wife had a miscarriage. I wasn't exactly thinking about work," Jamison said. There were still specks of pink blood on the chest of his shirt. If it weren't for the setting someone might have thought it was a design of some kind.

"I understand, but there were other options. You didn't have to call the ambulance. We could've taken her someplace else," Leaf said before lowering his voice a little to be sure Val couldn't hear him. "I mean, she'd already lost the baby."

Standing against the wall, Jamison banged his head back lightly. He heard little of Leaf's argument. He kept seeing red—in every shade, everywhere. He thought that must be what a broken heart looked like—torn apart inside and out.

"The press is all over this," Leaf said.

"Who's talking to them?"

"I don't know. Everyone? Your neighbors. The ambulance drivers. Who knows. You really should've called me. I can't get in front of a situation if you don't—"

Jamison looked up and the red was in his eyes. "Why do you care, man?" he shot. "What is it to you?"

"What? I'm your assist—" Leaf stumbled back toward the wall behind him as Jamison stepped closer to him with balled fists.

"No. No. You're always around. Always in the right place at the right time. There's something about it—something about you," Jamison charged with his mother's accusations, his suspicions, and all the pressure of all the days caving in on his corneas. "Why are you here? Why the fuck are you here, man?"

He'd cornered Leaf, and the young man, who had suddenly become a boy, was shaking in his alabaster skin.

"It's nothing. I'm just doing my job," Leaf suffered out.

"Fuck that. Who are you?" Jamison was so close up on Leaf the security guards holding back onlookers on either side of the hallway left their posts to break the pair apart. One got there just in time to stop the mayor from wrapping his hand around Leaf's blushing throat. "Who are you? Who are you?" Jamison repeated.

Mrs. Taylor came rushing down the hallway when she heard her son's cries. She'd been sitting nervous in the waiting room where she'd been sequestered since they arrived at the hospital and the doctors, noting how hysterical Val was, had advised that Jamison ought to be the only person allowed in the room.

Mrs. Taylor jumped right into the fight.

"What's this? You came here to start trouble?" she said to Leaf. "My son is mourning! Can't you see that? This is no place for you! No place!" She turned to the security guards holding Jamison back. "You let go of my son and remove this man here from this hospital!" She pointed at Leaf. "He does not need to be here. He is stressing my poor son out. And at this time!"

The guards followed orders from a woman who signed not one

of their checks. They released Jamison and escorted Leaf down the empty hallway.

Mrs. Taylor pulled Jamison into her arms. "It's okay. Everything's okay," she said. "I'm here."

❧ ● ☙

When I was five years old, my mother gave me this fat pink doll with short blond curls she got at the dollar store in the mall. It was supposed to be a baby, but my big sister pointed out that it had on blue eye shadow and streaks of lavender blush over the cheeks. I took it up to my room and looked at it. Pulled the clothes off. The paisley bonnet. Slid down a little square of floor fabric that was supposed to be a diaper. I held the doll up and looked at her pink body in the sunlight coming through my bedroom window. I could see right through her. Right through what was supposed to be her belly. Right through what was supposed to be her heart. Her brain. There was nothing inside. She was all a pink shell. But she was mine. My baby. Pink and empty. My mother told me to name her. I never did though. I hid her clothes in my sock drawer and set her on my bed. When my mother asked why she was naked and what I'd done with the clothes, I said she didn't have a heart so she couldn't feel the cold and I was saving my clothes for my real baby who could feel the cold. One day after school when I was bored, I cut off all of her cute blond curls and burned them in the backyard behind the shed. When my mother saw her bald head, I explained that my baby was stupid and she didn't need nice hair because she didn't know about nice hair. On another day when I was bored, I broke off one of her pink baby arms. On the next day, I broke off the other arm. Then the right leg. Then the left. When my mother saw the armless, legless baby lying on my pillow, she demanded that I put the arms and legs back on. "You're too young to be doing all this, missy! You're not ready. Something ain't right with you." I couldn't find the arms and legs, so she popped me on the butt ten times and asked if I could imagine how that baby might feel without her arms and legs. I cried. And when my mother left the bedroom, I grabbed that armless, legless pink baby, my baby, and held her up to the sunlight. She had no heart. No brain. What could she feel? The next thing I remember is getting my sister's art marker and writing all over my baby's body. I wasn't bored. I think I just wanted to make a point. I wrote every curse word I knew. And there were many. Over her forehead, I wrote Broken. I put her back on my bed and went outside to play by myself. When I came back into the house, my mother beat me again. She said I was being ugly and hateful. And that was the very first and very last doll she'd ever buy for me. She said the next baby I'd get would be the one I birthed on my own and she'd see how I treated that one.

All my life, I've only had broken shit. Broken. When it came to me that way. Or I made it that way. Broken. Old books from the thrift store with pages torn out the back. Freshly painted nails with beautiful red lacquer that smudged right after I walk out of the nail salon. Friends with no loyalty. Men with no hearts. A run up the back of my stocking. Rain anytime. And that's not what hurts. No, the broken thing being there doesn't hurt. I built up the expectation for it. I learned young that even if it isn't there, maybe I should find the broken thing. It is coming. For sure. Just like my father, found floating in an old swimming hole. It's coming. What hurts is forgetting that it's coming and soon secretly thinking maybe it won't.

When I was on the bathroom floor with that toilet filled with red broken things, I realized it was happening because of me. I forgot about the breaking. About how fragile every fucking thing around me is. No matter how hard I try to hold it together, it will fall apart. Even inside of me.

I should've expected it. I couldn't think Jamison would just suddenly love me. And then our baby would come and he would love the baby. And we would hold our baby up to the sunlight. And see that it had a heart and a brain. And it would stay together. And we would stay together. And never fall into pieces. I couldn't think that. But I should've.

When I woke up at the hospital, I felt an emptiness that let me know the doctors had sucked every living thing out of me, placed me in a bed, and covered me up in something white. At first, I was still pretending for myself. Maybe they'd saved the baby. I'd given birth in my sleep and my child, no bigger than my hand, was somewhere in a nursery under a blue light with white gauze pads covering her eyes. But I looked at Jamison and knew I had to stop. It was the first time he ever looked sorry for me. His eyelids were low. His lips were somewhere between smiling and frowning. He asked, "What happened?" I was about to tell him I didn't know, I didn't remember. But then I started remembering, going back past the bathroom floor and toilet. The wet mattress beneath me. My stomach hurt like someone was cutting me wide open from the inside out with kitchen knives. Walking up to my bedroom. Mrs. Taylor telling me to go lie down if I wasn't feeling well. My stomach hurting just a little bit—maybe gas. Sitting in the kitchen beside the new friend I'd found in a mother-in-law who insisted I eat a second serving of the summer soup she wasn't eating. Her laugh. A cackle.

And then I was about to answer Jamison's question—"What happened?"—I looked at him and saw a hand on his shoulder. Beside my hospital bed where I was lying all hollow was his mother.

I screamed like a freight train was rolling through the room full speed ahead, "Get her out of here!"

"Hell"

There was no funeral for the dead. You can't bury something with no name or thumb print. Maybe that wasn't true, but that's what Val told her mother when she'd called to say she was getting on a bus to Atlanta. "Don't come, Mama. Ain't nothing to come for," she'd said before collapsing into an honest cry Mama Fee never knew could come from her child.

The spectacle of screams sent a thunder clap through Mama Fee's soul. She dropped the phone on the bed where she'd been sitting and stood mechanically in a way that made clear she'd disconnected her every sense from the world around her.

"Mama? Mama?" her little girl was calling through the abandoned phone, but Mama Fee couldn't hear. Her feet took her to the old mahogany stained chifforobe willed to her from Val's great-grandmother, a swamp woman who'd had only the wooden clothing cabinet to her name when she'd died in a muddy abyss in a disregarded part of Louisiana struck hard by Hurricane Katrina. There, in the back of the top drawer that creaked and moaned when Mama Fee pulled the handle, was a little silver picture frame buried beneath a cabal of dried flowers with insidious names like the snake lily and devil's tongue and five candles burnt to puddles of bubbling wax. "Mama? You there? Can you hear me?" Mama Fee uncovered the silver treasure, wiped bits of the dried flowers from the glass covering the picture, and saw traces of an art she'd learned from the swamp woman as a girl—cut out holes where there had once been eyeballs belonging to those who'd meant to harm what was hers.

"Silver, silver, black and silver," she said to the holes.

Val could hear her chanting but couldn't make out what she was saying. "Mama?"

Mama Fee slid her hand back into the mess of snakes and tongues and retrieved a cold heavy weight, a silver candelabra. She pulled it from the mysterious soup, held it high over her head, and lowered it with force to break the glass over the picture to bits. She banged and banged and banged until glass dust was kicking up everywhere in a cloud.

"Mama? What are you doing?" Val was hollering then, but she knew. She always knew.

Mama Fee returned to the phone rewired, reconnected, and in a voice as clear and as calm as if she was floating in a pool of salt water, she said, "Get out of that house. There's nothing there for you."

Jamison was handling the loss his own way—which kind of meant not handling it at all. The mayor who'd abandoned his profession for so long Sunday morning pundits had questioned if the city once known as Terminus had a mayor at all and could have elected better replacements that included the newborn panda bear at the zoo and the Big Chicken on Cobb Parkway, dove back into his list of promises with a resolve that had his growing list of faceless enemies suiting up in armor that wasn't figurative and loading bullets that had a target in mind.

Jamison's participation in the ambiguous duel wasn't as methodical though. It was reborn in him in the way a cause was exhumed from the hearts of all great leaders who preceded him: a long hard look in the mirror to measure the man before him. It was time for him to answer to anything he thought he was. Even in the face of what he knew he'd lose. What the unburied thing had shown him was that loss was always possible. Inevitable. And sometimes you could lose things you didn't know you had. You didn't know you wanted. Or needed. But he wouldn't know that until he was tumbling to cold, pressed tar, no future in front of him, but a past of no regrets.

He called Leaf and told him to meet him in the parking lot behind Fox News. When Leaf got there, Jamison was standing on the side of his car, rubbing his palms into the sides of his slacks. Leaf was moving slower than usual, had the distant look of the accused in his eyes.

Jamison had expected this, so he started with something like an apology: "There's a lot going on. I don't know who I can trust, but I don't really believe those things I said to you at the hospital."

Leaf just nodded and looked up at the huge satellite bolted to the roof of the news station. "Why are we here?" he asked. "There's nothing on the schedule. Did I miss something?"

"I went to the jail this morning. Met with Ras and his attorney," Jamison explained, pointing to a stack of papers sitting in the backseat of his car. "Got a lot of information about why the police department—and I don't know, like the whole damn criminal justice system—seems to want to take him down."

"Why?"

"Because they want to take me down with him," Jamison whispered.

"Come on. You don't believe that. I told you—" Leaf started and then paused. "This isn't your fight. This is about Ras and his mess. You're just caught in the middle. Right? And so what if the system is trying to take him down? Shouldn't it? Isn't that what it's for?"

184 / *Grace Octavia*

Jamison was clearly ignoring Leaf's rationalizations. He opened the back door to get the papers.

"So, what? You're gonna go in there on the news and say the police are trying to arrest a drug dealer? What if all of this is a lie?" Leaf asked, trailing behind Jamison as he started walking to the station doors. "What if it has nothing to do with you and your friend is using you? You said already there's so much going on. You aren't thinking straight. You don't need to do this."

"I'm the only one who can do this," Jamison said when they got to the doors.

Leaf grabbed Jamison's arm to stop him from opening the door.

"Look, if you have something to do with this, tell me. Tell me now," Leaf said. "So I know what I'm dealing with."

Jamison looked at the hand so hard, Leaf let go.

"No worries, my friend," Jamison said. "No worries."

When he was turning to go into the station, his eyes caught a glimpse of silver rolling slowly along in the lot behind Leaf.

Jamison's stare lingered so long, Leaf turned too.

The silver was the top of a Maserati with limousine tinted windows rolled up to hide any inhabitants. The car slowed to a pace that might allow a gunman riding shotgun to steady his weapon. But just as Jamison and Leaf got any inclination of what could be happening, the car bolted forward with speed that indicated not an escape but a certain threat.

"You know who that was?" Leaf asked Jamison after looking long enough to see there was no plate in the back.

"I think I do."

It wasn't ever hard for an embattled mayor to get on television. A notable man with one hand holding a folder of secret files and the other in a closed fist was the kind of thing news stations lived for. An exclusive on a drama that had other news stations scrambling for leads meant any plans producers had from the local stand-ins to the national mother station were on hold. The only issue was that when Jamison and Leaf walked in, the in-house crew was preparing to shoot a segment about the importance of late-summer sun protection and the only camera-ready face in the building was that of the pixie-cute lifestyle journalist Alina Blue.

Her boss pulled her out of the bathroom as Jamison was being outfitted with a wire microphone.

"You're the only person who can talk to him," the producer said. "Opal and King are over a half hour away and he says he's going to another station with this if we don't move."

"But I'm not a *real* journalist," Alina said by mistake. "I mean, I'm not—this isn't—my thing."

"Doesn't matter. You went to school for it. It's your job."

Alina followed her boss to the set where she could see Jamison and another man looking over a stack of papers and seemingly practicing a statement.

"What does he want? What is he going to say? What should I ask him?" Alina asked, remembering the director of her department in college telling her she shouldn't even think of going into political journalism because she was too cute and no one would take her seriously.

"I have no fucking idea. And I don't really care," the producer said as a team of makeup artists finished off Alina's lipstick and added more blush. "All I know is he promised he'd only talk to us and only right now."

"Does he know I'm just a lifestyle journalist?"

"I don't think he half cares who you are. Look, just go and talk to him. Talk and take it from there," he said before nearly pushing Alina toward the little interview area where Jamison was already seated. "And, hey, try to get him to say something about his baby dying. Everyone's talking about that right now."

So, the important late-summer sun-protection story was scrapped and too-pretty journalist Alina Blue and her panicky eyes were sitting across from Jamison. She'd actually heard the rumors around the office that the mayor had something to do with Dax's death. It sounded like nonsense. Politics couldn't be that perilous. These were men in suits. Not gangbangers or mobsters who'd kill someone just for talking. Right?

Alina tried to smile. To catch her breath. To show her teeth.

Jamison looked at her and saw all of this debate.

"Just relax. This will be fast," Jamison said, and then the producer counted down to the camera taping a live broadcast.

"We're ready?" Alina said, looking at the cameraman, who pointed to the camera to let her know she was already on the air. "OH!" Alina refocused. "I'm Alina Blue and you're watching Fox Five News. We have a bit of a treat for you today. A special, exclusive visit from Mayor Jamison Taylor."

The shot widened to show Jamison sitting beside Alina.

"Welcome," Alina added, unsure of what to say next.

"Thanks for having me."

"Now, I understand you have some big news you'd like to share," Alina said, already sure she wasn't going to ask about the baby. She'd been through that same tough night with her husband.

"Yes, I do," Jamison said. "I want to take a moment to address my people, those who've supported me over the years, those who no longer support me, those who never supported me, all of them." The cameraman went in close on Jamison's face then. "I want to let everyone know about a violation of the law that's happening right here in this city where one man sits in a jail cell for weeks without having a bail amount posted and for charges that are without exigency and based upon an arrest that remains in question by his attorney."

"Excuse me, Mayor Taylor," Alina cut in. "Are you talking about the case concerning Glenn 'Ras' Roberson?"

"Exactly."

"Why are you interested in his case? Why should the people listen to you when there are actual reports out there noting your connections to him and inferring that perhaps you are connected to the crimes he's been charged with? Are you connected to him?" The camera caught Alina sitting at attention and poised with query in the way a mature anchorwoman might when set to interview a high-profile dignitary. And her tone was right on time. Throughout the state, viewers were switching over to see what everyone on social media was talking about.

"I am connected to him. He is my friend. My former college roommate. And that's why I can say beyond any doubt that this man is innocent. And the charges he faces are without merit, and the police and the district attorney, everyone knows that. But no one makes a move."

"Do you have proof of this?" Alina asked.

"I'm glad you asked," Jamison said. "In fact, I do. See, Glenn Roberson, a respected community man who has no record of criminal activity including selling drugs and is a known Rastafarian who smokes marijuana as a part of his religious rite, he says there were four men on the scene that night when he was pulled over. Now, the station report on that squad car notes that two officers were in the car when it left the station."

"Okay."

"But my friend says there were actually four men at the scene when he was arrested. Two men in uniform in the squad car and two men in suits in a car that was following behind the car, who identified themselves as detectives."

"Well, nothing there sounds out of order. Isn't it plausible to consider that maybe since law enforcement was already building a case against Mr. Roberson, they were simply following a tip and the detectives were on a lead?"

"But the detectives aren't in the police report." Jamison slid a copy of the police report from his folder and handed it to Alina. "And neither is the second cop."

"So . . ." Alina stalled a little as she read.

"A squad car left the precinct with two officers in it, but only

188 / *Grace Octavia*

one officer was noted in the police report that evening when it returned."

After eyeing the report for a minute, Alina looked back at Jamison. "Mayor Taylor, I see the discrepancy here, but this could amount to a simple clerical error. I'm sure if Roberson's attorney requested the information about the officer in question, it would be made readily available." She smiled gingerly.

"Well, it hasn't been." Jamison handed over a stack of papers. "Phone logs, copies of letters. More than fifty calls and certified letters. All requesting that information. All unanswered."

Alina thumbed through the logs and letters. With each turned page, it was evident she was becoming a believer, unknowingly nodding her head.

"Now, that makes you have some questions—questions any citizen of this fine state, even one who's behind bars, ought to have answered. Doesn't it?" Jamison pressed.

"Well . . . yes."

"And what are you wondering?"

"I'm wondering—"

"You're wondering," Jamison interrupted, "how in the hell we can keep a man in jail for this long with such an obvious error in a file related to his very arrest. Since when is it a secret who arrested someone?"

"I—I don't know."

"Neither do I!" Jamison said. "And you know what else you might be wondering, if you're smart—and I can tell you're smart," he added, noticing a little bulldog hanging from the necklace around Alina's neck. "What, you went to UGA?"

"Yes." Alina's neck blushed red.

"Then, you're a smart woman—go dawgs!" On pure adrenaline that lightens the pressure on the brain of someone on a winning team, Jamison pumped his fist in the air.

The anchorwoman met the enthusiasm for her alma matter with a matching fist.

"Now a smart person would wonder not only how this man could remain in jail, but also why someone might want him in jail," Jamison charged. "Those men whose names aren't listed, my friend claims they planted most of these drugs in his car."

"Why?"

"Yes—why? Why would major stakeholders, big names with deep pockets in my home state want to put this man in jail?"

"I don't know, Mayor. Why? Are you going to tell us?"

"I intend to do just that," Jamison said, turning from Alina to the camera. "Expose who's behind all of this. But that's all I have for right now."

Jamison stood and started removing the wired microphone from beneath his jacket.

"That's all?" Alina looked nervously at Jamison and then to the camera that was still recording and then back again. "That's all you have to say?"

Leaf saw his boss in a struggle and rushed on set to help him get untangled from the wire. When he freed Jamison, the mayor walked off set and left Leaf in front of the camera holding the wire. "That's all," Leaf said. "That's all."

The cameraman turned his lens back to Alina.

"A Fox Five News exclusive. I'm Alina Blue. Thank you," she said, realizing that the mayor's impromptu visit would be the rope that catapulted her to a height she'd actually secretly thought she'd never see. Months later, when she was being interviewed for a job at the desk at MSNBC, she'd mention that she saw in Jamison Taylor's eyes truth and honesty. It had broken her heart, and renewed her faith in the power of journalism. She hoped her viewers had seen the same thing. She had no way of measuring that. But they had.

Val returned home from a follow-up appointment with her doctor to hear harsh voices that sounded like arguing coming from inside her closed bedroom door. Stepping up, she was sure the source of the battle was the television she'd left on, or maybe the radio on her alarm clock had gone off. Jamison had hardly been in the bedroom since the long night in the hospital. Even after the maid cleaned the mess, he said he couldn't take the memories. But Val felt another way. She didn't want the memories from the bed and the bathroom, but being in the space where her baby had died made her feel in some way close to the lost soul. Feel that maybe the soul would find her.

She put her hand on the doorknob and was about to push in, but stopped when she heard that the angry sounds were familiar and coming from just one voice. She pressed her ear against the door and through the wood heard ricochets of anger from Jamison's tongue: "I know who he is . . . matters . . . mine . . . matters . . . my son . . . my son! You can try . . . won't win. . . . I'm tired too! You won't win. I'll get him . . . to Georgia . . . me. . . . Go ahead!"

Val kept her ear to the wood until there was silence and then she turned the knob.

The bedroom was dark, but Val could see Jamison sitting in a chair that he'd turned towards the window, so his back was to her. He turned his head a little to acknowledge her entrance and let out a deep breath.

Events had made of Val a woman who was short on pleasantries. She went right in with, "Who was that on the phone?"

Jamison exhaled again. "I tried to tell you," he said. "That night at Paschal's, I tried to tell you."

"And don't say it was Kerry. You wouldn't even talk to her like that."

"I'm not going to lie to you. I can't lie anymore. I can't lie to anyone else." Jamison got up from the seat in the dark and turned to Val. "It was Coreen."

"Coreen? Coreen? That woman in California?"

"We have a son."

"What? A son? But I—" The weight of the news made Val stagger for a seat on the edge of the bed. "I thought you—I thought she had an abortion. That's what you told me. What you said. Remember?"

"That's what she told me. But she never did. She had the baby on her own—I guess she was trying to get back at me for leaving. I don't know."

"All that money Leaf sends to L.A. every month—?" Val looked at Jamison for a response before she'd finish.

"Yes. It's supposed to be for my son; that's what we agreed. For him and for her to just keep quiet until I got things figured out here."

"This is crazy."

"But it's more than that to Coreen. Once she saw that we got married and then that you were pregnant on the news, she started asking for more money and her demands have only gotten worse. She threatened to kill herself. To kill me."

"What?"

"I don't think she's capable of that, but really, right about now, I don't know what she might do."

"I can't believe this. I can't believe you would keep something like this from me." The room fell in and out of focus around Val. It was long and then wide and then closing all in. She realized it was the tears in her eyes blurring her vision.

"I tried to tell you. It has nothing to do with you," Jamison said.

"Bullshit! We were going to have a child together. You can't keep something like that from me," Val blurted out.

"I didn't intend to. I didn't intend for any of this to happen."

"Fuck you. Fuck you and your intentions, Jamison. Who cares what you intended to happen? It did," Val said and she was speaking more about the present than the past. "Did you tell Kerry this? That her son has a brother? Have you even seen the boy?"

"Of course I've seen my son," Jamison said. "And I will tell Kerry when I'm ready to."

"Well, what's his name?"

"Jamison. His mother named him Jamison."

Val erupted in bitter laughter. Angry laughter. "She got you. Man, she got you good," she said. "You know, the game used to be to have an abortion and get him for the two hundred and fifty dollars, but I guess it's changed to have the baby and wait until he's mayor, so you can get two million dollars."

Jamison responded, "Is that the game you played?"

"It's the game we both played. I just got better at it."

"Well, it seems your game is over now," Jamison said coldly. "Don't you think?"

"Maybe it's better that way—that's what I've been thinking." Val stood up in front of Jamison. "Maybe everything that happened was what was supposed to happen. Because there's no way I could continue to live here. Not like this." Val pointed to the door where Mrs. Taylor was still taking up residence on the other side.

"You keep saying that—'I'm not safe here. I have to watch my back,'" Jamison repeated words Val had said in mumbles covered by the strength of the painkillers she'd been taking after the miscarriage when he brought her home.

"Why can't you see? Why can't you believe me?"

"Believe what?"

"That she killed our baby! Your mother! She killed our baby!" Val cried so loud it seemed like it was the first time she'd said it.

"You kept saying that when we came home from the hospital. It was just the medication talking," Jamison said. "You made it up in your head."

"I didn't make it up. I told you everything that happened that night. I remember it all."

"She made you dinner. That doesn't sound like a killer to me," Jamison said matter-of-factly.

"There was something in it," Val said.

"You said that before, but it's crazy."

"Why? Why can't you believe it?"

"Because it's crazy. Because she's my mother. And that was her grandchild. Why would she do that?" Jamison listed.

"Because she wants you to herself," Val said. "And she wants me gone. Just like she wanted Kerry gone."

"That's ridiculous. My mother may be a handful, but she just wants me to be happy. So, yes, she did want you gone, but that wasn't because of the baby. It was because of your actions." Jamison's statement took him back to the kitchen that day when his mother had come in from her walk talking about the car—the silver car. Then his mind went back again, way back to a darker time. A dark night with a silver car in it. The Rainforest. The silver Maserati in the driveway. It was the same car at the news station earlier that day.

"My actions? I didn't do anything! I've been—"

"Who was in that car?"

"What car?"

"That silver car. The Maserati." Jamison stood.

"No one," Val stumbled with her heart jerking forward in fear.

"Tell me," Jamison said. "Who was it?"

"I told you and your mother, it was nothing! I wasn't cheat—"

"I don't care about that—" Jamison grabbed Val's arms and started shaking. "I just need to know who it was. It's not even about you."

Val wrestled loose from Jamison's hold and his wild eyes and told him that name. The story. The past.

"It was over between us when I met you," Val said after telling. "And then he just showed up asking all these questions. That night at Paschal's—he had all these questions about you. And then he wanted to know what you knew about Dax's murder."

Jamison pushed away from Val and went to the window to look

at the shadows gathering in the ground at the promise of night coming.

"I knew something was up—something was going on, but I—I was afraid."

"Why didn't you tell me?" Jamison whispered.

"I was afraid. Afraid of what he'd do to you. To us," Val said. "He's dangerous, Jamison."

"You should've told me."

"For what? What are you going to do?" Val asked.

But Jamison didn't respond. He never would. He went to the nightstand to gather his keys and his cell phone and walked out of the bedroom, out of the house, away from Val.

"Enemy Territory"

Keet walked into the mayor's office the next day with a smile and a ginger step. He was in an argyle sweater and penny loafers. The visit came via an invitation from Jamison's receptionist, who knew only her orders and greeted Keet in the lobby.

"Officer Neales, welcome to Mayor Jamison Taylor's office." She shook his hand. "The mayor will be with you in a minute. Please know we don't allow recording devices of any kind beyond the reception area. I'll hold your cell phone up front. If you'd like a picture with the mayor, I can bring the phone back in after your meeting."

"Darling, I know the rules." Keet held out his hand. "No phone. No camera. No recording devices."

"Wonderful. I'll let him know you're here."

Jamison and Leaf had come up with the idea to invite Keet to the office over a beer at a bar the night Val had told her story. The plan was simple: talk—say what they knew and see what he'd say. Keet may have been dangerous—obviously he was dangerous—but he wasn't stupid. They could get him on their territory. Play by their rules.

"Brother Neales," Jamison said, standing at his desk when Keet walked in with his receptionist. He offered Keet a seat and excused the receptionist. Leaf was in the room adjacent to the office listening in. "I'm glad you agreed to come today."

Keet sat and opened his legs wide in comfort and ease, but the smile on his face had so many levels.

"I'm sure you know I didn't call you down here about a job," Jamison started. "I'm sure you know I know that was never your intention."

"Maybe it was," Keet said free of his stuttering. "Maybe that was my intention—a long, long time ago."

"Well, it's not now," Jamison said. "We both know that. You want something else. Something that has you following me around. Following my wife around. And, you know, I can say that because I don't think you want it to be a secret. I think you've been waiting for me to figure it out."

"Why would I want you to do that?" Keet asked.

"That's what I've been thinking about. What I've been trying to figure out all morning. All night. We know it's not that you want to be here. And it can't be that you want me in your pocket—I know there's already a list of people both of us know, who think they have me in their pocket."

"Really? Like whom?"

Jamison went on with his list. "And—and it can't be that you want both sides of your bread buttered. You'd be found out soon enough and, well, whoever's on the other side of this toast, they wouldn't take too kindly to that."

"So what if they do?"

"Humph . . ." Jamison rocked back in his big leather chair and weighed options he hadn't really considered yet. "Well, if they do, whoever they are, they'd probably get rid of you. Because they don't need you. For whatever they want to do."

Keet laughed to suggest that Jamison was wasting his time.

"You're funny as fuck, Mr. Mayor," Keet said. "Always have me laughing. Can't even watch the news without you having me laughing—you know, that performance you made on Fox yesterday. Pure entertainment."

"I'm glad you tuned in. I only wonder if whoever so desperately wants Ras behind bars was tuning in too."

"I'm sure *whoever* was," Keet said distantly before abruptly getting up from his seat.

"I'm sure they realized they don't have me in their pocket anymore. That probably made them very mad. Probably made them come down on the low guys on the totem pole." Jamison stood up as Keet had turned his back to walk out. "The low guys like you. The ones who do the dirty work."

"This is a joke," Keet said firmly.

"You think?"

"Yeah, it is. It's a joke if you think this little Columbo routine you're playing here is going to get you anywhere. You can go on any news station you want to. It won't stop."

"Why?"

"Because you're talking about men and money. And men and power," Keet said. "The shit that makes this motherfucker go around." He looked around the office. "All of it. The fucking reason you're here—in office. Contracts. Business. That mean green. You think you got here by chance? They made you. They fucking made you. And when you're gone, they'll just make another one. Another contract signer. Get them in. Get them out."

"How much are they paying you?" Jamison asked.

"What?" Keet laughed at what he'd selected as a joke and finally turned to leave.

"How much did they pay you to kill Dax?"

Keet stopped, and with his full back to Jamison, he answered, "I wasn't there the night Dax was killed, Mr. Mayor. You were."

Jamison's bubble of boldness burst with that mention. He hadn't told Leaf, who was listening in, about the night at the Rainforest.

Keet felt Jamison's hesitation and turned to attack.

"Don't you know they have that in their pockets? That you were there that night? You put in work. Right?"

"I didn't do—"

"No. No. No," Keet said. "We're both familiar with the law. You know you can't be in the room with a dying man and not take some of the blame. Your hands are dirty too. How much are *they* paying you?" He looked around the room again.

Jamison was stunned to silence.

"And look, you can tell that girl not to worry. Won't be bothering her anymore. I'm not into seconds. Plenty fish out here." Keet tilted his head toward Jamison in mock concern. "And I'm sorry to hear about her baby. Your baby. Right?"

When Keet walked out and Leaf walked in, Jamison felt that he was losing his step. He imagined Dax standing in front of him holding a microphone, smiling, youth alive in his eyes.

The good thing about losing my marriage was finding myself. Not me before Jamison and I got married fresh out of Morehouse and Spelman. Me with a bow and arrow. Me with heart and nerve. With fight in me. It's funny, because anyone who knew us back then knew that my weakness was part of why Jamison loved me so much. It was what made me available to him. What made him open so wide to me. Yeah, I was feisty—someone that had my mother for backup, but I was always falling apart and Jamison was always getting me together. Sometimes I look back and think maybe he felt like a needed thing. Like a hammer or wrench. A gun. But in the end, after the end, in the divorce, I, like most other women, learned to be my own hammer and wrench. Be my own gun. I didn't need him like I needed him before. I needed me.

Now, that's a whole lot of catharsis. Liberating language that came after years in the world by myself. Raising a son. Living alone. Realizing that, at the end of the day, the only person who was responsible for my life was me. But I didn't get there on my own. There were signposts I had to learn to read along the way. Friends who showed up and dragged me out to dinner. Lovers who made me feel sexy. Family who let me know I would trust again. A son who proved to me every day that it wasn't just about me.

Probably most influential in that journey was a place I found when I was way at the bottom of a barrel of misery. A place filled with other women who were going through the same thing and understood what I needed to understand. The women at Hell Hath No Fury House, an innovative counseling center for women going through divorce, held my hand and helped me over my hump. After I cut off my hair and everyone thought I was crazy, I showed up on the doorstep of the house and met with a counselor who said my sisters there were going to change my life.

And they did. As they listened, I felt soft, empathetic hands wrapped over my shoulders. It was more than a rebirth. It was a baptism there. I became addicted to the place. To the feeling I got from being helped and helping. I referred friends and family, anyone I met on the street, there. And soon I realized being at HHNFH was more than nourishment for my spirit, it was what I wanted to do with my life—to spend it helping others. Interestingly enough, I was already on that path when I started at HHNFH. I was working on my second degree in public health with hopes of opening a clinic for handicapped mothers. Somewhere that they could go to get help and basic services. Really, it was everything I could do at HHNFH—just with women dealing with a specific kind of handicap. So, I put my hopes on hold and joined the board of trustees at HHNFH. It's amounted to a career choice I don't get paid for. But I put in the hours anyway, knowing getting paid in no way measures up to a payoff.

"That little girl stays in some trouble. Doesn't matter what I do, Cheyenne will find a way to get in some trouble and drag me and her brother and the little ones right up into it with her. You know last week she told Reginald she didn't want him to be her father anymore? She said AJ is her real father now. Can you believe that? You know what kind of crazy phone call I got from her father after she made that little comment?"

I nodded along. I could believe every detail of the tale. I was sit-

ting at the front desk at HHNFH beside Dawn, one of my Spelman sisters who'd been having a hard divorce years ago when her room-mate from Spelman arrived at her doorstep one morning for a visit and left one evening with Dawn's husband in tow. It was a scandalous affair that had left Dawn on the brink, but I referred her to HHNFH and her brink experience became her calling for service. Now, she was in the vineyard at HHNFH working with me.

"You've got to give Cheyenne some space. Let her get some bruises," I said to Dawn. "And if her father was so hurt by what she said, he should've taken it up with her—not you. You didn't say it. What did he want from you?"

"Blood! I don't know," Dawn joked before smiling at a HHNFH sister who was walking in to meet with her divorce counselor. Neither one of us knew her name. None of us went by our real names at the center. Instead, we wore name tags highlighting the names of famous and infamous former brides (Ivana, Juanita, Jennifer, Elin, Star—there was even a Carol McCain) in an attempt to protect everyone's anonymity because there were some pretty rich first wives walking through that door in tears and with black eyes and broken hearts.

"Who do I write a check to?" the woman asked before picking up a name tag that read LisaRaye.

"Oh, no one," Dawn said. "You know all of your treatment here at HHNFH is privately funded through donations. There's no charge to you. Not ever."

"Oh, I know. I'm donating today," LisaRaye started as she pulled out her checkbook and a shiny silver pen. "I signed my divorce decree last night. I realized I never would've made it through that if it wasn't for everything I learned in this place. Who do I make the check out to?" She looked from Dawn to me sitting beside her.

"Oh, it's Hell Hath No Fury House, LLC," I said.

"Great." She knelt down and wrote before our eyes a check for twenty thousand dollars. She pressed the silver pen hard into the paper and drew a little heart over her name on the signature line.

"That's the last time I'll be using this name. We can all thank Mr. LisaRaye for this twenty-K. Bastard." She tore the check from the book and handed it to Dawn like it was a receipt from the supermarket.

"Enjoy your session," Dawn said to her back as she walked toward the steps that led to her counselor's office. The actual Fury House was really a house. A huge Queen Anne with a porch out front made for sitting. There were hardwood floors throughout. Pictures of beautiful things and beautiful words on the walls. Dawn's favorite was a Maya Angelou poem over the mantel in the group meeting room.

"Twenty thousand?" Dawn read the check, amazed. "Did she really just do that to her poor ex-husband?"

"Don't act surprised. I know you've seen bigger checks than that floating around here," I said. "And don't be sorry for her ex. I'm sure he earned every dime of that punishment. She wasn't wearing that name tag for nothing."

Dawn and I laughed. I took the check from her and went to put it in a locked file cabinet for the director.

Standing there, looking for the donations folder, I was talking about how it always seemed like the men were the ones messing up the marriages. The women weren't without fault, but somehow it seemed between the assistants, Facebook friends, old girlfriends, bad business deals, and poor financial decisions, the men carried the blame.

"I'm not trying to generalize and I might be a little biased, but I'll be damned it it's not true." I'd stuffed the check into the folder and closed the drawer when I realized Dawn hadn't said a word in a few seconds. I turned to the desk where she was sitting to ask what she thought and discovered why she was silent. Standing there with crossed arms was someone whose face we both knew.

"Can I help you?" Dawn asked awkwardly. While she'd never seen the face before her in person, like everyone else in Atlanta, she knew who it was.

"I need help."

I honestly thought she was there to fight me. There to start something. Get in my face about Jamison and call me out of my name. Why else would Val be at HHNFH?

I stood my ground. Two feet planted firmly to the hardwood. Ready to fight.

But then I saw the worry in Val's face.

I loosened one foot and wondered if maybe she was lost.

But then I saw the tears in Val's eyes.

I loosened the other foot and wondered if she was trying to be found.

I walked up behind Dawn, whose silence let me know she was actually waiting for me to say something.

"I'll handle this," I said to Dawn.

She looked up at me. "You sure?"

"Yes."

Dawn got up from her seat and patted me on the shoulder. "I'll be right in the back," she offered. "Call me if you need me."

"I will."

Val and I locked eyes in a conversation, and Dawn's heels clicking against the wood became more faint.

"Someone told me about this place," Val said, looking at a banner on the wall. "I didn't know you worked here. I wouldn't have—"

"I don't work here," I said, cutting off her frantic statement that seemed to make more tears spill out of her eyes. I handed her a box of tissue. "I'm a volunteer. Nothing between us—none of that matters here. How can we help you?"

Marcy has this saying she always uses when she has to do something really tough. She says, "It's time to put my big-girl panties on." Forever, I thought she was talking about the size of the panties and laughed just because the image she painted in my mind was so funny. But as I moved a chair to the table for Val and listened to her talk about how things were dissolving with her and Jamison, I knew the saying was about handling the big things and letting the *little things slide. Who Val was married to wasn't important. She and I may have had our differences in the past, but right there in HHNFH, she was another sister who needed help. She had nothing. Nowhere to go. No one to go to. She kept talking about how someone was going to come after her because she'd opened her mouth about something. She was scared.*

I had to make myself a bigger person to see a way to comfort her. Remind myself that she'd had nothing to do with my marriage falling apart. By the time she'd shown up, the ink on my divorce decree had been good and dry. For whatever reason, Jamison had chosen to let her into his life. And for whatever reason, I had chosen to be in the position to help women like her when their part in someone else's story was over. If my father and his military mind had been sitting there, he'd call it my "true test." How I moved forward would determine my grade.

"I felt so bad for you that day—the way she was talking to you in front of Tyrian," Val said to me, talking about Jamison's mother and how Val felt she'd only moved into the house to ruin her marriage. "I wanted to say something. I kept telling myself, 'It's your house, Val! It's your house!' But I don't think I ever really believed that."

"Well, you know the law is on your side with this. Right? You can stay in that house no matter what—at least until you figure out what to do next," I said.

"I can't. I won't stay in that house with that woman." Val leaned in toward me and wiped tears from her eyes so I could see she was speaking from her clear mind. "I think she did it—she killed my baby. I know it."

"Val, you're very upset, and I know Mrs. Taylor is a handful, but she's not—"

"She is. She is. She did," Val said harshly. "You tell me what else could make me come in here like this? See you and not walk right out the door? You think I want to sit here in front of you of all people and talk about how my marriage is falling apart?"

"No. I don't," I said.

"*I feel like everyone thinks I'm crazy and I'm running out of options. The woman killed my baby.*"

"*But it was on the news that you had a miscarriage,*" I said. "*How could she have anything to do with that?*"

"*She poisoned me,*" Val explained.

"*Come on, that doesn't happen in real—*"

"*Well, it happened to me,*" Val said, cutting me off like she'd heard my response a dozen times.

"*If you're sure she did, then did you call the police? Have her arrested?*" I imagined Mrs. Taylor being dragged out of Jamison's house in handcuffs. How much losing his grandmother would hurt Tyrian. How horrible his grandmother had always been to me.

"*I had the doctors at the hospital run extra blood work. They didn't find anything,*" Val answered.

"*Okay—so she didn't—*"

"*She did,*" Val said firmly this time and so clearly I knew she believed every word. "*Look, I'm not here to make you hate Mrs. Taylor. I know you have to live with her because of your son. I just want to know what my options are. You know, moving forward.*"

"*Well, I'm sure whoever sent you here told you this is a counseling services center for divorcing women. Our first priority is to keep our members happy. And we advocate that in every way. So, if you decide you don't want to get a divorce, we'll support you. If you do, we have legal services, counseling, scholarships, grants, group sessions. Whatever you need to make it through, we can arrange it,*" I explained. "*You said you don't want to go back to the house—I can get you a hotel room. And if you don't feel safe, you can stay here overnight. We have people here around the clock who can help you.*"

Val started crying again and the shock of her situation made her breathing heavy like that of a child who'd survived an angry beating. She rested her arms on the table and cried into the palms of her hands.

"*Val? Val?*" I called, trying to hand her a tissue. "*Lift your head.*

Look at me. Listen." I reached over the table to the woman on the other side and touched her gently.

She shook her head in defiance of my demand and I remembered just how young she was. Beneath all of that old attitude, she was still a growing thing. Just like I had been when I went through this.

"Val, you can do it. Look up at me," I said again. "Look!"

She slowly lifted her head and the full exhaustion was in every fold of her face.

"Good," I said. "Listen to me. Can you do that?"

She agreed with a nod.

"You're going to be the one doing the work here. You. No one else. We help. But you work," I said. "You remember that girl in the red suit and red heels and red lipstick and nails and phone I met in Jamison's office?"

"Yes," she said weakly.

"You're going to need her now. You're going to need her strength to get through this," I said and I was crying then too. "You're going to have to summon her up, so you can be fit for your fight. Now is not the time for being weak or being nice. Now is the time for you to stand up for yourself. Time for you to be a woman."

Val caught a smear of snot and tears on her arm and sat up again to look me straight in the eyes.

"Now, you say that woman did something to your child?" I said and honestly had no idea as to where that statement came from. "If that's true, you have every right to defend yourself. If it was me and someone did something to Tyrian—if I believed they did something to my boy—there'd be payment. And you have every right to collect."

Emmett Louis Till was murdered over a lie that he'd wolf-whistled at a white girl. After the little black boy's body was discovered in the Tallahatchie River in Mississippi with a seventy-pound cotton gin fan tied around his neck with barbed wire, his muddled remains were clothed, packed in lime, and placed in a pine box so they could be returned via train to his grieving mother in Chicago.

Like most black children growing up in the South, Jamison had learned the true story of poor Emmett Till during a Black History Month lesson when he was in middle school. While the other kids in the classroom turned away when the teacher, an ambitious recent Clark Atlanta University graduate with long dreadlocks who was determined to teach the children the truth of what happened to Till, showed them a picture of his battered body, Jamison cried and walked out of the room. When the teacher caught up with him down the hallway, Jamison said he was afraid that would happen to him someday. The teacher explained that she hadn't shown him the picture to scare him; it was supposed to illustrate what happens when people stick together. How Till's mother's insistence that every newspaper run pictures of her son's dead body had resulted in an international uproar about racism in the American South that eventually led to a trial in the most racist state in the union—a trial against two white men for the murder of a black boy. And though the men were later acquitted, the trial itself was a success because it sent a message to everyone that shining a light on injustice was the best way to get justice where none seemed possible.

Jamison remembered that moment in the hallway with his seventh-grade history teacher the morning he got the call that Ras was being released from jail. He knew that it was his work, his belief in his friend, dedication to finding any way he could to support him and shine a light on the injustice for all to see, that had led to Ras's release. The news story on Fox went viral like every other video of Jamison. The story and copies of police reports Jamison had left at the news station were picked up by the Associated Press, and soon every major outlet in the nation had a story about the names missing from Ras's police report. Every article had its angle. Some argued police brutality. Some for Ras's right to practice his religion. There were even the conspiracy theorists who felt the entire case was just the government's way of sending a message to militant men like Ras. So many voices. A threat of the Georgia Supreme Court getting involved. The local court had to act.

When Ras was released from the jailhouse later that morning, there was a swarm of local reporters, journalists, bloggers, protest groups, and plain old nosey folk waiting to hear what he had to say about his arrest. Who was he fighting? How would he fight back? And what would he do next? There were folks in Free Ras T-shirts and others handing out handbills with www.freeras.com printed on the back. There was an Internet campaign. A fund. Followers. Fans. Stringy-haired white women who'd vowed to name their children after this man. Stringy-haired black women who vowed to have children with this man. All aligning themselves with the likes of Mumia Abu Jamal, Fred Hampton, and even Malcolm X.

His lawyer pulled him to a podium where open ears were waiting to hear Ras's first wise words.

Jamison stood toward the side of the crowd with Leaf looking on.

"You think he has any idea what all of these people want from him?" Leaf asked Jamison.

"Yeah, he does. And I know Ras—he'll give it to them," Jamison answered as the crowd began to cheer, "No justice, no peace!"

Following revolutionary etiquette, Ras began pounding his fist at the podium. The crowd was enlivened and the chanting grew louder as supporters closed in tighter around the podium.

By then, Jamison and Leaf had already put together the pieces of the puzzle of Ras's arrest. Everything Ras had told Jamison was true. There were evil eyes all over that scholarship program. Even with Ras's release, suddenly none of the basketball players would talk to him again. And Jamison's biggest backers had made calls to his office to say they would pull out their dollars if the mayor did business with Ras. The siding with one team or the other was par for the course for a man whose main job was signing contracts, but the pressure made it clear the message was coming from somewhere up top. Keet was clear about that. Jamison just needed to figure out who it was.

"What I'm about to say isn't for anyone standing out here," Ras said when the crowd quieted. "Because if you're out here, you recognize truth. You know I stand for truth. You support the truth."

The crowd began chanting "truth," and Ras waited until the noise petered off.

"This message is for everyone at home. For those of you who are still trying to understand what is really happening here. I want you to know this is a war. A war these people are fighting against our children. Against our black children. Against our poor children. This isn't about them trying to lock Ras up. This is about them trying to lock your children out. Out of this process. You ever wonder why in nations like Demark and Germany and Brazil and Finland, a college education is free, but in this nation, the most wealthy nation in the world, poor children are either denied a college education because they don't have the money or they're forced into massive student loan debt they'll be paying off for the rest of their lives just to get a decent job? Why? It's because more and more in order to get somewhere in this country, you need a college education. If you don't have one, you can forget it. And if you don't have one they approve of, you can forget it. The system is forcing you out. Forcing us out. Forcing our children out. I, Glenn Roberson, was just trying to do my part to stop the educational caste system in this country. That's why I ended up here. Don't let anyone else tell you anything different. Look it up online. Find out the facts before you fall for the okeydokey. That's what they want you to do."

Ras threw up the peace sign and attempted to step back from

the podium, but people started yelling questions. The loudest was from Alina Blue, who was up front with her new camera crew.

"Ras, what do you want the people to do?" she asked. "What can they do to help you?"

Ras looked over the crowd as if he hadn't considered that someone would ask that very obvious question (though he had). Then he refocused and looked into Alina's camera, which was pointed at him.

"Go into your neighborhood and find a kid and make sure he knows what's coming. Make sure he's prepared," he said. "If he's not prepared, he'll lose for sure. And stop giving your money to these churches. If each of you donated your ten percent to a local scholarship fund to make sure the kids in your communities went to college, it would be a different place in four years. Put your money where your mouth is. Back your prayers for change with action."

The crowd dispersed quickly when Ras was stuffed into the back of his lawyer's black minivan. A few reporters lingered to ask Jamison questions about his support of Glenn Roberson and he engaged them with planned responses about seeking the truth no matter how many feathers he'd ruffled. He made it clear that the situation with Ras was far from over. While Ras couldn't face any charges concerning the guns because he had a license and there weren't any laws in the state of Georgia that stated how many guns he could actually own, he still faced felony charges for the marijuana and the police department still hadn't released the names of the other three officers involved in the arrest. When asked if the mayor's office would continue to follow the case, Jamison said it was his job to ensure the safety of Atlanta residents, so yes, he would.

Emmit was waiting beside Jamison's car. Standing up straight with a cell phone in his hand.

"Something about this car and parking lots," Jamison said, approaching Emmit with a grin. He'd already realized that Emmit was somehow connected to Ras's arrest and knew once he spoke out on the news, Emmit would come around with one of his warnings.

"Better to have people meet you here than at night in your bedroom, you think?" Emmit replied darkly, but then he quickly smiled. "Can't be too safe from the forces of evil."

"That's why I'm wearing a cape."

Emmit looked over Jamison's shoulder playfully. "Must be invisible."

"Just so the bad guys can't see it."

The two laughed uneasily.

"You a bad guy?" Jamison asked.

"Nah. I'm an old guy. What they call mature. Experienced."

"Is that so? I guess that's why it was so easy for you to kill Dax," Jamison said.

"Hold up now, son—"

"Don't call me son!"

"No one knows what happened to him. He played the game. He knew the rules. He broke them," he said.

"So, you killed him?"

"I've never killed a man in my life. Not even when I was at war. I'm smarter than that. Smart men have men killed. Right?"

"I didn't tell you to do anything—" Jamison exclaimed.

"You think you had any say in that, son? That all of that was for you?" Emmit laughed.

"Then who was it for? Who's pulling the strings?" Jamison asked. "Look, I get it. You didn't want me behind the scholarship fund; you were on the job to get me to support that WorkCorps proposal. That's all you kept saying. Trying to get me to bet on that horse. Did you think I'd be that predictable?"

"You're being predictable right now," Emmit spat. "Putting all your cards on the table like a cheap prostitute."

"You assume these are all of my cards," Jamison replied, opening his car door. "And you know what they say about people who assume."

"So, you think you have it all figured out?" Emmit asked as Jamison got into the car.

"No. But I think I have you thinking. All of you."

"I was trying to help you." Emmit held up the fraternity hand sign. "On the brotherhood, I was trying to help you. I'm your brother. Not your enemy."

"Yeah, well, with brothers like you, who needs enemies anyway?"

Val was driving down 20 West in that shiny new Jaguar two-seater with the top down, shaking something awful. While the sun was out and the flowers, all pleasant purple and happy yellow, were sprouting randomly out of the green grass on either side of the highway, setting an irresistible tone of happiness, her heart and mind and spirit were in dread. Someone, her mama or some wise woman with gray, kinky hair, should've been riding beside her in that car to tell her that this was what moving on felt like—contractions hard against your very soul on earth, pushing you forward no matter how much you wanted to stay behind. To stay small. The truth was that Val, with a heart so angry from birth, was about to begin a journey that would take her into her destiny. Someplace where she'd find the love she wanted in her own reflection. And that love would blossom into a beautiful life. There'd be a man, three babies, tall trees in the yard out back, and cooking and baking contests on Sundays. She'd be a rich woman someday, and not only in her heart. But she still had to survive this. And not knowing the end made this all the more painful.

While Dawn and another woman from the Hell Hath No Fury House volunteered to go with Val to get her things from Jamison's house that afternoon, she felt she should go alone. She wanted it to be quick and easy, and when Jamison answered his phone and said she could take whatever she wanted from the house without so much as asking where she was going, she thought she'd get just that.

She remembered what Kerry had said about her old red self when she pulled into the circular drive with the perfectly shaped creamy stones and purple pebbles. She'd thought about how she'd changed over those months trying to patch things up with Jamison—holding her tongue and watching what she wore and locking herself in the bathroom all day long. None of that was her, and while she didn't want this new self, she wasn't sure she wanted the old Val back either. She wanted the fighter, but even fighters get tired sometimes. When she stopped her car beside Jamison's, she wondered who she'd be when she got her things out of that house in front of her and turned the key in the ignition. She looked up at the windows staring down at her. In one rectangular pane that completed a series of windows toward the back of the dining room, she saw the fading face of her mother. She was wearing the dress she'd worn the day she came to Atlanta for the wedding. Val remembered that the rectangular pane was the very window Mama Fee had been standing in that morning when Jamison came home. While the image was fading in and out like an old vision, Val realized it wasn't her memory because she'd been sitting in the room when her mother had been standing there, and when she went down to greet Jamison at his car, she hadn't looked up. Mama Fee smiled at Val. She waved. She beckoned her daughter with a pointed index finger that slowly led her to the front.

Val didn't try her key. She turned the knob and the door opened right up.

Jamison was sitting on the couch in the living room, obviously waiting for her.

The fresco was already gone—compliments of Mrs. Taylor.

Neither Jamison nor Val knew what to say at that point, so they said hello to each other.

Though he had so many questions, accusations, and contentious exchanges in his thoughts, Jamison typed a few words on his cell phone in a decisive move to show he was busy and didn't want to be bothered with Val. If this was his "out" from this relationship, he'd take it. He'd already called a lawyer and planned to tell Val he'd pay for hers. He just wanted it to be over. His emotional landscape looked something like someone who'd been in a long-term relationship that shouldn't have made it past the first date. And that "someone" wasn't just Val—it was both of them. Days later, he'd look at Kerry and realize he'd never gotten over his marriage. He wasn't fit to date anyone, let alone get married. Maybe that was why he had been with Val—some kind of personal sabotage to make himself hurt so he couldn't feel his real pain. But, again, like Val, he didn't know the future and hadn't yet considered that, so he typed on his phone.

Val, who'd never really felt like more than a visitor in the house anyway, was made more nervous by his detachment. She readjusted her purse on her shoulder.

"Guess I'll go get my stuff," she said coldly.

"Do your thing."

Val turned to the staircase and found her foe looking down at her.

"No, you aren't. Only over my dead body are you coming up these steps," Mrs. Taylor said. She was wearing one of her sweat suits and one of her wigs and one of her attitudes.

"Have it your way," Val said, climbing the steps.

Mrs. Taylor started coming down toward her and they met in the middle.

Jamison was on his feet and begging his mother to calm down.

"Mama, I told you Val was coming to get her things," he argued.

"And I heard you. Don't mean I'm allowing it." Mrs. Taylor eyeballed Val from a step right over hers.

"Stop it!" Jamison went to the steps to come between the women. "You know you haven't been feeling well. You don't have any business being out of bed—let alone out here starting something. I told Val she could get her things."

Mrs. Taylor pointed at Jamison like he was a boy. "No way she's coming here."

"It's not that serious. You're acting like I'm here to steal something," Val said. "Ain't shit in here I want but my stuff."

"How do I know what you want and what you don't want?" Mrs. Taylor said. "Might get a case of the old sticky fingers like your mama."

"Don't you say nothing about my mama!"

And those were fighting words. Val had cocked back her fist and she had every intention of punching Mrs. Taylor in her mouth.

But the baby boy was there to hold the blow.

"Ya'll stop this, now!" Jamison said. "This is crazy. It's my house and I am not having this."

Val tried to pull away from Jamison, but soon she was calmer.

Mrs. Taylor wasn't budging though. She'd balled her fists and was ready to rumble.

"I ain't moving," she said to Jamison. "She ain't coming up here. She might've made a jackass out of you, but now she's at the bull and the bull gonna charge."

"Mama!" Jamison let go of Val's hand and pushed himself between her and Mrs. Taylor. "Look, what if we compromise?"

"What? How?" Mrs. Taylor asked.

"I can get Val's things for her and she can wait downstairs where you can see her," Jamison suggested. "That work?"

"Humph." Mrs. Taylor rolled her eyes to show she was still annoyed but softening.

"Val?" Jamison turned to Val.

"I just want my stuff," Val said. "I don't care if a blue leprechaun comes in here to get it, I just want all of my stuff."

"Okay." Jamison turned back to his mother and her rolling eyes and muttered expletives. "Mama? You okay with that?"

"I suppose."

Before going up to the bedroom with three trash bags, Jamison shored up his arrangement by leading Val to the couch and making his mother promise him she'd stay at the top of the stairs. It wasn't the best idea, but being a man who wanted this to just be over, it was all he had to work with.

Before he could get one bag filled, Mrs. Taylor found something she couldn't resist saying to the woman at the bottom of the steps. She felt it was okay to share her thoughts, no matter how ugly they were, as she hadn't broken her promise to Jamison— yet.

"Funny how you're making an escape in a car my son bought. Seems like you'd have your own car to drive off in. Was your name even on the lease for that car?" Mrs. Taylor teased.

Val didn't respond. She was becoming familiar with the bait.

"Oh, you don't have to respond, dear. Trust me, you don't. I'll find out. And I'll make sure my baby gets that car right on back." Mrs. Taylor laughed. "And where are you going?" She paused for a response, but only gave it a second. "Probably right back to the strip club where Jamison found you. Or maybe with the man in the gray car. Or maybe that man in the gray car is taking you to the strip club! Wasn't he your pimp?"

Something inside of Val came crumbling down when faced with a secret she'd whispered to Jamison when they were alone. The little comment took her right to her past. Put her back in that place where she felt like she was never going to get what she expected or deserved. Kept her believing she'd never been enough and never would be.

Mrs. Taylor was laughing loudly and going hard at Val about whatever came to mind and might tick the woman off.

"Yeah, you can sit down there and act like you don't hear me if you want to, but I'll tell you what, I made good on my promise, didn't I?"

Val didn't respond.

"I told you that night that I was cleaning house. Sure did. Didn't I?" Mrs. Taylor laughed. "Couldn't have my baby up in here with this bullshit. Had to make things right. Get things in order. That's what a real mother does. Guess you'll have to wait to find that out." Mrs. Taylor lowered her voice to something above a sigh, and Val thought she heard her say, "Glad I took care of that."

"What did you say?" Val shouted so loudly Jamison almost heard her in the bedroom. And had he been paying attention, he might've taken that as his cue to stop packing and take whatever he had in his hands downstairs to get Val away from his mother as quickly as possible.

But he was on the phone. Lazily throwing pieces of Val's wardrobe into a plastic bag with one hand and holding his phone with the other.

Ras had called to thank him for his support. To say he knew he'd had a brother in Jamison and he was happy to call him his friend. It was the kind of ego massaging few people could resist. And though Jamison tried twice to get off the line, Ras kept coming back with his future plans and stories about women showing up at his house.

Meanwhile, downstairs (because Mrs. Taylor was downstairs then), heads were about to butt. The son couldn't miss out on a kind word and mother couldn't miss out on the chance to deliver a mean one, so when Val demanded that she come downstairs to say what she'd had to say at the top of the stairs to her face, Mrs. Taylor rushed down the stairs like a six-year-old girl going to fight behind a school building.

"I know you stupid, but you ain't deaf!" Mrs. Taylor said, meeting Val toe to toe on a small landing between the living room and staircase.

"Whatever. You can save all of that. I just want to hear you say what you said, so we can get this all out in the open," Val said.

"I said, I'm happy you're getting your ghetto ass out of my son's house!"

"No, that's not what you said. You admitted it! You just admitted it. In your own evil way, you admitted it."

"Admitted what?" Mrs. Taylor asked, feeling a tingling in her right arm that went quickly to her shoulder.

"That you killed my baby!" Val charged and in a voice so low and hateful, Mrs. Taylor felt her resentment and vengeance vibrating through her eardrums. Suddenly, she was taller than her aggressor. Her eyes caught hold of Mrs. Taylor's pupils and any other word she had leveled against this woman shot right through to her mother-in-law's conscience. And guilt at being accused or maybe having acted sent that tingling quickly throughout the entire left side of Mrs. Taylor's body.

"I didn't kill anyone," Mrs. Jackson retorted, feeling her body jolt backward.

"Yes, you did! And you're going to jail," Val lied to scare the old woman and she was surely successful, looking over Mrs. Taylor's body as she fell to her knees.

"Jail? No! I didn't!" Mrs. Taylor wanted to call for her son, but she knew her body couldn't handle the strength she'd need to complete a sound that he'd hear.

"Yes, you did and the doctors found what you put in my food in my blood work and they're coming to get your old evil ass right now!" Val went on. "Remember, you said you were leaving here as soon as you got things right? Well, now you can go."

"No!"

The tingling made ice of every blood vessel and the freeze spread to her heart, where Mrs. Taylor's hands went to somehow catch the final kick that was tugging her to the floor. But it was no use.

She fell backward and her eyes rolled up at the ceiling. Her brain cut loose from her body and she thought she was calling for help, crying, laughing, singing, looking for her little boy who had always loved her. But she was just seeing shadows and half in and out of the world. She saw Mama Fee in her red wig, smiling in Val's face over her body. She tried to get away, but couldn't move.

And if she could've, Val wouldn't have stopped her. The freeze had come upon Val, as well. She couldn't move herself for a hold that went past fear or anger. She was under a shroud of sadness that had been born with her, in her, and that had grown into an iceberg that stood between her and the reality of a woman dying at her feet.

"You could've shown me kindness," she said in a low, creepy tone that would stay in the walls of that house.

"Jamison," Mrs. Taylor called out breathily. "Jamison, I loved you."

Upstairs, Jamison was off the phone and had gotten an inclination to drop what he was doing and run, run, run. It wasn't due to the noise. It was the silence. A nagging silence of doom, like the voiceless cries of fish flipped out of water onto a side of the strand where the waves would no longer roll.

He saw his mother's contorted body seizing at the bottom of the steps. Val standing against a wall a foot away.

"Mama!"

He was at her side, on his knees watching her eyes rolling fast, her hands still clinching her heart.

"Mama! Hold on! Hold on!"

He shouted to Val for her to call the police, but she was still against the wall calling for kindness.

"Mama, stay with me! Come on! Stay with me!"

He reached into his pocket and called for an ambulance. When the dispatcher asked for the matter, he said that his mother was dying. It was her heart.

He held this woman's head in his lap and felt the powerlessness men knew only in the face of God. The face that nature had imprinted in his mind as the safest place in the world—for he knew every line and gash and mole and the way it could say whatever it wanted—was leaving him. And this full man wanted to yell out to the world that he was not yet grown.

"Why couldn't you love me? Tell me!" Val whispered to Jamison's back from the wall.

"What are you talking about?"

Mrs. Taylor's eyes were slowing; her hands were loosening over her breasts. The freeze was leaving her.

"Why? I tried everything . . . and you just let her come in here and—"

"Mama! Mama, stay with me. The ambulance is on the way!"

The eyes stopped.

"I tried to tell you, but you wouldn't listen."

The hands fell to her sides.

"Mama? Can you hear me? Mama?"

The eyes rolled up at nothing.

"Look what you did to me, Jamison. Look."

There was no movement.

"I loved you," Val said.

"Mama! No! Mama!"

PART III

". . . until death do us part."

PART III

"There Are No Good-byes"

In a perfect world, Mrs. Taylor's son wouldn't have had to bury her. Well, in a perfect world, she would've died, yes—and maybe sooner than she had—but in that perfect world Jamison wouldn't have had to bury her. Burials, funerals, wakes, memorials, those were things people did who wanted to move on, who intended to let go. But Jamison wasn't one of those people. He wanted his mother back. And instead of planning her funeral, he'd spent most nights considering how he might do that. It was dangerous. He was a smart man. Not a crazy man. So he knew he couldn't revive the cold body he'd had to look at for a second time at the morgue on a rainy night after waiting for the perfect flash of lightning. There was only one way. The gun was in the nightstand. He lay in his bed for days looking at the oak box.

Mrs. Taylor's sisters showed up to bury their baby sister—three short bullets of women with wide hips and attitudes that showed they'd been raised in the same sandbox. They descended upon Jamison's home like a swarm of bees. Cleaning and cooking, whispering and making phone calls. They told Jamison planning a funeral was women's work. He didn't need to worry about a thing. They just needed his credit card—Mrs. Taylor hadn't had any life insurance. Calling him "baby boy" and vowing that they'd take care of him for the rest of his life the way their sister would see fit, they only pulled him from his bed for dinner and signatures.

One night, he called for water and no one came, so he went downstairs and found a party of women in his kitchen. There were pictures of his mother in various stages of life scattered all over the table. They were laughing. His aunt Belinda was in the middle of a story about the day her baby sister got saved and got to rolling all over the pulpit until the entire deacon board picked her up and carried her out. Jamison was still aching, so he pretended not to listen. He went to the refrigerator with a cup and pressed for water.

"Baby sister went a hundred percent on everything. She ain't never went half. All heart, she was," one sister said.

"Evil!" another said and they all laughed.

"Yes, evil, but decisive in her evility," another said, and everyone hollered.

"Evilina," another said.

"Queen Evilina!"

"Yeah, but only when you crossed her. Only when you hurt someone she loved."

One sister had quietly gotten up from her seat and taken a picture over to Jamison at the refrigerator. It was of him and his mother standing in front of the Grand Canyon. She rubbed her nephew's back but didn't say a word as he stood there looking at the picture like it was a vision right in front of him.

"She loved," someone said.

"Loved her family. Loved her son."

"Loved her son more than life itself."

There was a collective, elongated sigh that had been perfected by women gathered around kitchen tables for such purposes.

The funeral events—and that's what one would call them—were a mix of tradition and new money. Claiming always, "Baby sister would want it this way," the three sisters took Jamison's credit card and bought the biggest pink and gold casket they could find. They didn't wait for people to send flowers. They ordered twenty dozen pink roses to be delivered wherever their sister's body went (new ones at each stop). When they called the newspaper to place an obituary, they decided that the quarter-column statement the editor was offering was too small for the mayor's mother. They paid for a two-page spread—in color. A chartered bus went down to Mobile, Alabama, and picked up twenty-eight people, turned around, and made three more stops on the way back to Atlanta to gather whoever wanted to get to the funeral to mourn the dead. There were three choirs, two pastors, and a full reception with a band.

By the time they made it to the burial, the mourners were more psychologically fatigued than a group of freshman heading home from their first spring break in Jamaica.

Jamison's shoulders were so low. At some point, he'd stopped crying. Maybe his eyes were too swollen. At the burial, he sat in the front row with Tyrian beside him looking around awkwardly at everyone crying and tugging at his tie.

Once it was announced that in the order of all natural things, ashes had been returned to ashes and dust to dust, Jamison got up not knowing where he was or how he'd get home. Through the stops of the day, he'd been depending on a series of tugs and pulls at his sleeve explaining that his car was over there, it was time to get to the church, his seat was up front, he had to read the eulogy. But after the burial, it seemed everyone was dispersing back into their own worlds. The sisters with their promises of care now had their husbands and their children. The shipped-in mourners were getting back on the bus. Kerry came up and retrieved Tyrian, kissed her ex-husband on the cheek, and said she was sorry, she was really sorry. Jamison was about to say something to her—perhaps it was about the gun in the nightstand—but he decided not to.

When he thought he was all alone in the world, he turned and behind him was his assistant.

Leaf said, "I think I'll drive you home. I know you can't stand being in that funeral car. It's too damn slow. We can speed all the way to your house if you want. That cool?"

Jamison actually smiled and said yes before sharing a masculine hug with his new friend.

"Jamison, I'm glad I caught you!" an excessively friendly voice with the octave register of an older white man interrupted the moment.

"Governor Cade, how are you?" Jamison and Leaf fumbled these words into one big group greeting before taking turns shaking Cade's hand.

"Thanks for coming. I thought I saw you at the church earlier," Jamison said. He'd only seen Cade a few times since he'd been in office. They'd had lunch at the governor's mansion once, and Jamison thought he was a nice man, one who held his cards close to his chest and had eyes with secrets. There was nothing on him that made Jamison consider him one way or the other. They disagreed on policy, but they were from different worlds. That kind of polarity wasn't uncommon in Southern politics. It was actually what had made the transition through the ages.

"Yes, I had to come when I heard about your mother passing. Had to come and give my condolences in person," Cade said. "That's how we did it in the old days. None of this emailing and stuff. My wife actually sent a cake over to your house."

"Yes, I got it."

"I hear your mother was a good Christian woman. Had a church home. Served on the usher board for many years."

"Yes."

"Well, we know where she went then. Praise the Lord."

"Yes-yes," Jamison stuttered. "I'm sure that's true."

"Well, you rest in faith," Cade said, reaching out and clutching Jamison's shoulder. "Hey, can I talk to you for a minute?" He looked at Leaf with polite suspicion. "Alone?"

"Sure. Leaf, can you go and get the car? I'll catch up."

"As you wish," Leaf agreed.

Cade used his grasp to pull Jamison toward him.

"I know this isn't the best time," he said, "but I just wanted to make sure we're still on the same page about this WorkCorps thing."

"WorkCorps?"

"Yes. Judge Lindsey spoke to you about it, right? Now I know some time has passed and you've been through a lot with your mother and your child passing, but I hope I'll still have your signature on that. Right?"

"I haven't promised anything to anyone."

"Lindsey said you'd back it. Now that we got that other terrible business with Ras out of the way, we can move forward."

"Honestly, I haven't thought much about it. Where's the logic? Putting young men to work in minimum-wage jobs?"

"Any work is good work," Cade pointed out.

"Would you work for minimum wage?"

"I went to college, son. And so did you."

"Then where's the program for that?" Jamison asked. "Those young men will be grown men one day, with families and homes. They can't do anything with just a trade. Not more than the minimum. That's no way to set anyone up. I don't know."

"There are a dozen other programs just like this one," Cade said. "All around the country. We're not inventing anything new. I need your signature on that contract."

"I'll need to look it over again. I can't answer you right now."

"I'm telling you it's good, son. For your own good. I've looked it all over myself." Cade paused and thought a second the way a salesman does at the end of the day when he's speaking to the last customer on the floor. "Now Emmit bought into the company organizing the construction. His name isn't on the paperwork, nothing can come back to him. We have more space for another partner."

"So?"

"You want in? I can give you the same deal. Cash under the table."

Jamison just started walking away. He couldn't believe what he was hearing. He'd heard it before. It was rare that such deals didn't exist behind contracts in the city. The disappointment, the reason for walking away, was in the details.

Jamison's sudden departure made already ogling eyes turn toward the governor.

"All right, son," he said loudly. "We'll have lunch next week."

Jamison showed up at his ex-wife's house drunk, bewildered, and with no way home. In the car with Leaf on the way to his house, they'd decided that they needed somewhere to talk, to sift through the governor's offer in connection with rumblings down under that were no doubt in connection with the scene at the funeral. Of course, Cade knew about Dax and Keet and probably even the confrontation Jamison had with Emmit outside the jail. His position though wasn't to play as a man who was in the know. His visit with Jamison was a final plea. Or a warning. Still, there was no simple way to explain everything. They decided the best place to consider the chessboard from every angle was a bar. There they had drinks that turned to shots, and soon both men were so drunk they had to use each other as crutches to make it to Leaf's car.

When Jamison told Leaf to drop him at Kerry's house, Leaf asked if that was a good idea. Jamison hid behind a desire to see his son, but at Kerry's door it was a different situation.

"I can't go home. I can't," he said, lifting a ban on emotional exchanges he'd had in place since the day he'd realized he would have to see her as an enemy to move on.

Kerry looked out the door and noticed that she didn't see Jamison's car—or any car. Jamison had made Leaf drop him off at the head of the driveway.

"How are you getting home?" Kerry asked. She still hadn't decided if she'd let him into the house. Tyrian was with her mother and she was not in any mood to handle a drunk man after hours, who was coming from his mother's funeral.

"I'm too drunk to drive," Jamison muttered.

"Then how'd you get here?" Kerry asked.

"You going to let me in?"

Kerry backed up and let Jamison in the door. He smelled of smoke and scotch.

"Can't look at all those cakes. Everywhere," he half whispered.

"What?"

"Cake. Pots of collard greens. Fried chicken. All over the house."

"Here, come sit down," Kerry said, pulling Jamison to a seat in the living room. "You want some coffee?"

"There you go! Trying to make me feel better already," Jamison said laughing drunkenly.

"You say that like it's about you. I just don't want you to throw up on my floor."

"Humph."

Kerry went to the kitchen to get the pot of coffee started. She stood at the sink and stared out of the window at the pool. Somehow she wasn't so surprised that Jamison was at her door. She knew better than anyone that losing his mother meant he'd have nowhere to go with his emotional pile-up. Mrs. Taylor had always been his official unloading station, a voice that confirmed his divinity in any situation and cursed anyone who questioned it. Now, there was no one there to tell him everything would be okay and that this death didn't mean the whole world had come to conspire to kill him. Then Kerry considered that maybe Jamison thought she was supposed to be that someone. She looked over at the coffee machine, remembered opening her front door and letting him in, offering him comfort in her chair, offering him a drink for clarity. There she was, so quickly a fool. She decided not to put any

creamer in the coffee the way he liked it. She cursed herself for remembering that.

"My mother's dead, Kerry," Jamison said. He'd left the living
room and was kind of propped up against the wall in the entrance
of the kitchen. He'd been standing there watching Kerry at the
window for a few seconds before he spoke.

Kerry looked away from the window and at him. "I know."

"I knew it would happen someday, but, you know, that doesn't
make it easier."

"I don't think it's supposed to be easy. It's death," Kerry said.

"Oh, shit, don't tell me I'm supposed to learn something from
this." Jamison pushed up and attempted to stand on his feet for a
second, before falling back into the wall. "Everyone keeps saying
that."

"You learn something from everything. You know that," Kerry
said just when the green light flickered to signal that the coffee
was ready. She didn't rush over to it. "Jamison, I can't do—"

"I love you," Jamison cut in before Kerry could finish. Even in
his diminished state, he'd felt Kerry's concern.

"Don't do that. Don't go there."

"I always have."

"You're drunk," Kerry said. "And your mother just died."

"You don't think it's true?"

"I don't care if it's true."

Jamison recoiled like someone who'd been dismissed and sort
of smiled at Kerry's defiance.

"You love me?" he asked.

Kerry paused and looked at the green light.

"I'm out of creamer," she lied.

Jamison told Kerry about Governor Cade showing up at the
funeral. Shared with her every angle he'd considered with Leaf

through careful examination. With no contemplation, Kerry summed it up: "Shady son-of-a-bitch. It's greed. Nothing but greed. That's what this shit is all about."

"Well, money's always the motive, but that doesn't explain why there was so much heat on Ras," Jamison said. "That's the one piece that doesn't fit."

"You were doing business with Ras. Maybe they thought if you worked with him, you wouldn't work with them," Kerry said.

"Leaf and I considered that, too. But it doesn't add up. I could do both. I could do whatever I want."

The two of them sat and thought of other solutions, like time was running out on something.

There'd been a second pot of coffee and soon that creamer did come out. They'd already talked about Tyrian and how hard he'd taken his grandmother's death. Kerry revealed that he was now focused on her mother and had practically begged to go to her house after the funeral. Jamison told Kerry about Val leaving and how she had been there the night his mother died. Kerry didn't tell Jamison about Val showing up at HHNFH. Or their conversation. Or Val's plan to move back to Memphis to be with her mother.

And there was more to what Kerry was being silent about during the coffee chat that saw the sun set and had the exes sounding like old friends. She wasn't lying to Marcy when she'd said she'd stopped paying the private detective she'd hired. Only she never told Marcy why. It wasn't because she was over Jamison or trying to move on with her life. It was because of something the detective discovered on one of the recording devices he'd planted in Jamison's office—another detective planting a recording device. In fact, there were many voices whispering on the 3 AM. recording. "Sounds like the FBI. This is big shit. They're watching him," he'd said. Kerry told him to find out who was watching Jamison and why. The detective called in favors from all of his old friends at the Bureau and the result was a map that led to a probe that had Jamison at its center. She knew about Cade and the setup, but it didn't take long for the investigators to figure out that she'd been investigating them and when they did, they swore Kerry into silence, the lead investigator telling her that if Jamison wasn't guilty of any crimes, it was actually for his own good that he not get involved with the process and make any questionable moves. She'd have to stand down and wait it out.

But that wasn't all. There were other things that Kerry had been silent with Jamison about—the things about Coreen and Jamison's other child that Kerry had learned about and that she could bring up.

So when the conversation lulled and there were more pauses for sips of coffee than questions and solutions, and Kerry couldn't handle her avoidance any longer, she decided to broach the subject in a way that so many other women had, to bring to the surface information they already knew. "Jamison," she started slowly in a voice that Jamison knew and feared, "is there anything you've always wanted to tell me, but didn't know how?"

Now, it might seem that a secret child on another coast would be the most obvious response, but that wasn't how men like Jamison worked with such questions. Rightly so, he first considered what Kerry might know and be speaking about, as he'd heard this kind of question from women before and knew what it indicated. He thought of what Kerry might know and came up with nothing, so he answered with, "No."

"Are you sure? Anything you did in the past when we were married that maybe you need to tell me? Something maybe you're afraid to tell me? Something you—"

"No, I can't think of—"

"Maybe something you know of but that's not at the top of your mind right now?" Kerry's prompting was getting desperate. She wasn't pushing to get Jamison to fall into a fight with her, though that was all too possible. She'd already mourned the secret, the betrayal. She'd seen pictures of a little boy playing soccer, looking like Jamison and even Tyrian. She couldn't hate the boy with the soccer ball. Wasn't he Tyrian's brother? His little brother. Tyrian had a little brother who looked just like him. Those realities had come to her after she'd gotten an email listing the many flights Jamison had taken to Los Angeles after he'd found out about the boy. His teachers knew the Atlanta mayor as his godfather. He hadn't missed one school play, parent-teacher night, or concert. His Sunday school teacher told the detective that she thought Jamison was the boy's father and asked if he was. Then there was the information about the money being wired every week. How it had gone up to six thousand dollars and sometimes ten thousand dollars at a time. The detective made it rather clear what was going on between Jamison and Coreen. He was no counselor though, so he couldn't ask her how she felt or advise her on what to do with the situation. It was communicated like items on a shopping list.

"No. Nothing." Jamison became comfortable in his denial.

"Nothing?"

"Is there something you think I'm keeping from you?"

"Whatever." Kerry got up, frustrated, from the couch. "I knew you wouldn't tell me." She grabbed the two cups and went back into the kitchen for a refill. It was dark outside then. Her mother would be calling soon.

"What? What does that mean?" Jamison was following right behind her.

"What does what mean?"

"What you said."

"Never mind." Kerry threw the mugs into the sink.

"No more coffee left?" Jamison asked. "I wanted more."

"No."

"No?" Jamison looked at the opaque carafe. "You sure?"

"Just tell me!" Kerry leaned against the sink.

"Tell you?"

"About Coreen."

"What about her?"

"Don't mess with me, Jamison. Not right now! You showed up at my house drunk and you're in here drinking my coffee and I have to carry your ass home before my mother gets here with Tyrian and he's looking at us crazy because you're here."

"Shit!" Jamison said.

"Tell me!"

"Okay. You know about Coreen."

"Tell me."

"Val told you?"

"Why would Val tell me anything? How would I even talk to her?" Kerry said. "Just tell me."

"Why would I tell you what you know?"

Kerry crossed her arms and pressed her lips together. The steam coming from her brain was almost visible.

"Okay. Okay." Jamison gave in. He knew sooner or later he'd be having this conversation with Kerry. He'd planned it in his mind so many times, but never did his rationalizations sound right or the blows come easily to someone he was tired of hurting. "I have a son. His name is Jamison. That's all."

"Why didn't you tell me?"

"The same reason I didn't tell anyone else. I was ashamed. I wasn't raised to have children out of wedlock," Jamison said.

"So you were raised to have children in secret?"

"You don't understand. That's not how it was. Coreen—she's different. Worse than before."

Kerry remembered the psychotic break Coreen had had when her dwindling affair with Jamison had fallen through before she left Atlanta. She was a widow. A young widow. Her hurt and all the loss had led to a full unraveling, and Jamison's presence had been the only thing that kept her from suicide. That was how she'd lured him to California for those weeks. She'd needed him.

"What does Coreen have to do with you telling me about your child?" Kerry asked.

"I didn't even know about him. When she called to tell me about Jamison, he was already walking and talking. She just asked me for money. Said she didn't want me in his life. She just wanted the money," Jamison said. "Then, when I became mayor—"

"She's been blackmailing you?"

"Kerry, I wish it was that simple," Jamison said solemnly.

"I have time," Kerry said. "And I'm pretty smart."

"She's been, I guess, worrying me," Jamison got out uneasily. "It's like she's more erratic. Something about me marrying Val and the baby. She started threatening me. Said she's going to take me to court. Last month, I sent her twenty thousand dollars."

"What's the money for?"

"She keeps saying her son should live like my other son and she's not letting me get away with just abandoning him. It changes every day."

"Do you have a lawyer? Anyone looking into your options?"

"With everything happening with Val and the news and Ras, I just wanted to keep things low for a while. I've been trying to keep her calm, but it's getting worse. She wanted to bring Jamison here for the funeral."

"Why didn't you let her?"

Jamison looked at Kerry. "Because I hadn't told you yet."

Kerry laughed off his intimacy. "So you felt no way about telling me about Val's child, and even marrying her, and I'm supposed to believe you've been holding out on this because you hadn't told me?"

"I didn't want you to have to question again how much I loved you when we were married," Jamison said. "I didn't want to put you through that again."

"How do you know what I went through?"

"I don't know and I'll never know. But I've thought about it. And I think you must've wondered if I was lying to you. If I ever really loved you."

"I know you loved me."

"And that what I did in Los Angeles meant I loved you less. That it undermined it."

"No sense talking about it now," Kerry said.

"Why not?"

Kerry looked at the creamer on the counter beside the half-full carafe. "You ready for me to take you home?"

Jamison exhaled and shook his head. "Fine. Sure."

"I need to call my mother to tell her to wait to bring Tyrian back."

"Why is it so bad if he sees me here? I'm his father. I think it's healthy."

"Let's not do this. Look, I'm going to call my mother, and then let's go." Kerry walked out of the room so quickly she forgot her cell phone and had to call her mother from the house phone in her bedroom. Thirjane withheld her judgment and suggested that Tyrian stay at her house.

"Just don't be stupid. You've been doing so well," she said to her daughter, knowing Kerry wasn't listening.

"Sure, Mama," Kerry agreed. "Don't worry. I'm taking him home now."

When Kerry got back to the kitchen, Jamison was standing in the middle of the floor with his cell phone to his ear and his hand over his mouth. He looked worried, shocked, disoriented. Kerry's mind went to his mother.

"What's wrong?" Kerry asked.

"I just saw him last night, man. He was at the wake," Jamison said to whoever was on the phone. "He said he was going to call me on Monday. He was fine. He—It doesn't make sense. He wasn't like that!"

"What is it?" Kerry asked.

"Are they sure it's him?"

Jamison listened some more and then hung up the phone. He looked like he wanted to scream, or maybe he was screaming but Kerry couldn't hear it.

"What?"

"Ras. He's dead."

"What?" Kerry almost snickered.

"That was his lawyer. They found his body in his grandmother's basement. He shot himself. In the head."

"No. That doesn't—"

"This don't make sense, man!" Jamison started pacing the room. "No sense. He was—he was fine."

"Suicide? That's not like Glenn. He's not like that. Was he depressed?"

"Depressed? No. I just talked to him. He thought he was like the next Malcolm X. He wasn't depressed. Never. That wasn't him," Jamison said.

"I know."

"Suicide? No! It can't be. He wasn't—he—! No, man! No!" Jamison's pacing led him to a wall that he tried to push out of his way. "He wasn't—This ain't right. Suicide? No, Ras! Not like that."

"I'm with you," Kerry agreed. "It's not like him. You think"— she looked at him before choosing her next words with caution— "something happened to him?"

Jamison kept pushing his wall. It seemed like everything was behind it.

"They did this. They did this! They did this to him!" He pushed away from the wall and turned to the center of the room with a grimace.

"Who?"

"Give me your keys?"

"Who? My keys? Why?"

"They did this. I know it," Jamison said.

"They who?"

"I need your keys."

"You're not thinking straight," Kerry said. "I'm not giving you my keys."

"I can't let them get away with this. He was my friend. They killed him. I know it."

"They who? No, Jamison," Kerry said, trying to hold Jamison back from her keys on the counter. "You just left your mother's funeral. You're upset. You're not thinking straight."

"No, I'm clear. I'm very clear. I know what I have to do," Jamison said. "I have to stop playing fair. No one's playing fair."

"Fine. If you know who killed Ras, let's call the police. Let's try to—"

"The police won't do anything. They are the police," Jamison explained, wrestling past Kerry and grabbing the keys.

"Don't do this," Kerry said. "I swear, it'll all work itself out. You just have to be patient. Something is about to happen. I can't tell you what, but it's happening." Kerry tried to keep Jamison from the door. "If you go out there and get yourself in trouble, I can't help you."

"I don't need your help, Kerry," Jamison said. "I don't need anyone's help."

Jamison purposefully pushed Kerry to the floor to get out of the front door. He slammed it open and left it swinging behind him.

"Think of your son! Don't do anything stupid!" Kerry cried, trying to get up to catch up with him. By the time she made it to the front door, her car was heading up the driveway. She ran into the kitchen and grabbed her cell phone.

"He's gone," she said. "He has my car. I don't know where he's going, but it's not good. We have to move now! We have to do something!"

"Calm down," the person said. "I'll find him. Don't worry."

"Hurry. Just hurry, Leaf. Please hurry."

Jamison parked Kerry's car around the corner from the Rainforest. He'd stopped at his house to get the gun from his nightstand. He thought to change out of the gray suit he'd worn all day since his mother's funeral, but decided against it. Every familiar car was parked outside the old house with the fraternity bar in the basement. The silver Maserati was up on the grass.

Jamison pulled the gun out and held it behind his back with his hand on the trigger. The lock was off.

He descended the steps into the Rainforest. Kicked the door open and held the gun out in front of him.

No one was in the main room. The usual young bartender was standing guard wearing a fraternity T-shirt. He dropped a towel and a glass he was holding when he saw Jamison. Raised his hands and backed away from the bar.

"How many people back there?" Jamison asked lowly, shifting his eyes from the back hallway, where the doors leading to the bathroom and bedroom were shrouded in a blackness he couldn't see through.

"Three," the boy said nervously. "I don't want trouble. I'm in school. My father's—"

"Get out of here!" Jamison charged. "Get the fuck out of here."

The boy backed out of the bar with his hands up, facing Jamison. He started running as soon as he hit the basement steps.

Jamison thought he heard something coming from the corner where the old papier-mâché palm tree was now leaning against a wall. He pointed the gun at it and found nothing but dusty green leaves.

He crisscrossed slowly down the hallway with his gun pointed out, listening for footsteps or voices, anything behind or in front of him as he penetrated the darkness.

At the door to the bedroom where Dax had been held weeks ago, he heard men laughing heartily, talking in tones of victory.

"Militant X turned to straight bitch when he saw that steel. Begging for his life. What am I supposed to do with that?"

While Jamison had been waking from the original wrath that engulfed him when he'd heard the news about his friend's death and he was finally seeing where he was going and what he was doing with clear eyes, this bragging brought the vehemence back—and with more register.

Jamison took a deep breath and kicked the door open. There were two loud bangs as his shoe hit the wood and the door swung open wide to hit the wall inside the room.

The men inside stood fast. One tried to hide. Two went for their guns. But Jamison's barrel was in perfect position to commit to the swiftest action.

"Don't fucking move," he hollered. "Nobody fucking move!"

Six hands went up. Under the dim light Jamison saw Emmit, Keet, and Scoot. Keet was in a black hooded sweatshirt with his badge at his waist. Scoot and Emmit were in suits with their shirts unbuttoned halfway down, ties missing.

Jamison stepped deeper into the room, ordered everyone against a wall.

"Calm down, son. Think about what you're doing," Emmit tried in the wise voice he'd always summoned in Jamison's presence.

"Shut the fuck up," Jamison said, waving the gun to signal for the men to get in line on the wall.

"What are you going to do? Kill us all?" Keet said, and he was almost laughing, but still moving.

"That's the plan," Jamison said, closing the door behind him with his loose hand.

"We can work this out. Figure this out. If you tell us what you need," Scoot said.

"I want the truth. Before I kill all of you, I want the fucking truth," Jamison said.

"What truth, son?"

"I'm not your son, Emmit. You stop calling me that. Just tell me who killed Ras, which one of you did it?"

Scoot looked at Keet from his place against the wall.

"What the fuck? I killed him," Keet said. "I don't care. I ain't scared of this nigga and his gun. Because he ain't gonna use it. Are you? Come on. We can play this game and line up, but you ain't gonna shoot nobody. Too far from the SWATS for that. Right, Mr. Mayor?"

Keet laughed to settle his point, but Jamison raised the gun to his forehead and so much anger, so much weight from those days kept his moistening finger on the trigger. And he was about to pull it.

"I told you, you had to expect this," Emmit said. "That you had to be ready. You wanted to play, and here you are. This is what everything you wanted looks like from the inside. Ain't pretty, is it?"

Jamison moved the barrel to Emmit's forehead.

"I never wanted to play anything. Any games," he said.

"Can't have one without the other. What, you think those superheroes you read about in history books never got their hands dirty?"

"For money?" Jamison asked. "For kickbacks from a program you know isn't going to help anyone get rich but the corporations on top who already have all of the money anyway?"

"I'm wiped out. Retirement money is gone. Clara and these medical bills. What was I supposed to do?"

"Do right. That's what you were supposed to do," Jamison said.

"How's that working for you?"

"I'm not the one standing against the wall with a gun pointed at my head."

"So, you think this is going to solve something? Stop something?" Emmit asked. "You think you're the first super-nigga to try to stand up against the machine. Well, you ain't the first and you ain't the last. You kill us and we're dead and you're in jail and guess what, Cade's just moving on to the next deal. That's all."

"But it doesn't make any sense. All of this over a deal? Over WorkCorps? Ras had nothing to do with that. Why kill him? Over this?"

"More niggas, more money. How were those white boys going

to get a bunch of niggas to sign up for WorkCorps if you two were giving out scholarships in the 'hood like reparations? Everyone goes to college, no one goes to work. One less nigga to scrub toilets."

"No, no, man!" Tears Jamison hid behind his mission blurred his vision.

"He was cutting in on the profits. About to speak to the news about WorkCorps. Too much work was behind it. Couldn't risk it," Emmit said.

"How much?" Jamison asked. "How much were each of you going to get?"

"Five million each," Emmit said. "Five million each and more on the other side."

Keet and Scoot saw Jamison loosening his grip in his anguish. They silently organized a plan with side eyes based upon who was closest to the door.

"He didn't have to die. He was just trying to do right," Jamison cried, unknowingly lowering his gun.

Scoot took this as an opening and rushed to the door as Keet charged Jamison, but before Scoot could open the door, a boom came from the other side and the wood banged into his face before a line of men with guns drawn stormed the room with military precision shouting, "GBI! GBI!"

The four men in the room were quickly outnumbered, even Jamison, who was still holding his gun out in shock.

At the back of the line filing in was Leaf with a Georgia Bureau of Investigation badge on his shirt pocket, a gun held confidently in his hand. The other agents subdued Keet, Scoot, and Emmit, but Leaf stepped toward Jamison.

"Give me the gun," Leaf said. "It's fine. I know everything."

"What? What are you doing here?" Jamison asked.

"I'm a state agent. Just give me the gun," Leaf said, pointing at his badge.

"I was just trying to find out who killed my friend," Jamison said.

"I know. Give me the gun, man. I can help you."

And then, as Jamison slowly lowered his loaded firearm, his undercover assistant stepped in and removed the weapon.

The scene at the police station was like something out of a movie. Cade and all of his underlings tied to the WorkCorps plot handcuffed to chairs in different interrogation rooms. Big names. And small names.

All sat stunned when agents walked in with the chief of police in handcuffs.

Clara Lindsey sat in the waiting area with Countess beside her making phone calls to everyone she knew to get Emmit out of jail.

"Agents had been watching you since you got into office. We knew you were clean, but we needed your connections to make some footing for the bust. We knew it was only a matter of time before Cade got his hands on you." Leaf had explained this in different ways to Jamison over cups of bad coffee in one of the interrogation rooms. His entire demeanor changed as he unveiled all of the evidence he'd collected. "When Cade showed up at the funeral this morning, I knew we had him. Now all we need is your statement. We can put him away for a long time."

Jamison allowed the agents to record his statement about what Cade had said to him at the cemetery and everything that had gone down with Keet and Emmit. When he tried to confess his part in Dax's murder, Leaf signaled for the officer holding the recorder to stop the tape. He thanked Jamison for his time.

"I'm free to go?" Jamison asked.

"Agents will probably contact you in the morning, but you need to go home now," Leaf said. "Get some sleep. Call your lawyer."

"Okay," Jamison said. "So, what's going to happen to the other guys? You sure you have a case against them? Got everything you need?"

"It's a done deal," Leaf shared. "Funny thing is we thought we'd still need to push some of them to confess to Dax's murder, but once one broke, they all started singing."

"Who broke first?" Jamison asked.

"You'd be surprised. The hardest one. Keet Neales," Leaf revealed before telling Jamison that it was Keet who pulled in Governor Cade and every other name he knew in a tirade once he'd gotten into the interrogation room. Keet said if he was going down, everyone was going down with him. He told them about the five million he'd been promised to see the WorkCorps thing through, even how much money Cade claimed they'd lose if Ras and his program got a contract at the same time. He said his profits would be cut in half. That's when he ordered the hit on Ras.

Leaf went to open the door to let Jamison out of the tiny room.

"I can't believe all of this," Jamison said. "Who would've thought politics could be so ugly. So criminal."

"This isn't the worst case," Leaf said solemnly. "This isn't the last case."

"And you," Jamison went on, "I never would've thought you were an undercover agent."

"I'm good at what I do," Leaf joked.

"You were a good assistant, too," Jamison said. "A good friend."

Leaf and Jamison shared a laugh.

"Let me know if you ever want to switch careers," Jamison said as Leaf opened the door.

"I sure will."

Jamison found Kerry stepping in worried circles in the hallway. She jumped into his arms like someone who'd feared the worst.

"Oh my God!" she said. "I thought you were going to get yourself killed. You okay? Everything okay?"

"Yes, woman, I'm fine," Jamison said, embracing her.

"I was just thinking about Tyrian and your mother—this would've been too much for him." Kerry started crying and Jamison rubbed her back to reassure her.

"I'm fine. I'm right here," he said. "Not going anywhere."

"I know. I know."

"And what about you?" Jamison looked into Kerry's eyes. "You knew about this the whole time? How could you keep this from me?"

"I found out about Leaf early on so he had to tell me what was going on and he said it was best if you didn't know. Then he could protect you," Kerry explained. "You understand? I wasn't trying to betray you. I would never do that. I just wanted to protect you."

"I know," Jamison said.

One of the agents who'd been assigned to drive Jamison home stood at the end of the hallway.

"You need a ride?" Jamison asked Kerry.

"I'm fine. They brought my car here. I can take you home."

"I'm okay. Don't think I'll be going home for a while."

"Where are you going?" Kerry asked.

"Over to the Westin probably. You know my office has a room on standby there."

"Okay."

"I'll see you tomorrow," Jamison said. He kissed Kerry on the forehead softly and ran to catch up with his ride.

"His Third Wife"

I don't know what made me get into my car and drive straight to the Westin when I left the police station. Or do I know and what it was just remains too embarrassing to express in any weak word that would make me feel foolish or stupid? I tried to call my mother to talk me out of it. Only I didn't say that. I just reminded her that Tyrian had to be at camp by 7 AM the next day. She'd have to let herself into my house and get clothes for him to change into. He needed his swimming trunks and sunblock—he'd get such bad burns on his shoulders. She pointed out that it was 4 AM. She wasn't complaining. I know she heard something panicking in my voice. "You're a grown woman now," she said. "You make your choices. You pay for them."

I hung up the phone after saying good-bye, opened the car windows, and turned up the music. Peachtree is a brilliant spectacle of lights just before daybreak. Not anxious like Las Vegas or busy like New York City. Just random bursts of ordinary lights, a few up-to-date animated billboards and forgotten We're Open electric blue front-door signage. All of this glittering brightness dotting a sleepy strip that's so empty it dares you to race to the next red light. It's like the world is over. Like one of those eighties movies where you wake up and everyone's gone, stolen in the middle of your dream, leaving you alone to drift forever.

This old Faith Evans song was playing on the radio. I started singing along, trying to forget where I was going and hoping maybe I'd drive right past the Westin and get on the highway that led home, but the music pulled me back to somewhere that I'd been. It was a memory of Jamison and I riding in his car. With the windows open. Listening to this Faith Evans song. Maybe we were driving along Peachtree. But the sun was out. It shined into his old Cadillac from every window. I leaned my head into his chest and let his hand dangle over my shoulder. We'd just been married a year or two, so we must've been about twenty-three. The song was a little too fast for my mood, but Jamison sang along and I squealed at the torturous sound of his voice. Not even a sweet moment like that could make his singing voice sound good.

I was about to tell him to stop singing when he pulled the car over. He didn't park. Just pulled over and left the car running.

"What's this?" I asked. "Where are we?"

He said he wanted to dance with me.

"Dance? Here? Now?"

Jamison jumped out of the car and ran around to my side to open the door. "Come dance with me," he said. "We never dance."

I tried to keep the door closed, but I was losing, and laughing. "We always dance," I said.

"Okay. We do, but I want to dance right now," he said. He pulled me out of the car and I almost fell into him. He wrapped his arms around my waist and started singing again. "If you only knew, what you really do! . . ." He sounded like a wounded baby bird.

"Please stop!" I hollered, wresting away from him and that horrible sound. He wouldn't let me go though. He held me tightly in place in front of him and started humming the words in my ear. Soon, I stopped fighting and swayed with him. Right on the side of the street that may have been Peachtree.

I was crying when I pulled into the Westin and gave the valet my car key. There was no way away from my memories. From a whole past life with someone who was a part of me. A real part of me.

Someone who had ached with me and loved with me. Not even my
bitter heart could protect me from that.

Jamison opened his room door and saw my tears. He pulled me
into his arms like he had that day when we'd danced to Faith Evans
and told me everything was going to be okay.

We were both too tired to talk about what had happened at the
Rainforest or at the police station. The sun was threatening to shine
soon outside the window. We could talk then. We crawled into the
king-sized hotel room bed like it was ours and spooned just in case
we were dreaming and reality was to arrive with daybreak to sepa-
rate us again.

I was drifting into some restless sleep when Jamison whispered
in my ear.

"Would you marry me again?" he asked drowsily like he was al-
ready half asleep.

"What? Hunh?" I asked, though I'd heard him clearly in my ear.

"Marry me." This time his words sounded less like a question
and more like an offering.

"Marry you?"

Jamison laughed. "Why do you keep answering me with ques-
tions?"

"Because I can't believe what you're asking," I said more clearly
than I had before. "This is crazy. Too fast."

Jamison cleared his throat and turned me around to face him.

"Then I'll ask it slowly. Would you marry me?" he asked slowly.
"That work for you now?"

"I—That's not what I meant. I meant it's happening too quickly
for me."

"Quickly? You know I love you. I never stopped."

"What is that supposed to mean?"

"Another question." Jamison cupped my chin with his hand. "Do
you love me?"

"I—"

"Don't bullshit me. Don't give me the 'we're divorced and I have

to play from this side of the court' response. Just tell me. Do you love me, Kerry?"

"Yes," I said.

"So would you marry me?"

"I can't. I'm like, what—you're married."

"I'm getting divorced. You know that," he said.

"So, I'm supposed to just be your third wife? Marry you again and be your third wife?"

"Third time's the charm."

"This isn't a joke. Not if you're serious," I said and I heard a hunger in my voice that made me want to bite my lip.

"I am serious. We should do it. Move past all of this shit and just do it."

"It's not that simple," I laughed lightly at his planning. "We can't just get married and live happily ever after. We tried that already and failed."

"We were different people then—you, you were different. Now, you're—"

"What I am, you made me," I said harshly so he could feel for a minute my pain. I knew I'd changed, but I'd had to. Had to discover my two feet so I didn't fall down.

I expected him to apologize, but he didn't.

"What I am, you made me," Jamison repeated, and then for the first time I felt how my actions in the divorce and even before it had changed him. I knew of his darkness. But before I'd seen the suffering as a sign of my wins. Now I could see it as proof of his wounds.

I turned and found my restless dream with Jamison's arm wrapped around my waist.

When I woke up, the arm was gone. I turned and saw the light on in the bathroom.

"I'm not going to talk about this shit with you, Coreen," Jamison said. The door was only halfway closed and I could hear him clearly. "Well, you saw it on the news. Fine. It doesn't affect you. Do what you have to do. You do that and I'll do what I have to do."

There was quiet. Jamison was cursing, but I knew he was talking to himself. Then I heard the phone rattling and he was repeating, "Where? Where? Where?" Jamison started cursing to himself again and came out of the bathroom. He was still fully dressed. We both were.

"What's going on? Who was that?" I asked. "Was it Coreen?"

"Yes." Jamison went to put on his shoes.

I sat up in the bed.

"What did she want? Where are you going?"

"I need to handle this. I'll be back." He stood up and pushed his phone into his pocket. I could still hear it vibrating.

"What? Is she here or something?" I looked around the room like she could be hiding under the bed. I remembered seeing her at the house that night when I'd found Jamison there. The wild, crazy look in her eyes.

"Yes," Jamison said soberly.

"In this building? What does she want?"

"I don't know. I just need to go and calm her down. Get her to calm down. That's all," Jamison said.

"Calm her down? You think you can calm a woman who's traveled across the country and followed you to a hotel?" I asked. "Wait, does she know I'm here?"

"I don't think so. Look, just calm down, Kerry. I've dealt with this woman before. I know her. I know what she's capable of. She just wants to see me. And that's it. I'll be right back down."

"Down? From where?" I was frantic, looking around the room for my shoes.

I was about to get up, but Jamison stopped me.

"Listen, we're just meeting in the Sundial. It's the restaurant on the roof. I don't need a bodyguard. It's just a woman. That's all. Everything is fine. I've dealt with Coreen before. We'll have coffee. I'll give her some money. That's it."

"I think I should go with you."

"No. I'm fine," he said. "Everything is fine." Then he lightened

his tone a little. "We'll order room service when I come back. Sound good?" *He forced a smile.*

"Jamison, this isn't right," *I said.*

"Do you trust me?" *Jamison asked.*

"What?"

"Do you trust me?"

"Yes," *I said.* "I do trust you."

"Well, try doing it right now. I'll be right back. I promise."

Jamison was about to walk out the door. I noticed that his gray suit pants were wrinkled in the back the way they always were when we were married.

"Hey," *he called walking toward the door.* "You relax and take a little nap. And think about what you'd say if I ever asked you to marry me again. Like formally. Down on one knee, a ring, the works. I might even call old Thirjane and ask for permission."

"You serious?"

"Depends. Would you say yes?"

"I might," *I said.*

"Might?" *He laughed.*

"Yes. I'd say yes, Jamison. I'd do it."

Jamison grinned wide and Tyrian was in his cheeks.

The phone started rattling in his pocket again.

"I'll be right back," *he said.* "Right back." *He went to go, but then turned around suddenly and jumped in the bed with me, kissing me all over my face.*

"Stop," *I hollered, fighting him off.* "You're so ridiculous!"

He jumped back up.

"Gone for real this time," *he said.* "Be back."

I fell back into the pillows when the door closed behind him. Begged myself for an answer over what I was doing. I hadn't known I was going to say what I'd said to Jamison. I was okay with admitting where it had come from then. I loved him. That was it. And I didn't care anymore. I closed my eyes and tried to forget about everything.

But I kept seeing red. Coreen's red hair. The red in her eyes.

I opened my eyes.

I'd promised Jamison I was going to stay in the room and wait for him, but I kept looking at the door. And then I'd look at my shoes. And then I'd look at the door.

I did trust him. He knew more about Coreen and her ways than I had. She wasn't crazy. She wouldn't do anything crazy.

I looked at the door and then at my shoes.

But what if she could? What if she had? Well, what was crazy? Was it showing up at the hotel? Was it demanding he see her when the sun was hardly in the sky?

I closed my eyes again and promised myself I wouldn't look at the door anymore. I'd force myself to sleep. I'd wake up with Jamison back in the room on one knee with one ring.

I tried to keep my eyes closed that time, but there was the red again. Red like fire. Red like burning everything I loved.

And that was it.

I jumped out of the bed and into my shoes. I don't remember if I closed the hotel room door behind me.

When I got up to the restaurant, there was nothing but a cleaning crew there. Someone told me that they didn't open until noon and when I told him I was looking for someone he said that he'd seen a man up there and he was looking for a woman, but he left. I asked if there was another open section to the roof and he told me I'd need to take the stairs on the side of the restaurant where the rotator was that turned the floor of the spinning Sundial around over the city. "But you can't go up there," he said to my back. "It's not safe."

My heart was pounding as I climbed those stairs up the side of the spinning Sundial. It was early morning. The sun was up then and the wind was calm, but so high up the altitude had my head light and my skirt blowing up hurriedly. But I have to say, I wasn't afraid for myself. I was afraid of what I'd find. What Jamison was facing. In my mind Coreen had grown into a big red monster, horns and fangs, anger and resentment.

I kicked a door open that led to the little flat landing on the side of the restaurant. Jamison's back was to me. Over his shoulder was a woman in a dress. But it didn't look like Coreen. The person was bigger, had broad shoulders.

"I don't know who you are, but I came up here to meet Coreen," Jamison said with his arms outstretched in a "T."

"Well, that's good, because that's who sent me," the person in the dress said but in a voice I could tell didn't belong to a woman.

I tried to see why Jamison was standing back with his arms up and that's when I saw it.

"No," Jamison yelled. "Stay back!"

"What? What's that?" I looked at the gun in the man's hand pointed at Jamison and then at me. "He has a gun!"

"No! Don't point the gun at her," Jamison said, pulling me behind him. "She's not the one you're here for. It's me."

"Well, that's the issue with these kinds of situations. You can't have any witnesses," the man said.

"I can't let you do anything to her. She has nothing to do with this. If Coreen sent you here, that's it, but you have to let her go."

"Hurt you?" The man laughed. "You think I'm here to hurt you?" He cocked the trigger and straightened his arm. "I don't get paid for that!"

"Oh, my God," I screamed. "He's going to shoot!"

Jamison fell back on top of me to shield me from the bullet, but where we expected to hear a bang there was nothing. He jumped up and when he saw the gunman getting ready to pull the trigger again, he rushed toward him.

"No!" I screamed, feeling so alone and helpless there was no way I could imagine I was standing on top of one of the highest buildings in the most beloved city in the South. I would've looked around for someone to help. Would've called for someone to help, *but everything was moving too quickly. I was nowhere. On top of everything. All I could hear was the hum from the rotator behind me. "Jamison!"*

Jamison and the man wrestled with the gun back and forth, turning it in every direction their muscles could will in the struggle and then back to one another, aiming it at their chests.

Soon they were locked in a fight at the ledge that came up just beneath their waists and I kept hollering Jamison's name, but I knew he couldn't hear me. I looked around to see if I could find something to hit the man with, but there was nothing there. Just tiny stones and air vents. The rotator humming.

And when I looked up, there was Jamison, finally looking at me. Finally looking into my eyes. His arms were held out to me. He was smiling. Maybe. And that's when I realized what was happening. The gunman had Jamison bent over the ledge. And his arms reaching for me were just flailing at me.

He was falling.

Everything went white.

"Jamison!" I ran to him. "Jamison! Jamison!"

I probably should've noticed the man with the gun still pointed at me, inching in and threatening me. But I saw only my beloved, his legs, his shoes, go over the ledge as I ran to him, not thinking for a minute about what going over the ledge myself might mean.

I reached for him. Tried to catch him, but it was too late. He was flying. Already dead when he was still in the sky.

"Jamison!"

I left myself. Went to some safe little place in my body. Where else could I go? I didn't want to see. Or to hear. I didn't want to know anymore of the truth. Give me another lie. The lie from the day before. The lie from a week before. Anything but the truth of that moment. There was no wanting that moment. No knowing that moment. I couldn't be there. We couldn't be there.

The next thing I heard was the door I'd come through banging open again behind me. I turned around screaming for help thinking it was the gunman trying to get away, but when I looked at the door there was more than one gun pointed at me and the man was nowhere around. The men in front of me were in blue suits. Silver badges. Screaming. "Put your hands up!"

"Jamison! He—" I tried to point toward the gunman, but I was alone then on the roof. I pointed to the ledge. "He needs your help. He fell!"

"Step away from the ledge!"

"Okay, okay!" I tried. "I just need help. I just need your help." I stepped toward the officers and they came in toward me, one going for every limb to capture me. "Wait! Wait! What?" I hollered. "It's Jamison. He fell! The man was here! He pushed him!" I was pointing over the ledge as they pulled me into a circle where someone cuffed my wrists together. "Wait! My husband!"

"Are you Kerry Jackson?" a man with short gray hair asked Kerry.

"Yes?"

"We need you to come with us."

"What? Why? I didn't do anything," Kerry said.

Two other officers came funneling about the maze of faces around Kerry.

"Chief, we shut down the hotel. I spoke to the couple next-door to the room where Mayor Taylor was staying. They said they heard arguing. Cursing coming from the room not over an hour ago," one said. "And the valet downstairs confirms that Ms. Jackson checked her car downstairs late last night."

"That was Jamison on the phone—" Kerry tried to explain. "He was arguing with Coreen. That's who did this. Who sent the man with the gun here to kill Jamison. You have to find him. If you shut down the hotel. He's still in here!"

The other officer added, "A witness downstairs said she saw a woman on the roof right after Mayor Taylor was pushed. Some guy in the restaurant described Ms. Jackson as the woman who'd been up here earlier."

He pointed to the guy Kerry had talked to in the restaurant standing in the back of the crowd of blue suits pointing at Kerry.

"No! It wasn't me! I'm being set up," Kerry said. "There was someone else up here. You have to believe me. You have to find him!"

"Kerry Jackson, you're under arrest for the murder of your ex-husband, Jamison Taylor," the chief with the gray hair started. He read Kerry her rights and men led her down to the lobby, through the front doors of the hotel and into the flood of lights and eyes gathered in the middle of Peachtree Street. The ambulance that would carry Jamison's body was on one side of the spectacle. The car that would take who would've been his third wife to jail was on the other.

Coreen

I was never a wife. Not in Jamison's eyes. Not ever good enough to be that. But still he lied. He followed me to Los Angeles. Showed up at my doorstep and begged me to let him in. Told me Kerry was a crazy bitch. He was leaving her. Wanted to be with me. Start a life with me. I believed him. In what we could be. And when there was a new life growing inside of me, the only thing that could always keep him tied to me, I knew it was real. But then, when I got too comfortable, I was the crazy bitch again and he wanted to leave and go home to her. Back to her? Again? Come and go. Go and come. And every time I'm supposed to just take it. Bend over and spread and not do anything. I know every woman feels that way in her life with a man. Or maybe every person who's ever been fucked over by someone. But you can't play with people and not expect them to react. Reaction is nature. A pack of lions setting a trap. In revenge. In retaliation. Because sometimes you won't be all right. And you know it. And getting even—no, not just getting even—getting back what was taken from you will require a fresh kill. A reminder that you're flesh and blood. That you're a real person and you bleed.

I told Jamison that. Showed Jamison that. He only ever listened to himself. Only saw himself in my eyes and never cared enough to look and really see me. At once a pure heart now made into an angry bitch I never asked to be.

I was tired of being someone's not-good-enough. And when I realized a dead Jamison would mean I wouldn't have to keep begging to be good enough in his eyes and my son would be good enough to get his father's fortune, my decision was easy. And Kerry ending up on the roof, that wasn't part of the plan. That was luck.

Epilogue

There would be no casket at Jamison's funeral. The coroner, after shaking his head at the muddle of once living parts now dismembered permanently by the weight of the hardest fall, scratched his head at the mess of blood and guts and organs on his table and thought to suggest to the family that cremation would be most efficient. There was nothing for a mortician at a funeral parlor to string together of the man that once was. Only the bones. The skin, a bag burst open and spilling out memories.

When the next of kin was called into the room to see, to confirm by looking only at a single left hand that had survived the weight of the tumble downward and looked recognizable as something that wouldn't cause nightmares to any eyes set upon it, there was a tear and acceptance.

Only flowers, white and red and yellow, sat on the altar as the city mourned the demise of a man who could've been great. A procession of wailers and mothers with wide hips and long, silken handkerchiefs pressed to their swollen eyes, sat tight together in pews at the back of the chosen sanctuary right across the street from the crypt that held the body of Dr. Martin Luther King, Jr. In front of them sat the children. Little black boys in cheap suits commonly reserved for church whose mother's woke them up early that morning and said they were going to say good-bye to a man who'd wanted to do something to change the world they lived in. Closer to the front sat the dignitaries. Politicians. Brothers. And then family and friends. In the front, there was a mourner no one expected to see. His wife. The woman Jamison died married to. The new widow who now inherited his fortune. His story. Val. Beside her: Mama Fee.

By then, the headlines had turned the death of the Georgia son into a scandal of the haves taking from the have-nots in a consistent and deliberate and historical and traditional plot to stamp out progress from the under. From the west end. From the south end. From the would be's and seekers.

But little of this fight reached through the concrete walls and metal bars that became the home of Kerry Jackson. She'd been charged with murder and placed in a cage to rot as an example of how swiftly and efficiently the Atlanta Police Department could do its work to avenge the murder of its leader. The chief, the brother who'd been put in office by the mayor himself, congratulated his team on a job well done. He handed out certificates, medals, raises, and promotions and closed the book on the right side of justice.

While Thirjane said she'd never visit her child in jail, she all but had to when she realized there'd be no bail set for her daughter's return home and the only chance Kerry would have of seeing her son again was in short visits in tiny rooms. Kerry begged to see, to just smell Tyrian. To look at his smile. His eyes. Alive and a part of Jamison.

So, one afternoon, when the inmates had been called to the front to greet visitors who'd braved the touch and prodding of guards funneling them in single file lines to prepare them for a thirty-minute visit with their sequestered loved ones, she was sure she'd find Tyrian and her mother standing at the middle of the line with open arms and smiles. But that wasn't who she found.

In a familiar beige Chanel suit and thin-heeled red lacquer

pumps that seemed oddly placed in the unadorned, pale blue room that hosted the short unions, there was a female face found less sad than it had been the last time Kerry had seen it.

The women hardly said anything to each other at first. Awkward greetings and something less than a handshake. They sat and looked into each other's eyes.

"I'm going to get you out of here," one said to the other.

"They have evidence against me. So many witnesses who saw me on top of that building," the other said. "I didn't do it. I didn't push him."

"I know. And I know who did."

HIS THIRD WIFE

Grace Octavia

ABOUT THIS GUIDE

The suggested questions that follow are included to
enhance your group's reading of this book.

Discussion Questions

1. Jamison is Tyrian's hero in most every respect. Still, while he remains a constant in one son's life, there's a child on a different coast who bears his name but only sees him in bits and as his "godfather." Was Jamison just in his actions concerning the treatment of his unexpected child with Coreen or was he acting selfishly and only seeking to secure his political platform? What effect might this have on the child even if he has Jamison in his life?

2. Jamison is his mother's "baby boy" and he assumes all of the rights and privileges of this position in her life—even as a married adult male. Though he realizes his mother's wrongs, he vows to stick by her side because she's his "mama." Was he correct to do this? How might different decisions concerning his mother have changed Jamison's fate throughout this novel? In *His First Wife*? How does this interdependent relationship reflect any you see in reality?

3. During her final reflections on her relationship with Jamison, Kerry reveals that she's always loved him and because they shared so much together, it was impossible for her to move on. Do divorcees, especially those with long histories together and maybe even children, ever really move on from their pasts? Or was this a unique case of true love?

4. The politicians and community leaders in the novel just can't seem to keep their hands clean. Interesting in that much of what they do is allegedly to stop corruption and protect the public from criminals. Who's the biggest fraud in the story? While much of their dealings may seem out of this world, do the actions mirror what happens in local and national and international politics on a daily basis?

5. There are so many factions vying for power in the world of the novel. How do people maneuver to try to protect their elite status or gain it? What does this do to Val?

6. There are three women speaking directly to the reader in this novel. All are hurt by and in love with the same man. How do their stories differ? How are they exactly the same? What happens when the women look beyond their differences to see their similarities?

7. It is said that those who are hurting hurt others. Revenge is a major point of motivation for many of the characters in the climaxes in this book. How did a need for revenge control people's emotions, even in the face of clear wrongdoing on the part of the person seeking revenge?

Don't miss Jamison's scandalous beginnings in

His First Wife

Available now at your local book store!

E-MAIL TRANSMISSION

TO: Jamison.Taylor@rakeitup.net
FROM: duane.carter@hotmail.com
DATE: 3/15/07
TIME: 9:57 PM

Hello. If this e-mail works and it's Jamison Taylor, I think I
found your PalmPilot in front of my house this morning. All I
could find was the name Jamison Taylor inside and I
Googled it and found this e-mail address. If it's you, I have it.

E-MAIL TRANSMISSION

TO: duane.carter@hotmail.com
FROM: Jamison.Taylor@rakeitup.net
DATE: 3/16/07
TIME: 5:03 AM

You don't know how happy I was to get this e-mail. I had
my assistants running around all day looking for that thing.
Where are you located? Can I come pick it up?

Jamison

Foolish

October 26, 2007

It was 5:35 in the morning. I was doing 107 on the highway, pushing the gas pedal down so far with my foot that my already-swollen toes were beginning to burn. It was dark, so dark that the only way I knew that I wasn't in bed with my eyes closed was the baby inside of me kicking nervously at my belly button and the slither of light the headlights managed to cast on the road in front of me.

I-85 South was eerily silent at this time. I knew that. I'd been in my car, making this same drive, once before. I kept wiping hot tears from my eyes so I could see out of the window. I should've been looking for police, other cars on the road, a deer, a stray dog that had managed to find its way to the highway in the dewy hours of the morning, but I couldn't. I couldn't see anything but where I was going, feel anything but what I didn't want to feel, think anything but what had gotten me out of my bed in the first place. My husband.

Jamison hadn't come home. I sat in the dining room and ate dinner by myself as I tried not to look at the clock. Tried not to notice that the tall taper candles had melted to shapeless clumps in front me. Knowing the time would only make me call. And calling didn't show trust. We'd talked about trust. Jamison said I needed to trust him more. Be patient. Understanding. All of the things we'd vowed to be on our wedding day, he reminded me. My pregnancy had made me emotional, he said. And I was adding things up and accusing him of things he hadn't done, thoughts he hadn't thought. But I was no fool. I knew what I knew.

Jamison's patterns had changed over the past few months. And while he kept begging me to be more trusting and understanding, my self-control was growing thin. The shapeless clumps on the table in front of me resembled my heart—bent out of shape with hot wax in the center, ready to spill out and burn the surface. Jamison had never stayed out this late. And with a baby on the way? I was hot with anger. Resentful. I was ready to spill out, to spin out, but I held it in.

I helped our maid, Isabella, clear the table, told her she was excused for the night. Then I moved to the bedroom, and while I still hadn't peeked at the clock, the credits at the end of the recorded edition of *Ten O'Clock News* proved that any place my husband could be . . . should be . . . was closed. I wanted to believe I was being emotional, but that would've been easier if I didn't know what I knew. Maybe he'd been in an accident. Maybe he was at a hospital. Yeah . . . but maybe he wasn't.

I lay in bed for a couple of hours; my thoughts were swelling my mind as round as my pregnant stomach. I knew what was going on. I knew exactly where he was. The only question was, what was I going to do?

Then I was in my car. My white flip-flops tossed in the passenger seat. My purse left somewhere in the house. My son inside of my stomach, tossing and kicking. It was like a dream, the way everything was happening. The mile markers, exit signs, trees along the sides of my car looked blurry and almost unreal through my glazed eyes. The heat was rising. My emotions were driving me down that highway, not my mind. My mind said I was eight-and-a-half months pregnant with my first child. I didn't need the drama, the stress. I needed to be in bed.

But my emotions—my heart—were running hot like the engine in my car. I was angry and sad at the same time. Sometimes just angry though. I'd see Jamison in my mind and fill up my insides with the kind of anger that makes you shake and feel like you're about to vomit. And then, right when I was about to explode, I'd see him again in my mind, in another way, feel betrayed, and sadness would sneak in. Paralyzing sadness, so consuming that it feels like everything is dead and the only thing I can do is cry to mourn the loss. I wanted to fight someone. Get to where he was and kick in the door so he could see me. Finally see me and see what this was doing to us. To our marriage.

I didn't have an address, but I knew exactly where she lived. My friend Marcy and I followed Jamison there one night when he was supposed to be going to a fraternity function at a local hotel. But having already suspected something was going on, I called the hotel and learned that there was nothing scheduled. That night six months ago, before he left, I gave him a chance to come clean. I asked if I could go. "No one else will have their wives there; it's just frat," he said, using the same excuse he'd been using for three weeks. He slid on his jacket, kissed me on the cheek and walked out the front door. I picked up my purse and ran out the back where Marcy was waiting in a car we'd rented just for the circumstance. When Jamison finally stopped his truck, we found ourselves sitting in front of a house I knew I'd never forget. The red bricks lining the walkway, the yellow geraniums around a bush in the middle of the lawn, the outdated lace curtains in the window. It looked so small, half the size of our Tudor in Cascade where the little house might envy a backyard cabana. It was dark and seemed empty until Jamison climbed out of the bright red "near midlife crisis" truck he'd bought on his thirtieth birthday. Then, the living room light came on, my husband walked in. And through the lace I watched as he hugged her and was led farther away from me. I fell like a baby into my best friend's arms. What was I to do?

I promised myself I would never forget that house. So there was no need to look at the address. I knew every turn that had brought me there. I just couldn't figure out why.

Now, here I was nearly half a year later, dressed in a silk, vanilla nightgown at five in the morning, making the same trip, but with a different agenda. I knew why and where, and something in me said it was time to act.

I saw that red truck parked in the driveway when I turned onto the street. It looked so bold there. Like it belonged. Like nothing was a secret. *They* were the perfect family. There was no wife at home, no child on the way; our love, our love affair, was the second life he was living. *She* was his wife. I was just the woman he was sleeping with. Sad tears sat in my eyes, my anger refusing to let them roll down my cheeks. Every curse I knew was coming from my mouth as I held the steering wheel tighter and tighter the closer I got. My husband, the person I thought knew me better than anyone else in the world, had turned his back on me for another woman.

I pulled my car into the driveway behind Jamison's and turned off the ignition. The sudden silence hit me like the first touch of cold beach water on virgin feet. Without the hum of the engine, I realized I was alone. I'd gotten myself all the way there, but I didn't know what I was going to do. I knew I had to act, but what was I going to do? Burn the house down or ring the door bell and sell them cookies? And if she came to the door, what was I going to say? Ask another woman if I could see *my* husband? Curse her out? Scream? Cry? Should I hit her? I hadn't hit anyone in my life. What if Jamison answered the door? What if he was mad and told me to leave? If he said it was over?

The baby kicked again, but lightly, as if he was nudging me to go and get his father out of that house, away from that woman. Coreen Carter was her name. Marcy found it on a piece of mail she'd snatched from the mailbox when we followed Jamison. It was a simple name, but Coreen Carter couldn't be that simple. She had my husband inside of her house.

The anger let go at that thought and the sad tears began to fall again. What was I doing? What was happening with my life? I felt like I was being torn inside out. My baby was the only glue that was keeping me together. I felt so alone in that car.

I snatched my cell phone from the seat beside me and called Marcy. She picked up her phone on the first ring. She was an RN and her husband was an ER doctor, so she was a light sleeper.

"I guess little Jamison is about to make his arrival?" she assumed cheerfully, but I couldn't answer. I was sobbing now. Sadness was coming from deep inside and I was sure the only sound I could make was a scream.

"Kerry?" she called. "You okay? Where are you?"

"Here." I managed. There was no need for me to say where exactly. She knew.

"It's six in the. . . . He didn't come home?"

"No."

"Kerry, why didn't you call me? You don't need to do that right now. Not in your condition."

"I just want this to stop," I said sorrowfully.

"I understand, but right now just isn't the time. You have other things to take care of." She paused. "I know I sound crazy to you, but I just don't want anything to happen to you or the baby. You understand that, right?"

"Yes," I said, with my voice cracking. "But I'm just tired of this crap. I mean, what the hell, Marcy? Why? Why is Jamison here with this woman?"

"I don't know that. I can't answer that. Only Jamison can."

"Exactly." I felt a twist of anger wrench my gut. Again I went from feeling sorry for myself to being angry that I was there in the first place. Jamison was *my* husband and he was cheating on me and I wasn't going to just sit in a car and let it go on. I slid on my flip-flops and opened the car door.

"What are you going to do?"

"I don't know," I said. I really didn't. But, again, my emotions were driving. I was spilling out like that hot wax and before I knew it, I was charging up the walkway.

"Just don't do anything foolish," Marcy said before I hung up. Later I'd think about how crazy that sounded. How could I possibly do anything more foolish than what was already being done to me?

The little cracked doorbell seemed to ring before I even pressed it. It chimed loud and confident, like it wasn't past 6 AM and the sun hadn't already begun to rise behind me. It was quiet. The only noise I heard was my heart pounding, shaking so wildly inside of me that I couldn't stand still. I waited for another five seconds which felt like hours. My husband was on one side of the door and I was on the other. Our wedding bands and my large belly were the only signs we were connected. I looked at his truck again. It was the only piece of Jamison I could see from where I was and my heart sank a bit farther. The shine of the paint, the gloss on the wheels, it looked so happy, so free, so smug, so complete. Everything he wanted. I was tired of making this all so possible for Jamison. Making his life so comfortable, so happy. His perfect wife, carrying his perfect son. I was alone in my marriage and I was tired.

I began pounding on the door then. Ringing the bell and then pounding some more. My fist balled up and it pounded hard like a rock threatening to burst through. Someone was inside and they were coming out. If there were children inside, a mother and father, a dog, a parrot. . . . I didn't care. They were all getting up and out of that house.

A small, light brown hand pulled back the sheet of weathered lace covering the square at the top of the door. A woman's face appeared. Her eyes were squinting with the kind of tired worry anyone would have over a knock at the door at 6 AM. I'd seen those eyes before, and before she widened them enough to see who I was, my fist was banging at the glass in front of her face. I was trying to break it and if I could break it, I'd grab her face and pull her through the tiny square.

"Tell my husband to come outside," I hollered, my voice sounding much bigger than I was. She looked surprised. Like she never expected to see me or hadn't known Jamison even had a wife. I pressed my face against the window to see inside. To see if Jamison was there behind her. The flap fell back down over the little window and I heard heavy footsteps. I was beside myself. Had totally let go of whoever I was. My baby grew lighter, as if he wasn't even there, and a thunderbolt inside shocked me into action.

"Jamison!" I shouted heatedly. "Jamison, come outside!" I began banging on the door again. I couldn't believe what was happening. I knew it was her. Coreen Carter. I saw her only once before in my life. But when she came to the door that time to let Jamison in, I learned her face the way a victim does her victimizer.

She was what most men would consider beautiful. She had short, curly red hair. From the car I thought it was dyed, but up close I could tell it was her natural color. Fire engine red, like the truck, from the root. She had freckles of the same color dotted around her eyes and her skin was the color of Caribbean sand. Really, she looked nothing like me. In fact, we were complete opposites. My hair was so black and long, most of my friends called me "Pocahontas" growing up. My hair wouldn't dye and most days it wouldn't hold a curl of any kind. And if the skin of the woman in the window was the color of Caribbean sand, then mine was darker than the black sand on the beaches of Hawaii. My mother didn't like to talk about it, but my grandfather on my father's side was half Sudanese, and while he died long before I was born, my father always said the one thing he left behind was his licorice color on my skin and my perfectly shaped, curious almond eyes.

My cell phone began ringing. I opened it, certain it was Marcy making sure I hadn't killed anyone, but it was Jamison.

"Jamison," I said, looking again in the window to find him. What was this? What was going on? I felt far from him already. Now he couldn't even come to the door?

"Kerry, go home." His voice was filled with irritation.

"What?" I asked. "Are you kidding me? Jamison, come out-side." I couldn't believe what I was hearing. He sounded as if I was doing something wrong, like I was out of place.

"I don't want to do this here. It's not right," he said.

"Not right? Not right to who, Jamison? Her? I'm your wife!"

"I know that."

"No, you don't because if you did, I wouldn't be standing out here in my nightgown, eight months pregnant. Or did you forget about that?" I started banging on the door again. Thinking of my child made me furious. I wanted that door down. I'd forgotten all about where I was. People were starting to come out of their houses, but I didn't care. I wanted it to stop and Jamison being on the phone from inside the house wasn't making it any better.

"Kerry, she didn't do anything to you. Just go home and I'll be right behind you." He was whispering like a schoolboy on the phone with his girlfriend late at night.

"I'm not going home. You come out here now or I swear I'll bust the windows in your car and set it on fire if I have to." I couldn't believe the things I was saying, but I felt every syllable of them. At that moment I was willing to do anything, and Jamison must've felt it too. He hung up the phone.

The door opened fast, like he'd been standing on the other side the whole time. Jamison stood there alone, dressed in a pair of boxers I'd bought him.

"Did you really think I was going away?" I asked. Through the corner of my eye, I could see an old lady standing in her doorway next door wearing bright pink foam rollers in her hair and a flow-ery nightgown. I wanted to lower my voice, but I was beyond car-ing about embarrassing myself. "What is this? What is this?" I started crying again, but I didn't bother to wipe my tears. I just wrapped my arms around my stomach and held tight. The baby felt heavy again, like he was feeling the weight of the moment.

"I can explain it—" He stopped mid-sentence and reached for me. "It's nothing. I'm just . . ."

I stepped away.

"Just what?"

"Look, Kerry, I think you should go. I'll put on something and then come too, but I need to get dressed."

"I'll be damned if I let you walk back into that house with that woman," I hollered. "Does she know you're married? That you have a son on the way? Why can't she come out here and face me? Don't be embarrassed. I'm here now." I tried to push my way through the doorway, but Jamison held me back.

"Let me in," I said, pushing my way in farther. "I just want to see her. I just want to see her. I want to see the woman you chose over me."

"Don't do this," he said, pulling my arms. "Don't do anything foolish."

I pulled back and looked my husband in the eyes. We'd known each other for twelve years. He was my first love. The only man I'd ever imagined marrying. He looked so naked standing there in front of me. So defenseless. He had pale, milky white skin, looked almost white sometimes in pictures, and the centers of his cheeks were beet red, the color they turned when he was sad or angry.

"Don't do what? *Anything foolish*?" I cried. "*Foolish*? You jerk. You fucking jerk."

I practically jumped into Jamison's arms and started pounding my fists into his face. He was 6'5", well over a foot taller than me, but I was towering above him then. Every bit of anger and frustration I felt grew me taller. I was swinging and screaming and hitting to make him feel the pain I felt. I was beat down and beat up by his lies and now I wanted him to feel the same thing. It didn't stop what I was feeling, but it felt good, like I was releasing something. Letting go, or at least loosening up my anger.

"*Foolish*," I screamed. "I'll show you *foolish*."

"Ma'am, stop it!" I heard an authoritative voice before I felt a hand pull at my shoulder. "Ma'am."

My body was being lifted up. I felt two hands on both of my sides.

"She's pregnant," Jamison said, reaching for me as the hands pulled me farther back. I turned to see two police officers standing beside me, while two others were holding me. Suddenly, I could see the flashing lights from their cars in the street, the flickering blues hitting small groups of people huddled in different places along the curb. There had to be at least six cars out there, and all I could think was where they'd come from and who they were there for.

"He ain't worth it," one woman said in the crowd.

I turned to look at Jamison. There were so many people there, so many people I didn't know, and I felt like adding Jamison to the list. He seemed a part of this place, farther and farther away from me than I thought.

"Do you live here, ma'am?" one of the officers asked me. She was the only woman and she was so small the blue uniform seemed to swallow her up.

"No," I said.

"That's Coreen's house," someone called from the crowd.

Then, as if the person had summoned her, Coreen Carter came shuffling out the door. Her face was streaked with tears that seemed bigger than mine. Her eyes were red and she was visibly shaken. She stepped outside and stood beside Jamison in front of the door.

Seeing the cops had brought me back to reality, but seeing Coreen stand beside my husband sent me into what I can only call an out-of-body experience. Baby and all, I twisted out of the police officers' hands and charged after her. The word "nerve" was echoing in my head and if I had my way, I wanted to cut it into her chest with my bare hands. I was filled with rage. With disbelief. My life wasn't supposed to be like this. My marriage wasn't supposed to be like this. And love wasn't supposed to feel like this. All I could do was blame her for all three.

The female cop and another tall, white cop caught me and

pulled me farther down the walkway, away from Jamison and Coreen, who were standing together.

"Ma'am," the female officer said, standing in front of me. "I'm Officer Cox. What's your name?"

"Kerry . . . Kerry Taylor."

"Ms. Taylor, I can see that you're upset, but I need you to calm down, so I can talk to you and figure out what exactly is going on here." Her eyes were soft and brown like my Aunt Luchie's. The look on her face was sincere, kind, like she was the only person out there who understood what I was feeling. "Now we don't want anything to happen to your baby. You understand?"

"Yes," I said. I wiped a tear from my eye and looked over at Jamison. He was talking to two male officers, a fat white one and a black one who seemed like he was in charge. Coreen was standing beside him with her hand over her mouth.

"You don't live here?" Officer Cox asked me again.

I shook my head no.

"Were you sleeping here?"

"No," I said, looking at Jamison. He was looking back at me. Tears were in his eyes. The other officer was telling him not to come over to me.

"Is that man with you?" the other, tall officer asked me.

"He's my husband."

The weight of my words must've surprised both of them. Officer Cox stopped writing on her little pad and looked at the other officer.

"Yes," I said, confirming what they were both thinking.

"Hum," she said and looked over at Coreen. "He's here with her?"

"Yes," I said again.

"Should've told us that first," the tall cop said. "We would've given you more time on him." They both exchanged glances and a short, nervous laugh.

"I know what you're feeling. We see this all the time," Officer Cox said, writing again. "But you have to control yourself."

"And not let the cops see you hit your husband," the tall cop said.

"Cox," the officer in charge called, coming toward us as he adjusted his holster.

Jamison turned toward the house when the officer walked away, but I could tell he was crying. He punched the door so hard it sounded as if a gun had gone off.

"Ma'am, I need you to go on in the house," the white officer said to Coreen. "We'll come in and speak with you after we're done out here."

Coreen turned and looked at me quickly, her eyes still wet with confession. She went to walk into the house, reaching first for Jamison, who stepped away from her immediately.

The older officer signaled again for Cox to walk toward him.

"You just stand here, calm, and I'll be right back," she said, stepping away.

"What's going on?" I asked. I could see some trace of dread in her eyes.

"She's just talking to our captain is all," the other officer said. "Standard procedure."

"Am I in any trouble?" I watched as Officer Cox talked to the captain. Her eyes dropped and she placed her hand over her mouth just like Coreen had.

"Probably not," the officer said. "They'll probably let you go."

"Let me go?"

I looked back at Jamison.

"Baby," he tried, his voice filled with desperation.

"Sir, I'm going to need you to stay where you are," the fat officer said, putting his hand over his gun.

"Jamison?" I called. "Jamison."

"She's my wife. You can't take her." He kept coming toward us.

Two other cops ran to him and held him back from either side. Suddenly, there were at least ten cops between us.

"Take me? What's going on?" I asked. I looked back to Officer Cox. She was obviously pleading now with the captain, but he kept shaking his head, and then finally she looked me right in the eye and mouthed the word "sorry."

"Just be patient, ma'am," the officer beside me said timidly. "They'll be back over in a minute."

"Can't I just speak to her before she goes?" Jamison yelled. "She's pregnant. She can't go to jail."

"Jail?" I said. The word slapped me so hard my bladder dropped and urine came flowing from between my legs, wetting the front of my nightgown. "Jamison!" I cried. "Stop them!"

The female officer came toward me, pulling handcuffs from her hip.

"Mrs. Taylor," she said, her voice deep and throaty, as if she was forcing it to be stern. "I'm going to have to place you under arrest—"

"No," I hollered. "No! I didn't do anything. I was just here to get my husband. He's my husband." I began crying again. My adrenaline was wearing thin and the thought of being arrested for the first time in my life suddenly made me feel desperate and ugly. Not who I was. Not Kerry Taylor who'd grown up privileged, on the right street, in the right part of Atlanta. Not me. Jail? I looked at Jamison, for him to do something. To stop them from taking me away. This thing wasn't for me.

"Baby," he said, still being held by the officers, "just go with them and I'll come get you. I promise."

"But I didn't do anything."

"Mrs. Taylor," Officer Cox said, "because we all saw you assault your husband, we're going to have to take you in for domestic violence."

"Domestic violence?" I couldn't trust the echoes vibrating through my ears. "But he's here with that woman cheating on me."

My spine began to twitch as the baby shifted, panicking, from side to side.

"I know. But because we saw you and our captain is with us, we have to do this. If the captain wasn't with us, we could let you go, but we have to protect ourselves. You understand?" Her voice turned to reason for a second and she slid the cuffs on and began to read me my Miranda rights. The crowd, which had grown even larger, stood silent in fear and amazement.

"That ain't necessary, officer," one woman said. "She's pregnant. Just let her go."

"Yeah," other people agreed. But it was too late. My hands cuffed on top of my belly, I watched them all desperately as the officer began walking me to the car. I turned again to see Jamison still standing there, looking at me helplessly. He'd done this to us, to me. I was being sent to jail for hitting a man who had beaten my heart to a pulp.

"You'll be out quickly," the female officer said, helping me into the car. The rainbow of lights went shining again and we were off.

John Small may be a successful Wall Street banker, but at heart he's a country boy from the sleepy town of Nedine, South Carolina, with big dreams—but big dreams can bring big problems. John is about to learn some hard truths about money and power, love and loyalty—and the forces that connect us all. And when his future, and his family's legacy, is in danger, help will come from where he least expects it . . .

Don't miss Trice Hickman's

Looking for Trouble

On sale now!

Summertime, present-day Atlanta, Georgia

"Oh no," Alexandria softly whispered, trying to hide her discomfort. Her body tensed, anticipating the annoyance that was about to come. *This can't be happening again. Not now,* she thought.

"What's wrong?" Peter whispered back, still continuing to nibble on the left lobe of Alexandria's ear.

She moved her head to the side, trying to block out the sound that was making its way back into her mind. *Go away! Please go away and leave me alone!* Alexandria shouted to herself as she repositioned her nude body under the weight of Peter's muscular heft. She turned her head back to face him, releasing a low, measured sigh.

"You okay?" Peter asked; this time, there was a bit of concern in between his heavy panting.

"I'm fine," Alexandria lied. She hesitated; then slowly pulled him closer against her bare chest. "Kiss me," she demanded in a not-so-playful tone. She took a deep breath, closed her eyes tightly, and concentrated on her boyfriend's languid tongue as she tried to block out the voice—laced with a deep Southern accent—that was invading her head.

Although she knew that her love life with Peter was woefully lacking, and she couldn't remember the last time she'd had an orgasm, Alexandria had hoped that a quick roll between the sheets would give her mind a break from the recurring loop it had been stuck in. But instead of arresting her anxiety, the physical romp only seemed to kick her senses into overdrive.

As Peter's movements became more urgent, her desire began quickly to wane by the second, sinking into the background of the voice repeating itself inside her head. She tried to concentrate on the moment, but that didn't work, so she willed her mind to take her to another place. But that was no use, either. The harder she fought, the louder the sound of the voice grew. Finally she gave up.

"Peter, I'm sorry, but I have to go." Alexandria gently pushed him away, freeing herself from his hold.

"What?" Peter huffed, looking confused. "You've gotta be kidding me."

"No, I really do need to go," she said as she sat up and kicked her long, slightly thick legs to the side of his king-size bed. She ran her fingers through the mass of long, kinky dark brown curls atop her head as she slumped her shoulders in frustration.

"One minute you want me to kiss you and the next you're pushing me away. What gives?"

"I'm sorry, Peter. I don't mean to send mixed signals."

"Then don't." Peter paused as he moved in close, still trying to nuzzle his body next to hers. He leaned into her, giving her shoulder a light kiss. "C'mon, lay back down with me."

Alexandria ignored his coaxing; instead, she slowly stood to her feet as she spoke. "It's not you. It's me," she told him, knowing how off-putting and clichéd her response, albeit truthful, sounded. She could feel thick tension rise in the air as soon as the words left her mouth, so she tried to speak in a gentle tone. "There's a lot going on in my life right now. Things that have nothing to do with you, Peter."

"I don't believe this." Peter reluctantly reached for his boxers as Alexandria pulled her sundress over her head and then slid it down the length of her curvaceous body. "So where does this leave me?" he asked.

She wanted to tell him, *How the hell do I know? I can't even figure out what's going on in my own life, let alone yours.* But she knew this wasn't the time for such declarations, so she leavened her tone, inserting a measure of compassion in her voice. "I need to be alone tonight so I can think."

"Think? . . . Think about what, Alexandria?"

"Life, and what I'm supposed to do with mine. Like I said, there's so much going on right now. I hope you can understand."

Peter shook his head in dismay. "I've been trying hard to understand you, especially over the last couple weeks. I've been patient when you zone out on me, and I've tried to be understanding when you say you have a lot going on, like now, even though you never give a clue about exactly what the problem is."

Alexandria looked into Peter's dark brown eyes and nodded, knowing he deserved to hear the full truth: She was so scared about what was happening to her that she didn't have time to focus on their relationship. But at the same time, she knew Peter's primary focus was really on himself and his feelings—because not once had he asked her what kinds of things were bothering her.

She'd met Peter two years ago while working as a summer intern at Johnson, Taylor, and Associates, one of the largest law firms in the Atlanta Metro area. She'd been in her last year of law school at UPenn, and somewhat ambivalent about pursuing a career in the legal field. Peter had just graduated from Yale University School of Law, was an ambitious first-year associate at the firm, and was already rumored to be a rising star within the ranks. Although he was a bit uptight and a little too formal in his attitude than what Alexandria liked, Peter's tall, muscular physique, smooth dark chocolate skin, and handsome face had all attracted her to him. They had spotted each other during the first day of new employee orientation and had gone out for drinks during happy hour a week later.

They'd both been seeing other people at the time, but neither had been seriously involved. Their casual lunches and long dinners slowly turned into much more. They kept in touch after she returned to law school for her senior year, and they saw each other whenever time permitted, which wasn't often. Once she graduated the next summer they started dating exclusively, and had been together ever since.

"Who is he?" Peter asked.

"What?"

"Please, Alexandria," Peter said, looking at her with an accusatory glare. "Don't play me for a fool. If you're seeing someone else, I'd appreciate you being up front with me instead of feeding me excuses."

"Oh, like you and Monica?"

Peter let out an exasperated sigh. "I told you, that was nothing."

"Yeah, right."

"I can't help it if the woman showed up on my doorstep out the blue."

"Excuse me, but it makes a difference when *the woman* you're referring to, just happened to be your ex-girlfriend! And for someone who mysteriously showed up unwelcome, you sure did make her feel at home," Alexandria said, returning his accusing stare. "I got here and found you two drinking wine and laughing, acting all cozy."

"Number one, we weren't cozy. We were simply talking," Peter said in a direct tone. "She was depressed because the guy she was seeing had just dumped her. She needed someone to talk to and—"

"And you were the first person she went running to," Alexandria countered. "I think that's very strange, especially given the fact that you dumped her, too. So why on earth would she come to you for a shoulder to cry on? It didn't make sense then, and it still doesn't make sense now."

Until last month when Alexandria had caught Peter and his ex in that precarious situation, he hadn't given her much reason to question his fidelity. He was a pragmatist who preferred diplomacy over drama, and he avoided the latter at all costs. Having extra women on the side only upped the ante for chaos, and Peter wasn't one for the kind of trouble that fooling around could bring. He was the dependable type, almost to the point of being predictably annoying. Because of his anal manner, a small part of Alexandria believed that even if Peter wanted to stray, it would be challenging for him, given the fact that he also spent most of his time at the office.

Peter routinely worked twelve- and fourteen-hour days, sometimes six days a week, all in his self-imposed race to climb the ladder of success, following in his mother's large and looming footsteps. She was a circuit court judge and was currently being courted to run for one of Georgia's congressional seats. She was a demanding overachiever, and Peter wanted to make her proud, which meant working insanely long hours and forfeiting a social life beyond networking functions, where he could make business connections. When he wasn't at the office—which was hardly ever—he was either working from home, working out at the gym, or spending what little time he had left over with Alexandria.

But Alexandria also knew that just because Peter was a busy, regimented man, that didn't mean there weren't opportunities for him to cheat, or that he wasn't capable. Experience had taught her that regardless of one's work schedule and personal demands, a man or a woman could make time to do anything he or she really wanted. The only reason she hadn't followed up on the suspicions lurking in the back of her mind was because of the voice that had been penetrating her thoughts, forcing her to come to grips with a part of her life she'd been trying to avoid since she was five years old.

"I know it doesn't make sense to you," Peter said, "but that's exactly what happened when Monica came over here. Nothing more, nothing less. I'm telling you the truth."

Alexandria shrugged. "Whose truth?"

"If I wanted to sleep with her, I could've done that a long time ago."

"And that's another thing. Why do you still keep in contact with your ex-girlfriend?"

Peter let out another frustrated sigh. "We only talk once in a blue moon, like at the holidays, just to wish each other well."

"And why is that even necessary?"

"It's not. It's just a polite gesture. Besides, if I was trying to hide something, trust me, you'd never know that I'd had any contact with her at all." Peter pulled his T-shirt over his broad chest and taut waist. "But listen, my ex—whom I have absolutely no interest in—isn't the issue. Let's talk about our relationship."

"What I'm going through right now has nothing to do with our relationship. Like I told you, it's about me."

"Cut the shit, Alexandria." Peter smirked. "Call me 'crazy,' but I thought that when you're in a relationship with someone, everything that involves you involves the other person, too."

Although she knew Peter's comment was absolutely right, she didn't like the sarcasm or nasty tone that was planted behind it. Deep down, she knew that he only half-meant what he'd just said. She'd slowly come to realize that he was a bit selfish, hence his "Where does this leave me?" remark. So she knew what he was saying now was clearly meant to draw out a reasonable explanation that would put his mind at ease about the possibility of her cheating on him.

"I hear what you're saying," Alexandria responded, slipping on her turquoise-colored thong-toed sandals, "but this really is about me, and only me."

"Okay, then what's bothering you?"

Her eyes widened with surprise. "This is the first time you've asked me about *me*."

"No, it's not, but I won't waste time arguing that point right now. Tell me what's going on with you?"

She wanted so bad to call him on his lie, but she knew it would be a fruitless cause. "For one, I'm not happy with my career. I feel like I'm settling." This part was true, and she didn't hesitate sharing it.

"You graduated in the top of your law school class and now you're a fast-rising associate at one of the most powerful lobbying firms in the city. You work closely with one of the senior partners, and they even handpicked you to present and testify before Congress last year, which got you that major raise you're enjoying now."

"You act like you're giving me information that I don't already know."

"Okay, since you already know that, you also know how many people would kill—and I mean that literally—to stand in your shoes."

Alexandria looked down at her neatly polished toenails, then up at Peter. "I'm not concerned about other people. I'm talking about me, and what I really want. Being a performing artist is my calling. I've always known that, and now, every day, I feel it more than ever."

"Why did you work so hard in law school if this wasn't what you wanted?"

"That's just it. I didn't work hard in law school at all. It came easy for me, just like high school and undergrad. I went through the motions and I did what I was expected to do. But now, I'm ready to pursue my passion like my mom did."

Peter looked up at the ceiling. "Here we go with that again."

"I'm one of the best spoken-word artists in the city—hell, in this region. Whenever I perform at the Lazy Day, people pack the house to hear me."

"You know that's not a sustainable profession, don't you? What do you make doing that? Fifty dollars a night?"

"You know what . . ." Alexandria drew in a deep breath. "Never mind, I'm leaving."

Feeling tired and frustrated, Alexandria didn't say another word. She gathered her handbag, picked up her leather overnight duffel, and walked toward the door.

"Hold on," Peter said, gently clasping his hand around Alexandria's slender wrist. "I don't want you to leave like this . . . upset with me."

"I'm not upset with you. Like I said, I need to be alone right now so I can clear my head." She leaned into him, planted a small kiss on his right cheek, and told him she'd come by the next day.

Twenty minutes later, Alexandria found herself sitting alone on her couch in her small one-bedroom apartment, devouring a small bowl of Ben & Jerry's chocolate ice cream and three dark chocolate truffles from her Godiva box. Whenever she felt down and out, ice cream and chocolates always seemed to lift her spirits. The cold, chocolaty sweet taste tickled her tongue and almost made her forget about the voice that kept repeating the same words inside her head: *"I'm ready for the fight."* The words were fragmented bits and pieces of a longer sentence that Alexandria couldn't fully understand.

"Stop it!" She hissed into the stillness surrounding her. "I don't care about your fight. All I want is peace and quiet. Leave me alone."

She rose from her couch and went into her bathroom. "This has got to stop," she said as she pulled her long hair back into a ponytail and reached for her facial cleanser. "I can't take this any longer. Why can't I block out this voice, like I can the others?"

After washing and exfoliating her skin, Alexandria looked into the mirror and studied the nude face that stared back at her. She hadn't inherited her mother's chocolate hue, but her light caramel-colored skin—compliments of her white father—was smooth and so even that she looked as though she were wearing foundation. She appraised her sultry brown eyes, perfectly arched brows, and full, bow-shaped lips. She was thankful that despite her stress, she still looked good.

"This is taking a toll," she said, crawling under her soft, cool bedsheets. She prayed for a restful night's sleep, but she could already tell that wasn't going to happen because of the buzzing that just returned to her ear. Hearing voices and seeing visions—which no one else could—was nothing new for Alexandria.

She'd experienced her first encounter when she was just a toddler, playfully talking with the spirits of children from bygone years. Her imaginary friends were as real as the ones she played with at school. As she grew older, she developed the ability of premonition. When she was five years old, she predicted her father's heart attack before it happened. A few months later, she drew a picture of her younger brother, Christian, before he was conceived. It had startled her teacher so much that she'd called Alexandria's parents. From that point on, she stopped drawing the things she saw happening in her mind.

Growing up the child of a black mother and a white father, Alexandria was taught by her parents that she came from extraordinary people on both sides of her family. But there was another dimension of who she was that she knew her parents would never be able to understand—let alone teach her about—so she made up her mind early on to bury the mysterious haunting that often gripped her in her sleep.

Over the years, she'd developed the ability to tune out voices when they tried to roar inside her mind. For some reason, though, she couldn't do it with the woman who was now drumming words into her ear. When she'd started hearing whispers a few weeks ago, she immediately knew there was something different about this new voice that was contacting her, and the spirit of the person to whom it belonged.

As she sat alone, finishing the last spoonful of chocolate ice cream, Alexandria heard the voice again. This time, the sound came in a little more clearly: *"Look for the diamond, 'cause the one who has that is the one who's gonna help save you."*

"What the hell does that mean?" Alexandria said. She set her empty container of ice cream on the coffee table in front of her. She knew that whether she wanted to or not, she would soon find out.